J. A. Hunter

Viridian Gate Online: Cataclysm

J. A. Hunter

DEDICATION

For all the crazy-amazing readers out there, who pay me to write these kooky stories. You guys and gals are seriously the best.

J. A. Hunter

VIRIDIAN GATE ONLINE
RECOMMENDED READING ORDER

VGO: Cataclysm (Main Series Book 1)

VGO: Crimson Alliance (Main Series Book 2)

VGO: The Jade Lord (Main Series Book 3)

VGO: The Imperial Legion (Main Series Book 4)

VGO: The Lich Priest (Main Series Book 5)

VGO: Doom Forge (Main Series Book 6)

VGO: Darkling Siege (Main Series Book 7)

<<<>>>

VGO: Nomad Soul (The Illusionist 1)

VGO: Dead Man's Tide (The Illusionist 2)

VGO: Inquisitor's Foil (The Illusionist 3)

<<<>>>

VGO: The Artificer (Imperial Initiative)

<<<>>>

VGO: Firebrand (Firebrand Series 1)

VGO: Embers of Rebellion (Firebrand Series 2)

VGO: Path of the Blood Phoenix (Firebrand Series 3)

<<<>>>

VGO: Vindication (The Alchemic Weaponeer 1)

VGO: Absolution (The Alchemic Weaponeer 2)

VGO: Insurrection (The Alchemic Weaponeer 3)

Viridian Gate Online: Cataclysm

J. A. Hunter

ELDGARD

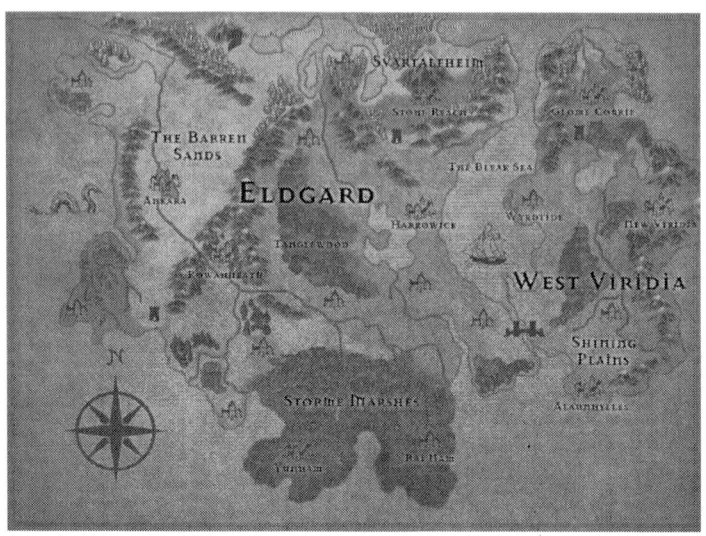

ONE

BEGINNING OF THE END

I TOOK ONE LAST GLANCE AROUND MY APARTMENT. A tiny studio flat, just under five hundred square feet, which still cost me a sizeable chunk of change every month. It didn't help that the cost of living had skyrocketed over the past few years while my meager paycheck had remained rock steady. Which is to say, *low*. Being an EMT doesn't pay what it used to, not that it's ever really been a lucrative career field—kids flipping burgers at most fast-food joints made what I did, despite the demands of the job. Working grueling shifts. Saving lives. Watching people die.

Still, even in spite of the pay, it was good work. Fulfilling.

My little slice of paradise had a small kitchen, a nearly microscopic bathroom, and a living room that doubled as my bedroom, office, dining room, and pretty much everything else. I'm something of a minimalist, I suppose. Someone less *generous* might say I was poor. Everything I owned was old, worn, and just this side of broken: a dented stove, a bulky white fridge that'd certainly seen better days, a used brown sofa I'd picked up from Goodwill a couple of years ago. The couch was heavily stained, the cushions deeply creased and sagging. A full mattress in the same condition bordered the far wall, near the door to the bathroom.

The TV was nice at least—a hulking seventy-five-inch Shintaro with a nano-crystal screen and multi-zone backlighting. My VR headset, a matte black helmet with a sleek viewing screen, sat on the floor next to the massive television. I smiled looking at it. Lots of good memories.

For a moment, I stood there staring, swaying slightly on my feet. I frowned, trying to decide what to do next. As an EMT I know what shock looks like, and I had it bad, but there wasn't anything I could do. I briefly considered going around my apartment and unplugging the appliances, just to make sure the place didn't catch fire and burn to the ground. No point in that, though. A house fire was the least of my concerns at this point.

So instead, I shrugged numbly, readjusted my bathrobe, shuffled over to the cramped kitchen, and poured myself a cup of day-old joe, strong enough to knock teeth out.

The coffee was tepid at best, so I stuck the mug in the barely serviceable microwave, hit the auto start, and headed over to the front door. The only door. The only way in or out, save the windows, but I was four stories up, so that wasn't a huge concern. I checked the lock for what was probably the hundredth time. Still shut nice and tight. The deadbolt was engaged, the hanging chain in place. Then, I rechecked the shoddy wooden chair I'd jammed up under the knob—in case someone decided the lock wasn't enough of a deterrent.

That was fine, too.

The microwave sounded, *beep-beep-beep*, letting me know my formerly lukewarm coffee was ready to go. I retrieved my cup, now steaming, took a few tentative sips, and headed over to the far window overlooking the street below. I didn't open the blinds—didn't want anyone to see my apartment was occupied, since that might mark me as a target—but instead peeked through one of the plastic slats. A quick gander. It was getting dark, and the streetlights were starting to kick on; not that the streetlights needed to be on, what with the fires raging all over the city. Sooty orange-and-yellow light littered the skyline, plumes of smoke drifting, rising, visible even against the darkening sky.

A man in a hockey mask strode by on the street below, a pump action shotgun clutched in his hands, a bag of looted toilet paper slung across his back in a duffel bag. The strobing lights of an empty police cruiser washed over him in splashes of red and blue. *Toilet paper. His prize loot is toilet paper. Maybe the world deserves to die.* I shook my head, then took another sip of coffee, letting the bitter liquid wash down my throat and hit my belly with a surge of delicious warmth and caffeine.

I turned away from the window and fixed my gaze on the brand-new, state-of-the-art NexGenVR capsule—a coffin of glossy black plastic and sleek chrome. Really, it looked more like a high-tech suntanning bed, but, all things considered, it sure *felt* like a coffin. A host of tubes snaked away from the capsule to a hefty generator powered by a renewable hydro-cell. The capsules drew far too much power to operate on the city grid, so they needed their own private source, and that generator could keep my VR capsule up and running for a solid month. Not that I needed a month.

Seventy-two hours would do it.

I paused and ran a hand over the surface of the capsule, feeling the smooth plastic. Honestly, I was lucky to have the thing—a good friend of mine from college was a program developer at Osmark Tech, and she'd hooked me up big time. Of course, that'd been before the news about Astraea. I tapped the surface, fingers drumming out a staccato rhythm as I took another sip of coffee. Almost time. I brought the cup away and realized my hand was trembling. Yep, almost time. But not yet. I still had a little longer. Long enough to finish my joe—it'd be the last cup of coffee I'd ever have, so I figured I should really enjoy it.

I turned, refusing to look at the capsule, feeling a wave of guilt rise from my gut and claw its way upwards. I shoved the feeling away and ambled over to the couch, plopping down on the well-worn cushions just like I had a million times before. *Just survivor's guilt*, I reminded myself; there was no reason to feel that way. I hadn't done anything wrong. This was the end, and I needed to do what I could for me. I didn't have a girlfriend. My parents were across the country, and with air services shut down they'd never make it out here. Not in time for it to matter. We'd already Interfaced and said our goodbyes.

I took another swig and glanced down, realizing my cup was already half empty. I swirled the mug, watching the black liquid dance. Better make it last.

"Sophia," I said.

"Yes, Jack, how can I help you?" The voice, polite, vaguely British, and female, resounded from a small black speaker shaped like a hockey puck attached to the side of the television. Sophia was a limited AI controller—an automation system that ran my home.

"Turn up the thermostat to seventy-two and please put on Cartoon Network."

"Of course, Jack, my pleasure." The heat kicked on a second later, a rush of warm air flooding in through the vents while the TV blinked to brilliant life. They had classic reruns on: Courage the Cowardly Dog shrieked, his eyes bulging out as a talking tree spouted sage advice. I wasn't in the mood for Courage, but neither did I feel motivated to look for something else, something better. Most of the stations would be covering the flaming death-ball anyway, and I sure as heck didn't feel like watching any more of that circus.

So, I sat and watched Courage's shenanigans, chuckling tiredly as I slowly polished off my drink. Enjoyed every sip. After half an hour, though, my cup was empty and the anxiety was coming back with a vengeance. "Sophia, find me news coverage," I said reluctantly. The channel switched in a blink. Courage was replaced by a pair of news anchors, one a forty-something guy with too-white teeth and well-coiffed hair, the other a cute black woman with a short bob cut and a pink blazer.

"We here at Channel 9 will continue to monitor the news right up until the very end, folks," said the woman in the blazer. A countdown timer in the corner of the screen spun merrily away: nine days, four hours, and thirty-two minutes left until impact. "Scientists from NASA," she continued professionally, "along with astronauts and researchers from the US-European think tank AIDA—Asteroid Impact and Deflection

11

Assessment—are working around the clock on a viable solution to either destroy or divert asteroid 213 Astraea, the nine-mile-wide chunk of rock and ice currently predicted to land in the North Atlantic near the coast of Greenland.

"Although few specific details have been released about AIDA's plans, our sources say the best hope we have is to nudge Astraea into the stable orbit of the Moon. With that said, we are told scientists and government officials overseeing the project do not seem optimistic at the prospect. Local A.R.C. lottery winners are being directed to rally at the Osmark Football stadium as quickly as possible. But any travelers, be warned, looters are out in force and you will need credentials, two forms of identification, and Lottery vouchers to get past the Guardsmen holding the stadium. All vouchers are nontransferable and are invalid without proper identification."

"In other news," said the man with the well-coiffed hair, "Osmark Technologies is still accepting people at their secure facility in the Silicon Valley. Those slots are limited, however, and are filling up quickly, so if you're prepared to make the leap into Viridian Gate Online, you shouldn't delay any longer. The company is urging private citizens with access to NexGenVR capsules to stream live as soon as possible. According to our sources inside Osmark Technologies, complete interface integration usually takes seventy-two hours, but apparently it *can* take longer, so they are advising people not to wait.

"For those without A.R.C. vouchers and no plans to upload into Viridian Gate Online, the National Guard is recommending you get to a secure basement and store at least one gallon of water per person per day for a minimum of five days. Also ensure you have any necessary life-saving medications on hand since emergency services will likely be off-line for quite some time after—"

"Turn it off, Sophia," I said, with a wave of my hand. The TV died with a single final flash of light. Then darkness. A preview of the world to come: one big bang, then black.

I set my mug down on a stained and scratched coffee table and rubbed slick palms along the legs of my sweatpants. My hands trembled noticeably. No point putting it off any longer—there was nothing left for me to do now, and if I had any chance of surviving Astraea, it was going to be inside that capsule.

I stood with a groan, went over to the NexGenVR, and reverently touched the machine, keying the manual power button on the control console. Immediately, it hummed to life, accompanied by a strobe of neon-blue light the color of a bug zapper. I swallowed hard, my hands now shaking so badly I wasn't sure if I'd be able to operate the controls. Thankfully, Sophia would help with the rest. I flipped open the lid and placed a modified version of the familiar VR helmet on my head, before carefully lowering myself onto the stiff memory-foam mattress lining the capsule's interior.

The lid automatically closed, leaving me in a cramped space filled with a pulsing light. My heart labored in my chest, thumping against my ribs, beating a million miles a minute. At this rate, I'd have a coronary, which would put me down long before that stupid meteor ever got here. *No, I'll be fine.* All I needed to do now was give Sophia the command, tell her to initiate Viridian Gate Online, and that would be that.

Except, I couldn't make my lips form the words.

Once I did, I'd be committed. And I might die. That was one thing they *weren't* telling people on the news: one in six who attempted full integration died during the process. And those that did "survive" would live on as virtual avatars in a virtual world. Was that really even living? I didn't know. I also didn't know if I had the guts to pull the trigger—this was like playing Russian roulette.

I shuddered. Shivered. My brow broke out in claustrophobic sweat.

Yeah, this process might kill me. *Might,* I reminded myself. When Astraea hit, though, I'd be one hundred percent dead. No question in my mind about that. "Sophia," I said, voice quivering, "please run Viridian Gate Online."

"Of course, Jack," she replied calmly. "Please lie as still as possible."

The machine let out a *click-buzz*—the lid locking mechanism—followed by the *whoosh-whoosh-whoosh* of a whirling MRI. Abruptly, everything went black as the VR headset engaged, but the black was soon replaced by a white loading screen. A video popped up in front of me, filling my vision, featuring a man with shaggy hair and wire-rim glasses, wearing black slacks and a dark navy turtleneck.

"Hello, I'm the CEO of Osmark Technologies, Robert Osmark, and I'd like to personally welcome you to Viridian Gate Online," he said, "the most advanced full-immersion video game in the world. Viridian Gate Online is truly the first of its kind. And that's not the typical hyperbolic language so cavalierly tossed around in tech circles. No, I can assure you, I truly mean this is the first of its kind.

"Our revolutionary work with massive memristive neuromorphic computing systems has created a paradigm shift in AI technologies, and the result is an experience second to none. Moreover, through Osmark's patented NexGenVR capsule you will experience a whole new world as though you were there in the flesh. Even the pain is real."

There was a pause—Robert froze with a stupid grin on his face. "Patch 1.3 update announcement," Sophia intoned.

The screen blinked and Robert resumed speaking. "If you are watching this," he said gravely, "it means you have a very real, very hard choice to make ahead of you. The imminent arrival of asteroid 213 Astraea has changed everything. Though it's possible, likely even, that human life will continue in some form or capacity after the asteroid's impact, many, if not all of you watching this, will die. That's a somber, hard truth, and at this stage it's a truth which shouldn't be sugarcoated. But there is another way. A way that you *might* live— and I'm extending that invitation to everyone watching this.

"Our NexGenVR capsules work by injecting microscopic nanobots into your bloodstream. The nanobots migrate north and map out your mind in precise detail. These extraordinary mechanical marvels survey each of the major portions of your brain—the cerebrum, the cerebellum, and the brainstem—and chart each of your neural pathways, which is no small feat. They're the secret behind our system's full integration: they actually stimulate the nerves in your brain, allowing you to experience the game with lifelike sensation. The information gleaned by the nanobots is then uploaded to one of several deep-earth servers, located in secure bunkers all across the globe.

"Truthfully, that's far more candid than I ever expected to be about how the process works, but this is the end of the world." He offered a tired, lopsided smile. "The system is perfectly safe—under the right conditions. During our clinical trials, we discovered that if this uploading process continues for longer than seventy-two consecutive hours, the body shuts down and the physical brain goes into a state of catatonia. After that, without proper life-support measures, the body simply dies."

He folded his hands, lips pressed into a tight line. "But that map the nanobots uploaded," he continued after a beat, "will continue to exist indefinitely within the game server. And that map is, for all intents and purposes, you. It's your thoughts, emotions, experiences, personality. A digital copy of you within the game world of Viridian Gate Online. Originally, we installed neural inhibitors into all the capsules, which automatically logged players out after six hours of game play, but Patch 1.3 has changed all that. The neural inhibitors have all been disabled and, after twenty-four hours of in-game time, the logout button will permanently disappear, leaving you stranded in the game.

"If you choose to upload yourself to Viridian Gate Online, you have a chance at surviving Astraea, at least in a digital form. Now, let me take a moment to address some of the concerns circulating around the internet rumor mill. First, I can personally assure everyone listening to this message that Patch 1.3 is our last major update—the game is locked and all essential functions are now being administered by the AI controllers.

"Second, contrary to what some fearmongers have reported online, once you are uploaded, no hacker or Osmark Tech employee will be able to delete your profile. All permanent user profiles are immediately encrypted using asymmetric key cryptography and then circulated continuously and randomly through all of our linked databases, ensuring no person will ever be able to access your digital identity. Not even I could manage to do it. And really, this is as much for our protection as yours—we don't want a way to delete players because that's a two-edged sword, which could easily be wielded against us.

"No, I can assure you, once you've successfully transitioned to a digitized form, you'll be safe and secure for as long as V.G.O. exists. With that said, I won't lie to you, this process isn't without risks. Not everyone successfully transitions. There is a one in six chance you will die during the process. One in six. But for the vast majority of you, there is a one hundred percent chance you will die if you fail to take the risk. By watching this warning, you hereby remove all liability of damages from Osmark Technologies, its corporate owners, and its subsidiary entities. Would you still like to proceed?"

His terrible question hung in the air, heavy like a storm cloud. *Did I want to proceed? Would existing in a video game really be better than dying? Than seeing what came next?*

"Yes," I said. "Proceed." The machine kicked into overdrive, the whirling picking up in intensity. *WHOOSH, WHOOSH, WHOOSH, WHOOSH.*

J. A. Hunter

"Traveler," boomed a hard-edged male voice, "prepare to enter Viridian Gate Online!"

TWO

V.G.O.

THE WHITE LOADING SCREEN GAVE WAY AND, IN an eyeblink, I found myself standing on the rocky slope of a gigantic mountain, snow and ice underfoot, a tremendous valley stretching out before me. The sight was breathtaking, amazing—the lush forests and rolling plains below so lifelike I could've sworn I was standing high in the Rockies or maybe the Swiss Alps. A slapping wind bit at my hands and face, plastering crude, scratchy, homespun garments to my body. I reached tentative fingers up to my cheek, feeling the prick of rough stubble running along my jawline.

Wow. I dropped to my ass, my legs too weak to support me. The chill from the snow instantly hit me as water soaked into my threadbare pants—I scrambled back to my feet in a hurry, eager to be away from the cold. I glanced down and saw a divot in the fresh powder. *Wow.* This was incredible. I'd been involved in VRMMORPGs for as long as they'd been around, but there'd never been anything like this. Never. Not even close. The graphics quality was unmatched, indistinguishable from IRL, even. The frigid snow and the blades of grass poking up from below were as real as the saggy couch in my apartment.

And the sensations …

I could *really* feel here. I wasn't sure what I'd expected when I'd first heard about the NexGenVR capsule's NerveTech features, but it hadn't been this. I could smell the fresh pine wafting from the towering spruces and sprawling evergreens dotting the mountainside around me. On a whim, I bent over and scooped up a handful of powder and took a bite—cold, faintly flavored with ozone and cedar. The snow melted in my mouth, water trickling down my throat and hitting my belly with a cool splash. Robert Osmark certainly hadn't been exaggerating—this was definitely a first-of-its-kind game.

Still, as amazing as this was, could I live here forever? Guess I didn't have much choice at this point.

That thought vanished as a semitranslucent display popped up. A hazy image of myself—an average looking guy with sandy brown hair, a medium build, and a slightly pinched faced—floated in the air. Except, I was no longer wearing my ratty old bathrobe and sweatpants; now, I was sporting a tattered burlap-looking tunic with rough stitching, a pair of equally uncomfortable trousers, held up with a length of rope, and some fur boots that weren't doing much to keep the chill out. An interface bar with a variety of options—race, build, sex, face, name—trailed down beside my floating avatar.

I glanced up at race, and immediately a new options menu appeared on my right, hovering in the air like a specter. A list of available, playable races. I scanned the first one, Hvitalfar. Immediately, my avatar's image changed; sandy brown hair was replaced by platinum blond locks, and my skin took on a golden hue while my ears elongated, slimming to narrow tips. It was still me, though, my face and body providing the underlying framework for some new and strange costume. A prompt popped up and lingered at the bottom of my vision:

Hvitalfar (Dawn Elf): The elves of the Shining Plains, also known as Hvitalfar, make excellent Clerics and Sorcerers. Due to their natural affinity for spellcraft and the restorative arts, they receive a 5% bonus to starting Spirit. With their affection for nature and close kinship with animals, they also make admirable Rangers, excelling in the Shaman kits.

I immediately scrolled down, gaze landing on the next race in the list—Dokkalfar. My avatar changed again, this time the skin darkening to a dusky gun-metal gray, my hair going a glossy raven's-black, which looked almost blue from a certain angle. This race also had pointy ears and I could tell they hailed from the same family as the Dawn Elves I'd just looked at. After a moment, a new text box appeared:

Dokkalfar (Murk Elf): The Murk Elves of the Storme Marshes are a tough and often unlikeable people. Many Dokkalfar prefer to keep to their own kind and rarely venture outside their boggy home lands. A lifetime of living in the dangerous and predatory swamps of Eldgard makes them excellently suited to be Rangers. They also excel in the Rogue class—particularly as assassins, *Sicarii*, since they possess a 20% resistance to poison and disease—or as mysterious Dark Templars, the enforcers of the Shadow Pantheon.

There were several other races to choose from.

The *Svartalfar*, short and squat, who resembled the typical dwarf and excelled in Smithing, Enchanting, and Merchant-craft. They also sported a hefty 50% resistance to fire, probably on account of their forge work. Next came humanoid creatures with dark, Middle Eastern features and pronounced wings jutting from their backs. They looked like living angels. The *Accipiter*, who could fly apparently, had a few race-restricted specialty classes, and a sizeable bonus to Dexterity.

Two varieties of humans followed: the Imperials—vaguely Roman looking with short, wavy hair and Mediterranean complexions—and the Wodes. The Wodes, big and blond-headed, looked like the Germanic barbarians of ancient history. Neither of the human races had any extra racial bonus or resistances, but there was a note, which read, "humans can assume any profession or nonrestricted class without penalty," which was probably a big advantage early on.

Last came the Risi—a meaty looking humanoid loaded down with thick muscle, faintly green-tinged skin, and a pronounced underbite studded with protruding fangs. Some variety of Troll or Ogre, if I had to guess. The Risi, more than any other race, appeared excellently suited for heavy melee combat and tanking, but I knew without hesitation I wouldn't be going that route. First, I found brawlers and fighters were great early on, but were often lacking at higher levels. And second—the more important factor—I refused to look like that *monster* for the rest of my life, no matter what racial bonuses might sweeten the pot.

I quickly went back through my options, eliminating the Dawn Elf and the Dwarf—being a glass-cannon mage didn't suit my play style, and I certainly wasn't a crafter by nature—which left the Murk Elf, the bird-winged *Accipiter,* and the two human races. I saw a wiki icon and immediately brought up a search menu. "Look for class kits," I said.

"Certainly, Jack," Sophia answered, which was a pleasant surprise. Hearing her voice was a small point of comfort. Unfortunately, the search yielded a whole bunch of nothing, so I closed out and went back to my character creation screen.

Usually, in MMORPGs I played as a Cleric/healer, but a mixed class like a Paladin or Dark Paladin might serve me well in this new frontier where I didn't have a clan, didn't know the rules, and might have to go it alone for a while. I paused, rubbing at my chin—Rogues were also highly versatile for lone wolf players, so that might be an option to consider, though that certainly wasn't my preferred class.

Finally, I scrolled over to the Murk Elf.

That 20% poison and disease resistance was too good to pass up. Plus, superficial as it may have been, he looked *badass* and the only other character I could reasonably see myself as was the Accipiter—except I wasn't so great with heights. So, I selected the Murk Elf, then scrolled through the other creation features, tweaking my appearance a bit—adding some extra muscle here, opting for a short beard there, picking a few swirling tribal tattoos—before finally selecting the "create," option. A new screen appeared asking me what name I'd like for my character. Jack didn't seem like an appropriate name for a high-fantasy elf, but it was *my* name, and I was hesitant to give it up.

Everything else was changing. My face, my body, my world. But I could keep my name, or at least a variation of it. Grim_Jack was my gaming handle, so if I went with that, it would kind of be the best of both worlds. "Grim Jack," I finally said, decided.

"Are you sure you would like to create Grim Jack the Dokkalfar?" came the booming baritone voice from before. "Once you create a character, you will not be able to change your racial identity or name. Please confirm?"

"Yes," I said again, trepidation mounting in my stomach, not knowing what came next.

THREE

CLASH OF KINGDOMS

I WAITED FOR A BEAT, THEN TWO, FOLDING MY ARMS. I was on the verge of saying something else, maybe telling these guys to get a move on it, when music exploded around me like a thunderclap. An epic score, with pounding drums, clanging cymbals, and a host of stringed instruments, conjured images of noble kings and fierce battles, clashing armies, and world-shaking magic—

"The year is 1095 A.I.C.—*Anno Imperium Conditae*," the disembodied announcer bellowed over the music. "Dark power and the stirrings of war ride upon the winds of Eldgard, the provincial outpost of the Great Viridian Empire."

Something streaked across the sky, a burst of fire that reminded me all too much of the meteor and the world I was leaving behind. The streak of light disappeared, blocked from sight by a thicket of pines, then exploded back into view a hundred feet away. A massive scale-covered body with huge, pumping wings flashed across the field of view, trailing fire from crushing jaws as large as a T. rex's. A golden eye, big as a dinner plate and slit down the middle with a slash of black, regarded me

25

coolly for a second. Then the creature ascended into the clouds above. Gone.

The breath caught in my lungs. A dragon. A fantastical monster of scale and fangs and flame.

"Imperial legions," said the announcer, "allied with the forces of light, march from the east, bringing the natives of Eldgard to their knees through flame, magic, and steel. Bringing progress. Building roads. Cities. *A kingdom.* Civilizing the dark-natured Wodes, the swamp dwelling Dokkalfar, and the Accipiter of the far-western deserts, enlightening them in the ways of the ever-victorious empire." On the stretching plains below, I watched in awe as a sprawling force of humans, elves, and Risi—men and women—all clad in gleaming metal and oiled leather, swarmed across the ground like a plague of locusts. Banners rippled in a far-away breeze while foot soldiers hauled towering catapults and other savage siege engines.

"But the natives of Eldgard are not so quick to give up the old ways—to heel for foreign masters. Though the rebellion is yet small, they fight on. Hour by hour, day by day ..."

Suddenly, I was floating, drifting high above like an eagle. The encroaching army vanished in a swirl of black smoke, and I found myself overlooking a marshy swamp filled with twisted trees and murky water. Dusky-skinned Murk Elves clad in dark leathers and crudely stitched robes fashioned swords and fletched arrows ...

The scene exploded in a shower of light as a flock of the birdlike Accipiters cut through the air, banking hard right on outstretched wings before unleashing a volley of arrow fire on the invaders below ...

Then, the scene faded, shimmered, resolved: blond-haired Wodes forged armor, battle-axes, and heavy maces in a roaring furnace, the sound of steel hitting steel ringing out like a battle cry...

"But, in the far flung North, another threat looms," came the announcer's voice as the Wode encampment vanished, giving way to a domineering peak capped with icy white. "The reclusive, mountain-dwelling Svartalfar have unwittingly burrowed into the prison of a dusty and long forgotten god. A monstrous being of true dark, eager to return to the land of mortals once more. The breach is small, but large enough for Serth-Rog, Daemon Prince of Morsheim, to call acolytes to his cause... Imperial. Rebel. Light. Dark. Living. Dead. Which side will you choose?"

The towering mountain erupted in a swirl of opalescent light and violent motion, wind beating against me with gale-force fury as I fell. Tumbled, end over end, arms wheeling, legs kicking, stomach rising into my throat. *This shouldn't be happening*, I told myself. *I shouldn't feel this way.* But the logic didn't do much to ease the fluttering in my belly. I flipped once more and caught a set of burning eyes, green and deeply malevolent, watching my meteoric descent with amusement —

I smacked against cold stone with a thud, pain shooting from my back, elbows, and skull. Man, the Devs had taken this whole *realism* angle very seriously. Maybe a little *too* seriously. My head began to pound with a dull throb, and I restlessly ran my hands over my stomach, impulsively searching for broken ribs. When I was finally satisfied that nothing was irreparably damaged, I pushed myself up and leaned back onto my elbows. I blinked sporadically, squinting against the dark, trying to figure out where exactly I was. What had happened.

The lighting was terrible—gloomy and provided by sparse, sooty firelight—but after a few minutes, everything took on a ghostly blue tinge.

Racial Ability Unlocked: Night Eye

Night Eye allows you to see even in the poorest of lighting conditions, casting the world into a blue haze. Hvitalfar (Dawn Elves), Dokkalfar (Murk Elves), and Svartalfar (Dwarves) automatically use Night Eye in dark environments.

Ability Type/Level: Racial, Passive / Level 1

Effect: 8% vision improvement at night or in poor lighting.

I read over the gained skill and smiled. That was a nice little bonus they hadn't mentioned during character creation. I dismissed the alert with a nod, and resumed my scan. The ground was gritty stone, and I immediately noticed thick steel bars around me—I was in a cage. A shoddy prison cell. I gained my feet, dropped into a crouch, and stole forward, searching for the door. It didn't take me long to find the exit, but it also didn't take long to find the thick iron lock, which refused to budge an inch when I yanked at it.

Well, this didn't seem like a good way to start things off.

I let the lock go and pressed my face against the bars, searching for an NPC—non-player character—or any sign of what I was supposed to do. I was in a rectangular chamber in some sort of underground cavern; formidable stalactites and stalagmites jutted from the ceiling and floor like the wicked teeth of a monstrous, slumbering beast. In the center of the room was a grisly scene that made me immediately rethink the wisdom in choosing Viridian Gate Online as my emergency life raft.

A rudimentary wooden table dominated the space, and strapped to that table were bodies. Pieces of bodies, in most cases. As an EMT, I'd seen a lot of awful scenes—high speed car wrecks were frequently stomach churning—but I still wasn't prepared for the graphic display. Amputated limbs. Strings of gray intestine. A glassy-eyed head, devoid of a body. There were also other tables littered with cruel-looking tools, hooks, pliers, knives, and clamps, plus a variety of machines and contraptions that didn't look friendly.

An open metal sarcophagus, outfitted with foot-long metal spikes, was particularly gruesome.

I swiped the back of my hand across my forehead, wiping away the cold sweat dotting my brow. I didn't know what they had planned for me here, but it couldn't be good. I immediately turned my attention back to the lock, holding it up and giving it a thorough examination. I thought about slamming it against the bars in hopes of breaking the thing, but quickly dismissed the notion. That wouldn't work, plus there was a good chance it would alert whoever was running this nightmare dungeon, and I wasn't keen to meet them.

Not as a newb, stuck in a cage, with no weapons, no armor, and no skills.

I turned back to my cramped cell, scurried over to a simple pallet of furs in the corner, and began to frantically search for a key or lockpick. The Devs wouldn't start you out in a cell if there wasn't a way out. There had to be something. I pulled aside a rough blanket and tossed the furs. Something metallic clinked against the floor. A glint of light revealed a piece of bent black metal. A makeshift prison shiv, maybe. Or a lockpick. Certainly not an elegant lockpick, but that had to be its purpose. I headed back over to the lock and slipped the thin length of metal into the keyhole.

I jiggled it around for a bit, pushing, prodding, rattling it this way and that. In most MMORPGs there was an auto-assist mechanism to help with the lock picking aspects of game play. I didn't get any kind of notification, however—no prompt telling me how the system worked—and I certainly didn't get an assist. After a few minutes of fruitless struggle, I pulled out the pick and slammed it against the ground in frustration. Then, I froze. The soft rustle of moving fabric caught my ear. I wasn't alone.

Someone, or something, was in the room with me.

FOUR

CUTTER

I SURVEYED THE MAIN CHAMBER AGAIN, BUT SAW NO one. Marching off to my right, though, were more heavy cages, identical to my own. I slipped the pick into a crude pocket on my trousers and crawled toward the source of the noise.

"Hello," I called out in a harsh whisper. "Is anyone there?"

A blurry shape materialized from the shadows two cages over.

A man, garbed in the same plain clothes I was in, was leaning against the bars, his arms folded, a faint grin lifting the corners of his lips. A human with the wiry build of a street brawler, short blond hair, and a strong jaw riddled with stubble. "It's harder than it looks," said the man. "Lock picking, I mean. People think they can just shove a spit of metal into a lock and *pop*"—he snapped slim fingers—"she opens right up." He shook his head.

"It takes skill. Finesse. You have to understand how the tumblers work. You have to *feel* the spring mechanism. Have to intuit the pin placement." He

31

paused, examining his fingernails. "If you're interested, I could walk you through the process, show you how to get that door open."

"Yeah," I replied. "And what would you want for that?"

"What would I want?" he asked, his face a portrait of shock. "What I want is to get out. You're a Dokkalfar, so I assume you see all that butchery on the table. I certainly don't want to end up like that."

I glanced at the table again, at the congealed blood and strewn body parts. "What are they doing here?" I asked, tearing my eyes away from the display.

"Not entirely sure," the man replied, shrugging one shoulder. "It's not good, whatever it is. There's some kind of dark priest running the show, an acolyte of *Serth-Rog*—at least that's what I've been able to glean through half-heard whispers. Not exactly a friendly, talkative sort, that fellow. All I know is he's experimenting on people.

"Trying to change them somehow. Sometimes, the change takes and he lets them go, other times ..." He trailed off, then waved a hand toward the table. "I'll tell you this, though. I don't want to undergo his experimenting. So, I could show you how to open that lock, in exchange for my freedom, or you could just toss me the shiv, I'll pop the lock on my cage, then come over and bust you out. Sound fair?"

"If I give you the pick," I said, "what's to stop you from just breaking free and leaving me here to rot?"

He sighed and rolled his eyes. "Obviously, there's nothing to stop me—except for the fact that we're both in an awful situation. I could do that, but at my core I'm a lover, not a fighter. Well, not a *fair* fighter, anyway, and it seems like we'd have a better chance escaping together than I would alone. I always say, why make an enemy when you can fashion a *tool* instead. Besides, worst-case scenario, I help you out, you distract the guards, and I slip away in the shadows and leave you for dead. You being free is a win all around for me."

I pulled the pick from my pocket and regarded it. As much as I didn't trust the shifty man in the cell, I didn't particularly feel like taking another run at the whole lock picking thing, even with instruction. I nodded, resolved, stuck my hand through the cell bars, and tossed him the pick. He snatched it from the air with practiced ease and immediately set to work on his cell door. He proved to have an awfully deft hand since the lock came away a second later—the guy made it look downright easy.

He pushed his door open, took a tentative look around to make sure no one was coming, then beelined for my cell, setting to work without a word. My lock came away even faster than his had.

I looked around my cell one last time, making sure there weren't any beginner items I was supposed to take. Nothing. "Thanks," I said, pushing my way to freedom. "I'm Jack, by the way. Grim Jack."

"Cutter," he said with a nod. "Now, how about we save the bonding thing for after we find a way out, eh? You can tell me your whole stupid life story over a pint of ale, friend, but until we make it to an inn, let's keep our minds focused on escape."

Cutter took the lead, dropping into a slight crouch and stealing across the rectangular chamber, giving the table at the center a wide berth. I followed behind, mimicking the man's posture and working to keep as quiet as possible. It was hard to do, though, what with my heart pounding like a drum.

There was a tunnel at the far side, a twisting thing that ran straight for a few feet before abruptly snaking right and out of view. Cutter halted at the tunnel entryway, putting up a hand, a gesture that told me to *stop*. To *wait*. He dropped to a knee and ran his finger over the floor, gaze flickering back and forth.

"What are you doing?" I asked, my curiosity getting the better of me.

"Traps," he muttered absentmindedly. "This seems like a good place to set a containment ward, but I'm not seeing anything." He stood and moved over to the wall, pressing himself against the stone. "I don't suppose you're the sneaky sort, are you?" he asked, glancing over his shoulder at me.

"If it means getting out of here in one piece, I'm absolutely the sneaky sort," I replied.

"Good, good," he said with a bob of his head. "Crouch a little." He bent his legs in demonstration. "And when you walk, move heel to toe, heel to toe— none of that tiptoeing nonsense. You want to evenly distribute your weight over your whole foot. Takes a little getting used to, but do it enough and it'll become second nature. Now, keep to the shadows, stay quiet, and walk Just. Like. Me." He turned and set off, ghosting forward on silent feet. As he moved the shadows almost seemed to reach out to him, to embrace him, blurring the sharp lines of his body, rendering him fuzzy, indistinct.

I followed, practicing the odd walk as I slipped along behind him. A prompt appeared a second later:

<<<>>>

Skill: Stealth

Stealth allows you to creep through the shadows, making you harder to detect by hostile forces. Successful attacks from stealth mode activate a backstab multiplier for additional damage.

Skill Type/Level: Active / Level 1

Cost: 10 Stamina

Effect: Stealth 7% chance to hide from enemies.

Nice. Even if I didn't end up playing as a Rogue class, Stealth was always a useful skill to have, especially at lower levels. That backstab multiplier could level the playing field for a relatively weak starting character.

Cutter and I continued down the winding hallway, moving from one pool of inky shadow to another, avoiding the light from the flickering torches mounted at sporadic intervals. After a hundred yards or so the tunnel connected to a rough circular cavern with a pool of stagnant black water loitering at its middle. There were no torches here, but a soft crimson glow emanated from thousands of rough crystals lining the vaulted ceiling above.

The chamber looked to be some sort of central hub. Two sizeable hallways, each constructed of smooth sandstone bricks, connected here.

Cutter tentatively crept out toward the water, but stopped as the sound of heavy footfalls drifted into the room—coming from the sandstone tunnel dead ahead.

FIVE

MERCY

CUTTER GLANCED BACK AT ME, EYES WIDE, AND jerked his head toward a narrow gash in the rock wall on our right. Both of us sprinted for the tight crevice, slipping in between the rocks, then went still as a group of *somethings* strutted into the room. As they drew closer, a caption appeared above their heads: [Lesser Fiend]. They were hulking creatures, eight feet tall, with blue, pebbled skin, wearing long shirts of black chainmail. Each clutched a deadly weapon—some held towering halberds, while others carried wicked flails— in claw-tipped hands. The creatures walked upright, but had inverted knees and cloven hooves, which *clack-clack-clacked* against the stone.

I counted six of the things—way too many for us to fight.

The lead creature paused as it entered the room, barking a harsh command in some unintelligible language, then raised a wolf-like muzzle, its black nose sniffing. Sampling the air. Sensing our presence. I held my breath, afraid the slightest motion might give us away. After what felt like a lifetime, though, the creature lowered its snout and shrugged beefy shoulders, *false alarm*, then led the rest of his squad down the other sandstone hallway, vanishing from view. I let out a ragged sigh of relief and wanted to fall over and call it quits.

This game was intense. Too intense. Being in here was less like playing an RPG and more like going to a haunted house—sure you knew the monsters weren't real, but that didn't stop them from scaring the crap out of you. Not to mention, in here the horror-house monsters could not only scare you, they could attack you and, more importantly, *hurt* you. "Ready to move," I whispered, turning toward Cutter. He was behind me, but I immediately noticed something behind him: the rough outline of a hidden door set into the wall.

A new alert appeared, and the outline of the door began to glow faintly purple.

Ability: Keen-Sight

A passive ability allowing the observant adventurer to notice items and clues others might not see.

Ability Type/Level: Passive / Level 1

Cost: None

Effect: Chance to notice and identify hidden object increased by 6%.

I rubbed a hand over my jaw in thought, feeling the unfamiliar bite of facial hair. I'd always wanted a beard in real life, but I'd never been able to grow one. At least not a good one—it always came in uneven and patchy. I dismissed the stray thought and reread the notification. Keen-Sight. Hmm, that seemed like a handy passive ability to have in my back pocket, though I had to imagine most players probably acquired this skill, since it wasn't tied to race and it was awfully easy to come by.

At this point, though, I'd take any freebies I could get.

"Door," I said, pointing to the wall behind the Thief.

"Good eye," Cutter said with an approving nod. "In my experience, someone doesn't go through the trouble of installing a hidden door unless there's something *worth* hiding. Let's take a little look, eh?" He moved forward, hands outthrust. He lightly ran his fingers over the surface of the stone, gently probing. Exploring the nooks and crannies, carefully feeling out every dip in the wall. "Ah, there she is," he said with satisfaction as the door *clicked* and retracted, pulling back, sliding into the wall. The room beyond was some sort of lab—a variety of long shelves sat against the wall, heavy-laden with various test tubes and glass vials.

I put them from mind, focusing instead on the corpse of a haggard old Murk Elf strapped to yet another wooden experimentation table.

She was rail thin, nearly naked, and all sharp, protruding bone. Her grayish skin looked as worn and frail as cheap toilet paper. She had several long scars crisscrossing her belly and arms, which had been crudely stitched up. Poor old gal. Cutter immediately rushed into the room, slinking around, presumably searching for traps, while I headed over to the body. I knew she was just an NPC—more likely a part of the scenery than anything else—but part of me felt like I should find something to cover her with so she'd have a little dignity in death.

Instantly, I recoiled when her chest rose and fell; a rattling gasp escaped from her throat like the rustle of wind through barren trees. I shivered at the awful sound, and the EMT in me immediately began chattering away, demanding I check for vitals and start CPR.

"Cutter—this lady is alive," I said. "She's alive, we should do something. Help her."

The Rogue turned from his thorough search, giving the woman a quick once-over followed by a sniff and a sneer. "There's nothing to do for her. She's one stiff breeze away from keeling over as is. And even if we could help her, why would we? She's not going to bring anything to the table. She's going to be a liability to our survival and escape. If she's not an asset, she's as worthless as a wingless bird."

"What?" I asked, appalled. What kind of guy was I dealing with here? "Okay one, maybe if we help her she could tell us something—like what they're doing here. And two, even if she can't help us, we can't just leave her here to die. To suffer more. That's cruel. We need to help her. It's just the decent thing to do."

Cutter stopped, frowned, then came over and placed a hand on my shoulder. "Listen, you seem like an alright bloke, so I'm gonna level with you. Eldgard's a hard, cruel world, friend. Kindness won't get you far here, I'm afraid. That's a lesson you best learn now if you hope to survive here. To *thrive* here. If you really want to help her, kill her. Put her out of her misery. Then, once you're done with that, cut her scalp off and stick it in your bag. She's a Maa-Tál—a Murk-Shaman. The Viridians pay well for Maa-Tál. Her scalp will fetch you a gold piece, I'd wager, which is nothing to scoff at. Easy money as far as I'm concerned."

"What? No. That's awful," I replied. "Seriously. Terrible. And I thought you were a Wode?" I asked, eyeing his pale skin and blond hair.

"I am," he replied, a confused look flashing across his face. "What's that got to do with anything?"

"I thought the Wodes and the Murk Elves were supposed to be in some sort of alliance against the Viridian Empire."

"Pffh." He rolled his eyes. "Sure. The rebellion. But here's another life lesson about Eldgard: you need to look out for you. The rebellion is for the feebleminded and the easily manipulated. For suckers. Me? I'm only worried about my coin purse, and that there"—he hooked a thumb toward the withered, half-dead woman—"looks like a gold piece to me. End of story."

I shook my head. "I'm not like you, I guess. I can't just leave her here like that."

"Fine." He waved his hand dismissively. "If you really feel *compelled* to help, check your inventory—which you can access by saying or thinking *inventory*—while I finish searching the room." He paused, gaze distant. "There has to be something in here besides this old bag. Has to be."

He turned away and resumed his quest.

Inventory, I thought, and a semitranslucent interface screen appeared. Aside from the extraordinary graphics on display, the system was remarkably similar to other MMORPGs I'd played.

A lifelike image of myself as a Murk Elf floated off to the left, slowly rotating, showing off my gear, which was *extremely* basic at this point. On the right was my inventory bag, displaying the items currently in my possession. The inventory wasn't a slot system like in some games; rather, it looked like I could carry as many items as I wanted, so long as I didn't exceed my maximum carrying capacity, which was displayed in the upper right-hand corner of my screen.

I didn't have much to my name, though. Rough tunic (shoddy); rough trousers (shoddy); worn fur boots (shoddy). I did have a few copper coins, though, and I also had one minor restoration potion—worth a whopping 12 silver pieces. I wasn't sure how far 12 silver pieces would go in this game, but I imagined for a lowbie it was probably a hefty price tag. Maybe Cutter was right. Maybe I should put the old lady out of her misery, then collect her scalp and the bounty that came with it.

Put myself first.

That was the smart thing to do. The practical thing to do.

I only hesitated for a moment. I pulled out the potion, popped the cap, and poured the luminescent red liquid into the woman's slack mouth.

Maybe I was being a sucker, wasting my time and money, but I couldn't bring myself to murder and scalp an old lady. Call me superstitious, but that seems like a good way to get irrevocably cursed. Plus, what kind of person would do that? A guy like Cutter, I guess. A Thief or Assassin. And though this *was* technically a game, this was also far more than a game—this was my life now, and I didn't want to start my new life as a killer.

The potion emptied quickly, but for a long spell, nothing happened. She just lay there, unmoving. Just when I was about to give up hope, she gasped in pain, her back arching as her arms thrashed and hammered against the table. It was like watching *The Exorcist* in real time.

SIX

QUEST ALERT

I LURCHED BACK AS THE WRINKLED MURK ELF SHOT up, her eyes wild, her back straight as a board. She stayed that way only for a moment before toppling back to the crude wooden table with a *thud*. She didn't look good—the healing potion certainly hadn't cured all her ails—but she was alert now and her breathing sounded cleaner, easier, less forced. She stared at the ceiling for a long time, her lips flickering open and closed, as though she were talking or maybe praying, but no words came out.

"Good job," Cutter said, his words radiating sarcasm. "I think she's worse now. You broke her. On the plus side," he said with a grin, "look at this." He smacked an unadorned section of wall with a curled fist, and the stone clicked and disappeared with a shimmer of light. A secret compartment guarded by an illusion. "A secret room is one thing, but a secret room *inside* of another secret room is something else entirely. And it means one thing. Loot."

"You go check it out," I said absentmindedly, waving him on. "Bring back what you find. I need to figure out what I can do for her."

Cutter stared at me, eyes narrowed, forehead creased, head cocked to one side. "Obviously there's something wrong with you. I said there's loot. Free stuff. Like weapons, armor, gold, jewels—the things that help you to not die. But you're going to let me, an obviously dishonest thief, go poke through the goodies on the honor system?"

Cutter was right—I was being a moron—but I still edged closer to the semi-lucid woman. "You do what you need to do, Cutter. This is what I need to do."

He shrugged and muttered a halfhearted "have it your way, idiot," before disappearing into the secret room. Vanishing from sight.

I placed a hand on the woman's neck, checking for her pulse. It was there, but reedy and erratic—always a bad sign. "Can you hear me?" I asked, reaching up and gently slapping at her cheek. "Hello, can you hear me?"

She sputtered for a moment longer, then turned her head, fixing me with rheumy, clouded eyes. "You stopped for me," she said breathlessly. "Why? This is a bad place. An evil place. Why risk your escape, your survival, for an old woman?"

"Well …" I stumbled, caught off guard. I wrestled to come up with a good answer, but there wasn't one. At least not a logical one. "Because I couldn't just walk by," I finally finished weakly. "It seemed like the right thing to do, I guess."

She regarded me, her cataract-covered eyes boring in, holding me firmly in their steely grip. The strange spell was broken as she fell into a fit of violent coughing, her body tensing as frothy blood dribbled from between her pale lips. "Very well," she said as the coughing fit subsided. "Regardless of your reasons, I thank you for your generosity, traveler. I fear your efforts are too late for me. The black priest of Serth-Rog has been thorough in his work, and I won't leave this place. Not alive. Perhaps, though, you would do an old woman a final mercy?"

She reached a shaky, arthritic hand toward her throat and pulled out a leather-corded necklace from beneath her stained and tattered shirt. A strange bronze talisman the size of a quarter hung from the end of the necklace. The coin burned with a subtle, shadowy light— emanating from the image of a raven gouged into the metal. "Please help me," she said with a grimace as she worked to sit. "Help me get it off."

As gently as I could, I used one hand to lift her and the other to slide the leather strap over her head, ruffling brittle hair. I dropped the necklace into her wrinkled palm.

"This"—she held up a shaky hand, the talisman dangling from the leather strap—"is a sacred artifact of my people. The mark of a Maa-Tál. Please return it to the chief of my clan, Kolle of the Ak-Hani. Of all the six named tribes, my people are the wariest of outsiders, but you are one of us—even if you are of the Lost Tribe— and with my talisman around your neck ... well, they will spare you." Despite her reassurance, she didn't actually sound all that sure they *would* spare me. "Take them the talisman and tell them what you saw here. What the black priests of Serth-Rog are doing. What they did to me."

"I'd be happy to let them know," I replied, "but I don't have a clue what they're doing here. Can you tell me anything that might help? Why these people captured me? What they want? Why they're doing these awful experiments?"

She smiled sadly, her eyes fluttering closed, her breathing labored again. She shook her head, the effort clearly a terrible strain. I bent over and urgently checked for a pulse again. I found it—barely there and fading fast.

"In truth," she wheezed, visibly fighting to open her eyes, "I cannot say what designs Serth-Rog has, because I do not know. But his intentions are truly insidious, this much is plain. Perhaps, if my people know about this place, about the experiments, they will be able to discover Serth-Rog's purpose. Put an end to the abominations being committed against all the people of Eldgard. Please, do this for me. Take the talisman." She thrust it toward me, the metal coin bobbing from the tremor in her hand. A prompt followed:

Quest Alert: Plight of the Maa-Tál

Help a dying Murk Elf Shaman by delivering her sacred talisman to Chief Kolle of the Ak-Hani clan in the Storme Marshes. Deliver the news concerning the shaman's untimely fate as well as the experiments of the black priests of Serth-Rog.

Quest Class: Rare, Class-Based

Quest Difficulty: Moderate

Success: Deliver the Talisman and survive Chief Kolle

Failure: Fail to deliver the Talisman or be killed by Chief Kolle

Reward: Class Change; Unique, Scalable Item; 15,000 EXP

Accept: Yes/No?

My jaw almost hit the floor. This was one heck of a quest for a level one player to get fresh out of the gate. In most MMOs I'd previously played, the only quests you got early on were common, generic quests that revolved around killing rats, running pointless errands, or gathering asinine amounts of ingredients for various NPCs. And the rewards for those quests were just as generic and boring. Marginal experience bumps, some common items, and access to other, slightly harder quests.

The quest the old Murk Elf had offered me was an absolute home run compared to the normal lot. I accepted immediately and grabbed the talisman from the woman's outstretched hand.

"Thank you," she murmured, smacking her lips, working moisture into the dry skin. I selected the talisman and saw it offered a few bonuses: +5 to Spirit, +1% Spirit Regeneration, +5% to Shadow-Based Skills. I wasn't sure what Shadow-Based skills were at this point, but I knew this amulet was bound to be better than any of the loot Cutter was turning up in the back room—certainly worth more than a gold mark, which is what I would've received for killing the Murk Shaman.

I felt a flash of hot joy—my act of kindness had already paid major dividends.

"My time is short," the old woman rasped, blinking her eyes open, complete exhaustion evident in every line of her frail body. "But let me offer you one more parting gift—a final thanks for your mercy. Within you, boy, is the Shadow-Spark."

Her hand lashed out, uncannily quick, and latched onto my arm. "I'll awaken it inside of you." Her fingers pressed down into my skin like drill bits, her flesh growing cool, then downright cold. Arctic, even. Icy power soaked through my skin, into my bones, and spread through my body like wildfire. Running along my nerve endings, my body shivering, my teeth clattering in response.

SEVEN

LOOT

THE CHILLY ENERGY GREW PAINFUL, AND MY FLESH cried out in protest as my head began to ache, to pound. Then, in a flash, the hurt was gone, snatching the bone-searing cold with it. The woman's hand dropped away, her muscles slack, her face lifeless, her eyes clouded with death. I glanced down—on my forearm was a black handprint, branded directly onto my skin like a tattoo. Another new notification popped up, drawing my gaze away from my burned flesh:

Ability: Shadow-Spark

Only a handful of Eldgard's natives possess the inborn Shadow-Spark needed to harness the ancient power of the *Umbra.* Fewer still have that inborn talent unlocked. With Shadow-Spark unlocked, you now have the ability to draw on the Umbra and learn a restricted class of Shadow-based skills.

Ability Type/Level: Passive / Level 1

Cost: None

Effect: Umbra unlocked. All Shadow-based skill stats are increased by 3% per Shadow-Spark level.

I read and reread the notification, then dismissed the screen and pulled up the in-game wiki. This couldn't be normal, could it? I quickly scoured logs and forums, rapidly scanning heading after heading, but so far the information available was severely limited. Not totally surprising, since the game had only been online for a handful of days, and the material world was also on the edge of an extinction-level event. Plus, I had a sneaking suspicion that Osmark Technologies might be suppressing info in a bid to prevent metagamers from taking an unhealthy advantage of the apocalyptic situation.

The scrape of boots over stone floated in from the secret room, and I immediately dismissed the notification before quickly slipping the woman's talisman around my neck, tucking it beneath the rough fabric of my simple tunic. As helpful as Cutter had been so far, he seemed like the type of person that'd knife me in the back if he thought it would benefit him. He strode out of the narrow opening a minute later, a big grin splitting his face. A wooden shield lay across his forearms, and piled on top were weapons and gear.

He scooted through the doorway and set the precariously balanced pile of loot on a nearby worktable, then let out a groan of relief. He turned, his eyes tracing over the body of the dead woman. "Didn't work out so well, eh?" he said with a nod to the Murk Elf. "I tried to tell you, kindness is a surefire path to being destitute and dead. But cheer up, friend." He turned and swept out an arm toward the pile with a flourish. "Maybe your venture in altruism turned out to be an utter pile of rubbish, but I hit pay dirt. Almost didn't find this stuff. Someone stored it in a chest behind a false wall, but I am *damned* good at what I do.

"Now obviously," he continued, regarding me through squinted eyes, "I'm not going to let you claim everything, what with you being a do-gooder dupe, but I'll let you select a weapon and some armor."

"Gee, how generous of you," I replied offhandedly, heading over to the pile.

"Think nothing of it," he said with a sniff. "Literally. In truth, I'm not doing it to be generous. If you're equipped, there's a better chance you'll make it out alive, which means there's a better chance *I'll* make it out alive." He tapped at his temple. "Remember, I'm always thinking of number one."

I grunted noncommittally, otherwise ignoring him, and accessed the gear pile, which immediately brought up my inventory screen on the right and a list of lootable items on the left.

The pile of gear on the table looked deceptively small, especially considering the gigantic number and range of items I could choose from. There was something for just about everyone: bows and arrows, blunt-headed maces and spiked flails, swords and daggers in an assortment of flavors, plus armor. Everything from fur-lined leathers to rusted scale mail. None of it was good, just the crude junk beginners usually got, but it was better than running around weaponless and in tattered linens.

"We don't have all day," Cutter said, folding his arms. "Those guards are gonna come back, and it'd be best if we were equipped and long gone by then. Personally, I'd suggest a pair of daggers and some light leather armor. The very best for sneaking and backstabbing, but that's just me. Which is to say, someone who is smart, capable, and much better looking than you. But you pick whatever you want, friend. You do you, as I always say."

I regarded the weapons for another second.

True, light armor and daggers would be great for a thief, but the more time I spent with Cutter, the less I thought I'd enjoy his profession. Besides, the idea of taking on one of those massive halberd-wielding [Lesser Fiends] with the equivalent of a kitchen knife wasn't comforting. My hand hovered over a single-handed bastard sword; the sword was *the* epic-fantasy weapon. The weapon of heroes. Of knights and warriors. I didn't know much about Viridian Gate Online, but I *knew* there'd be some awfully cool swords later on in the game.

Guaranteed.

I frowned and finally decided against it—swords took skill to use, and that was something I didn't have. Instead, I picked up a one-handed warhammer with a meaty, blunt face on one side and a cruel spike on the other. The warhammer looked brutal and rather straightforward: smash the blunt end into someone's skull. Not much skill involved in that.

Exactly my speed.

Next, I selected a simple wooden buckler the size of a large pizza, which slipped over my left forearm with leather straps. Not much of a defense, really, but if one of those guards came swinging for me, I wanted something to shelter behind. For a heartbeat, I considering picking the heavy armor for the same reason—better protection in case I got hit—but eventually opted for light brigandine armor with a pair of worn leather boots and a shoddy black cloak. So far, the Stealth ability seemed pretty beneficial, plus in light armor I'd have a much better chance of outmaneuvering and outrunning a big, lumbering opponent in battle.

I certainly wasn't above running if that's what it came down to.

Cutter looked at me quizzically, gaze flickering between the light leather armor and the heavy warhammer and shield. "Yep. You're an odd one, alright," he declared. "First that thing with the old woman, now this. Are you sure I can't talk you into something…" He trailed off, lips pressing into a tight, judgmental line. "A little more practical?"

"I'm good," I said, equipping the items in my inventory screen. "Now let's move. I want some answers, and I want to get out of this nightmare factory."

"Fine." He shrugged and ambled over to the table, retrieving the rest of the gear, then donned leather armor similar to mine. "But if you die horribly, don't say I didn't try to warn you."

We both dropped into Stealth and headed out of the secret room, pausing momentarily at the entrance to the circular room with the large pool of water at its center. Once we were certain there wasn't a guard patrol in the immediate vicinity, we stole forward, clinging to the shadows and hugging the wall, which turned out to be a smart move. As we neared one of the two sandstone hallways leading away, a fat black tentacle, studded with barbed hooks, broke the surface with a ripple, before dropping back into the black waters.

Cutter and I moved just a skosh quicker after that.

We took turn after winding turn—stopping twice to hide from roving patrols—and eventually found ourselves crouched in the entryway of a rectangular room. On the far side was an exit. Probably. I couldn't be sure without getting closer, but I'd played enough MMORPGs to know a freestanding portal shimmering with cerulean light had to be important. Unfortunately, the room between me and freedom looked to be a guard barracks. Massive beds of wood and straw lined both walls with crudely made footlockers waiting at the end of each.

Worse, the room was occupied.

EIGHT

BRAWL

A TRIO OF GUARDS–LESSER FIENDS IDENTICAL to the menacing goat-hoofed creatures we'd seen on patrol several times—milled about. Two sported heavy mail shirts and held beefy poleaxes topped with wicked, curved axe heads, which looked equally well suited for blocking an incoming blade or goring an enemy, spilling ropes of intestine to the ground. I blanched at the thought of going up against those monsters, even if this was only a game. The third guard lingered in the back, near the portal. Instead of mail, this one wore rough-stitched robes, a deep cowl drawn up around its inhuman visage. It held a short bronze dagger in one hand and a gnarled staff in the other.

A spellcaster of one variety or other, then.

As formidable as the two poleaxe-wielding creatures looked, I knew the sorcerer in the back was the biggest threat. If we could get to him, he'd probably go down quickly, but at a distance he'd lay down some serious firepower. Maybe literally, if he had access to any flame skills.

"Ready for a brawl?" Cutter whispered, his mouth inches from my ear.

"Can't we just sneak around them or something?" I asked, quiet as I could manage.

He squinted and rubbed at his chin. "Naw. We need to take this lot. No way around it. So how do you want to play it?"

I stared at the scene. With the heavy beds lining the walls, it would be awfully tough to slip past the poleaxe sentries and take out the caster first … Unless, of course, I caused a distraction, opening the way for Cutter to make a move.

"This is what I think we should do," I said, leaning into him and outlining my plan. He nodded along in agreement, but a seed of worry bloomed in my chest as I spoke, my eyes unwaveringly fixed on the Lesser Fiends in the next room. I sort of liked Cutter, but I didn't trust him. Not even a little. My plan might work, but only if Cutter didn't leave me high and dry.

And he might leave me high and dry. He'd said as much earlier on.

I stamped down that doubt, because really there was no other way. He would come through for me or he wouldn't. And if he didn't … Well, I guess I'd find out what dying in Viridian Gate Online was like. "Sound like a plan?" I finally finished, an edge of uncertainty in my voice.

He nodded, slipped a long black-bladed dagger from a sheath at his waist, then shot me a wink as he crept forward, disappearing after he was a few feet away. I had to admit, that Stealth ability was pretty incredible. Because he was a friendly, a ghostly blue glow outlined his moving form, showing me his location, but that was all I saw. He angled right and padded in as close as he could get to the guards, before slipping between a pair of heavy beds and shifting into a low crouch. Ready. Waiting.

I took a deep, shuddering breath, readjusted my grip on the warhammer, then stole into the room, likewise cloaked in Stealth. I inched closer to the guards, step by stressful step, whispering a silent prayer that this all went well. I was about four feet from the nearest guard when I saw the blurred form of Cutter stand—there was a subtle flash of movement, followed by the resounding clang of metal on stone. Both of the hulking, mail-clad figures before me turned to investigate—only to find a cheap knife lying in the center of the room.

Sleight of hand at its finest.

I leapt forward while both guards had their backs turned, lashing out with the hammer, aiming right for the side of a misshapen skull. The heavy face of my weapon slammed into an unprotected temple, clipping the guard on the right with a sickening *crack*. I'd played a little baseball back in high school and that *crack* sounded just like a Louisville slugger slamming into a well-placed fastball.

The Lesser Fiend staggered left, a harsh bark escaping its throat as it dropped its poleaxe and groped at its head—trying to stem the sudden flood of rancid black blood. It looked badly wounded, but it wasn't dead, which is what I'd been hoping for. I raised the hammer again, preparing for an adrenaline-fueled follow-up strike—only to have a stupid notification flash in front of me, obscuring my field of view:

Skill: Backstab

Those who rely on the backstab skill know fighting *fair* is highly overrated. Dead is dead, and a blade from the shadows is often far more effective than a sword blow to a well-prepared opponent.

Skill Type/Level: Active / Level 1

Cost: 20 Stamina

Effect: A brutal backstab attack can be activated while an adventurer is in Stealth. 5x normal damage with a knife; 3x normal damage with all other weapons.

Effect 2: 5% increased chance of critical hit while backstabbing.

I glanced at the screen and dismissed the notice in a second, but a lot can happen in a second. When the notification finally disappeared, it was immediately replaced with the sight of an incoming axe blade heading straight for my face. The first guard was still reeling from my surprise attack, but the second one was all over me. With a squawk, I dropped below the incoming weapon, the blade whipping over me with a *whoosh* of displaced air. I felt frantic, panicked, but I knew I couldn't afford to hesitate.

So instead of simply turning tail and running, I darted in, swinging my hammer.

Somehow, my weapon had twisted in my grip, and the railroad spike of metal on the opposite side slammed into the creature's unarmored knee. Not what I'd been planning, but the move was viciously effective. Bone snapped, blood spurted, and the horned guard dropped with a howl. The wooden shaft of its poleaxe caught me across the forehead, followed by a flare of pain, but I managed to scramble away before the fiend could get me with the bladed bit. Without thinking, I pulled my hammer free and brought it whirling around in a devastating arc.

Busted-Knee collapsed as I caved its head in; the Lesser Fiend dropped fully to the ground with a wet thud. Dead. Of course, yet another notification filled my vision.

x2 Level Up!

You have (10) undistributed stat points

You have (2) unassigned proficiency points

This one I dismissed without a second look. "Deactivate notifications during combat!" I shouted into the air.

"Alert," came Sophia's ever-familiar voice inside my head, "notifications have been deactivated during combat."

"Down," Cutter shouted, bringing my attention firmly back to the present.

I looked up just in time to see Cutter sink his black-edged weapon into the back of the spellcaster near the portal. Unfortunately, he didn't do it before said spellcaster unleashed a roaring column of flame my way. I threw my body left, flopping gracelessly onto my side, narrowly avoiding the blast of raw power, which blanketed my skin with unpleasant heat. I landed at the hooves of the still-staggering guard I'd clocked with my stealth-attack blow. Its pointed ears quivered in manic motion as it turned its muddy gaze to me, confusion evident on its blood-splattered face.

I tried to roll left, away from its hooved feet, but I wasn't quick enough.

This isn't gonna be fun, I thought as a cloven foot crashed down into my belly, connecting with the force of a car crash. A dull pain exploded in my ribs and radiated into my chest and lungs, making it hard to breathe, hard to think—the sheer intensity of the sensation was almost blinding. A red-tinged bar materialized in the upper right corner of my vision. On top of being horrendously painful, that nauseating stomp had also cost me a quarter of my available hit points.

The guard raised its foot, ready to curb-stomp me again—

I acted without hesitation, my survival instinct kicking in. I swung my hammer upward, throwing every bit of strength I could muster into the blow. The blunt face of my weapon collided painfully with the Lesser Fiend's tender bits, assuming it had tender bits, which had to hurt worse than stumbling face-first into a hornet's nest. Predictably, the creature lurched, stumbled, lost its footing, and toppled forward as it groped its nether bits.

Unfortunately, it landed right on top of me.

The mail-wearing fiend hit me like a rockslide, its immense weight crushing my chest, its rank stink—a combination of old meat and wet dog—filling up my nostrils. I struggled to fight back, flinching away from its teeth-filled jaws, but quickly realized it was already dead. All hail the cheap shot. Still, even dead, the creep weighed about half a ton, and struggle as I might, I couldn't get the corpse off of me. My health bar flashed again—my hit points were now down by more than 50% and dropping by the second.

This thing was literally going to crush me to death.

"Hold on, Grim Jack," came Cutter's voice as I strained against the corpse, working to flip it off. My health was still falling rapidly and I felt light-headed, probably because I couldn't breathe. Cutter's face flashed into view a second later, and then the weight on top of me shifted. Cutter grunted and cursed as he worked. "Am I the only one doing anything here? How's about you push, princess," he grunted. I gritted my teeth as black crept into my vision and threw everything I had left at the beefy body. Finally, slowly, the creature slipped to one side, and suddenly I could breathe again.

NINE

ROWANHEATH

THE INRUSH OF AIR WAS FOUL WITH DEATH, metallic blood, and old sweat, but I greedily pulled in great lungfuls. The corpse still pinned my legs to the floor, but after a few more seconds of wriggling, I managed to free myself and gain my feet. My health bar was at a quarter now and flashing a brilliant red—*warning, warning, warning* it seemed to scream—but at least its meteoric descent had halted. In fact, it actually looked to be replenishing. Replenishing at the pace of a snail stuck in frozen molasses, but replenishing.

"Thanks," I said to Cutter, nodding at the blood-covered Lesser Fiend.

"Welcome," he said curtly, then planted a kick into the corpse's ribs. "No good, heavy bastard. These things don't even have the good grace to die without causing trouble. Arseholes all the way to the end. All things considered, though"—he glanced around, a smug grin on his face—"we did pretty good. Nice work with the distraction. That spellcaster didn't see me until I slipped a blade into his kidney. Now, best we loot this room and move on before any more of these beasties turn up—

can't imagine we'll fare too well against five or six of 'em."

Cutter and I quickly broke apart, raiding the three bodies, then ransacking the footlockers at the end of each wood-framed bed.

I'm not sure what Cutter picked up—he was strangely covetous of loot, which seemed odd since I was still fairly certain he was an NPC—but I made out alright. I found a bunch of coins, 40 copper pieces and a handful of silver, plus a few low-quality gemstones. On top of that, I scrounged some crappy starting gear, which I could hopefully sell off to pad my wallet. Lastly, I scored a plain silver ring with a +1 Vitality stat from one of the chests and a rough-worn cloak with a 1% bonus to Stealth from the guard that'd nearly crushed me to death.

Those last two items, I equipped in an instant.

After pilfering what we could, Cutter and I mentally prepared ourselves for whatever threat might be on the other side of the shimmering portal, then jumped through, weapons at the ready. Part of me was expecting the portal to drop us off at the entrance to some new dungeon, full of new enemies we'd have to battle past. I was pleasantly surprised, however, when we ended up in a shallow cave, which exited onto the rocky slope of a forested mountain overlooking a walled city in a valley below.

And it *was* a city. Not some no-account, backwoods town, but a sprawling metropolis.

A broad river meandered through the valley; scattered farms and small wood-walled homes dotted the green landscape to either side. Beyond those rose a fortified stone wall—an enormous thing, which formed a giant horseshoe across the front of the city proper. The rest of the sprawling city sat in a natural valley formed by a series of treacherous mountain peaks, which effectively enclosed the place in a ring of formidable stone.

Looming high above the rest of the buildings, casting a long shadow over the homes and shops below, was a hulking fortress: all hard lines, gray stone, high walls, and domineering circular turrets carved directly into the mountain face itself. At a glance, the city seemed designed for practicality instead of extravagance. A stronghold built for defense. For war. There was nothing particularly beautiful or majestic about it, but there was a certain harsh beauty to everything.

"Thank the great gods above," Cutter barked, before giving a rough laugh.

"Good news?" I asked, stealing a sidelong glance at him.

"You'd better believe it, friend. Eldgard's a big place, after all. That portal could've dropped us anywhere. Maybe even someplace over in West Viridia. Yet, fortune smiles on us, because Rowanheath"—he swept a hand toward the sprawl of buildings—"is *my* home. She was a Freehold city until a couple of years ago when the Viridians finally breached the walls, but she's still a good place to be. One of the best. About as far from the Viridians' grubby mitts and *unreasonably* high taxes as you can get without ending up in the Storme Marshes or the Barren Sands." He clapped me on the shoulder, then gave another little laugh. "Staring at it won't get us there, friend. Let's get walking, eh?"

It was early evening by the time we finally made it past the outlying farms and through the main gate. It'd been a long march—easily four hours of hard walking, which spoke to the sheer expansiveness of the game world. I'd have to find a horse or some other kind of way to speed up travel; there had to be the medieval equivalent of a bus system. I was sure of it.

A mean-looking NPC guard, a [Legionary], sporting vaguely Roman-looking lorica armor—segmented, overlapping leather plates in dark reds and blacks—and a crested centurion helmet, stopped us at the gate. A few quick words for Cutter, followed by a suspicious monetary exchange, almost certainly a bribe, saw us past the looming gate and into Rowanheath.

From above, the city had appeared well organized and orderly, but up close, the place was a chaotic warren of twisting cobblestone streets and dirty alleys. Most of the buildings stood two or three stories tall and were built in a sporadic, haphazard fashion, many leaning drunkenly to one side. The place was a patchwork of homes and shops—some smooth stone, others rough wood, a few a pasty white plaster—which reflected a wide array of backgrounds. Rowanheath certainly wasn't like any other MMO city I'd ever been to. But despite the chaos, the clutter, and the slapdash clash of cultures, it felt brimming with life and possibility.

So incredibly *real*.

Cutter took off with a goofy grin plastered in place, his movements sure, confident, and comfortable. He was a man coming home after a long time away. I followed, weaving through a constant throng of foot traffic, mostly composed of burly Wodes in rough, fur-lined clothing and what I assumed were Viridians—men and women with olive skin and Mediterranean features, many wearing long robes trimmed in purple, red, or gold. But

I also caught the occasional glimpse of dusky-skinned Murk Elves, like myself, and a spattering of the other races I'd seen during the character creation process. The strangest thing, though, was that I couldn't tell which characters were players and which were NPCs.

Cutter led us down the main thoroughfare for a few minutes before slipping into a narrow alley, which connected to a smaller side street of dirt and gravel. We trudged on while hawkers cried their wares—meat pies, knives, skill training, potions, and just about everything else under the sun. For the most part, the vendors ignored us, instead focusing their attention on characters with gleaming, expensive-looking armor or the occasional robe-clad Viridians. With our cheap gear, Cutter and I probably didn't look worth the effort.

After a few more minutes, we hooked right, cutting through a claustrophobic cross-street, which dumped us onto a wider boulevard of paved stone worn from hard use. Carts lumbered along, drivers flicking crude whips at snorting horses or passersby that didn't move out of the way fast enough. Open storefronts adorned this section of city; there were tailors, weavers, apothecaries, grocers, fletchers, bakers, and blacksmiths. Wooden signs, decorated with pictures displaying each shop's purpose, hung above rough doorways.

An anvil and hammer on one, as though the resounding ring of metal on metal weren't enough. A pair of scissors and a bolt of fabric adorned another.

Cutter paused at the mouth of a shadowy alley, waiting with his arms crossed as a band of soldiers, attired like the Roman sentry at the gate, passed by, escorting a covered sedan chair. Cutter pulled me over and watched the little procession with a phony smile, bordering on a sneer, as the covered chair swayed and bobbed through a sea of grimy bodies. "Worthless, pompous Viridian bureaucrats," he grumbled under his breath. "Probably some braindead Quaestor, thinks he's better than everyone else." He bent over and spit onto the dusty street. "Only thing their kind is actually good at is raising taxes and putting on airs. Stuck-up pricks."

Despite Cutter's earlier assertion that he didn't care about the rebellion, there was obviously a great degree of animosity simmering under the surface. Maybe, buried somewhere deep, deep, deep down in Cutter's soul, there was a glimmer of human decency—a hope that he wasn't *quite* as selfish as he seemed on the surface. Or maybe he just really hated bureaucrats.

Once the procession turned a winding corner and disappeared from view, he grabbed my shoulder and dragged me into the alley, steering me toward an unmarked three-story building of plaster with a black door.

"Welcome to the Broken Dagger, friend."

TEN

THE BROKEN DAGGER

DESPITE BEING UNMARKED AND NOT HAVING A sign, the Broken Dagger was clearly some sort of tavern or inn. A very questionable one, filled with very questionable looking men and women. The interior was murky, thanks to the absence of windows, illuminated mostly by a roaring fire at the far right-hand side of the room. Blue-grey smoke drifted lazily around in great billowing clouds, and the smell of sweat, dirt, tobacco, and stale beer clung to everything. Rough, dirty patrons packed every bench and table—talking, laughing, gambling, drinking—while servers whisked through the crowds bringing full glasses and removing empty ones.

A fair-haired woman with the golden skin of the Hvitalfar, in a gown so sheer it left little to the imagination, sang some jaunty tune in a language I didn't know, accompanied by the sharp trill of a flute. Cutter draped an arm around my shoulders and dragged me through the muddled interior to a long wooden bar, presided over by an innkeeper with a balding head and a prodigious gut. Cutter shot the man a wink, but then guided me toward a whip-thin guy in black leathers, perched on a stool in front of a door leading to the back.

"Cutter, you sod," the leather-clad man exclaimed, slapping a hand against his thigh. "Thank the shadow— everyone thought you were dead. It's been weeks, man. Weeks. What happened?"

"Not dead," Cutter replied with an easy smile. "Who could possibly shuffle me off this mortal coil, eh? I'm far too good for that. Besides, the gods won't let me die— I'm too damned handsome to end up in a shallow grave where no one can see my pretty face. As to what actually happened … well, I'll need to see Gentleman Georgie about that. But my friend and I could use a few drinks first—maybe a bite to eat. But in a *private* room if you take my meaning." He nodded at the door behind the man.

"Sure, sure," the guy said, bobbing his head. "Not a problem. Georgie's out, though," he said with a dismissive sniff, "won't be back for a few days. Still, you and your friend are welcome back." He stood, pushed open the heavy wooden door, and ushered us through.

We headed into an unadorned hallway, then took a set of stairs down to a basement. My jaw nearly dropped when I saw what could only be a training facility. An expansive complex which featured a sparring area, complete with straw practice dummies, and a full archery range. But those weren't the only training areas: there was also a room off to the left near bursting with doors and chests, tons of them, lining the walls and littering the floor.

A handful of hooded men occupied the space, fiddling around, deep in concentration.

"Lock pick training," Cutter said, noticing where I was looking. "All the doors and chests have different levels of difficulty. Good practice for those who are interested. We have everything an aspiring thief or cutthroat might need here." He swaggered forward as he talked, leading us deeper into the training complex. "In the back, we've got a shadow room, designed for practicing Stealth abilities. We've got pickpocketing dummies. Heck, we even have our own blacksmith and a fleece who'll buy and sell stolen goods—for a markup, of course."

"Is this the thieves' guild?" I asked as we made for a wooden table in the corner, flanked by a pair of chairs.

"Naw," Cutter said with a grimace. "*Guild* is too official sounding. More like a thieves' union, really. Sort of a loose coalition of likeminded people. Everyone here is concerned with themselves first and foremost. With that being said, it's a cold, hard world out there, and we recognize there's a certain strength in numbers. So, from time to time, we work together for mutual benefit and survival. When it suits our individual goals, obviously."

"Obviously," I replied. "And who's this Gentleman Georgie you wanted to talk to?" I asked, plopping onto one of the chairs near the table.

"Well, we're definitely *not* a guild," Cutter said, "but *if* we were a guild—just supposing for a moment, understand—he'd be the head honcho. At least for Rowanheath. He owns the Broken Dagger, works out petty squabbles, bribes the guards, and takes care of city officials. That kind of thing. Generally, he keeps everything running smooth as a good pint of ale. And speaking of good ale—"

A haggard brunette with purple bags under her eyes stopped at our table bearing a thick platter filled with mugs and plates of food. She dropped them off without a word, then simply stood there, expectant, staring at us with one hand placed on a cocked hip. "Just put it on Georgie's tab," Cutter said, then made a little shooing gesture.

Her eyes narrowed into hard slits and her lips turned down in a scowl of disapproval.

A needle of guilt jabbed at me, so I reluctantly reached into my bag and removed a silver mark, which I passed into her hand with a polite smile. She took it, arched an eyebrow, then gave me a gap-toothed grin. "Need to toughen this one up, Cutter. Poor boy is softer than a newly hatched gosling. Thanks all the same, boy-o," she said, disappearing the coin with practiced ease, before shuffling back toward the kitchen.

Cutter regarded me solemnly for a second, then snorted and took a huge chomp of mutton chop. "Sucker," he muttered through a mouthful of pulped food. A slight blush crept into my cheeks. Instead of replying, though, I picked up a chunk of seared meat and regarded it suspiciously. The Broken Dagger wasn't a five-star restaurant by any stretch of the imagination, and I was a little worried the food might give me the VR version of dysentery.

But, as suspect as the meal looked, I was surprised to find I was hungry. Really hungry. Famished, actually. I'd expected there to be food in V.G.O.—most MMORPGs had that feature—but the hunger aspect was definitely a shock. With a grimace, I chomped down on the greasy meat and blinked in surprise as an explosion of flavor ran through my mouth.

Tangy, salty, rich.

Absolutely delicious.

Better than the best steak I'd ever eaten. I grabbed a pint of the copper-red ale the waitress had dropped off and took a big swig. I've never been much of a beer drinker, but the sweet, malty flavor with hints of honey tasted like a slice of alcoholic-heaven. A notification window popped up as I savored the food and drink:

Buffs Added

Mutton: Restore 75 HP over 21 seconds

Broken Dagger Mead: Restore 25 Stamina; Damage Stamina Regeneration 30 points over 60 seconds

Well-Fed: Base Constitution increased by (2) points; duration 20 minutes.

"Good, isn't it?" Cutter asked as he tore off a crusty chunk of bread, which he promptly used to wipe through a greasy smear of meat juice on his plate.

I nodded, mouth too full to speak. We ate in silence for a while, polishing off the heap of food and our ale.

"Now it's time to get down to our real business," Cutter said as he finished, pushed his plate away, slumped back, and issued an eye-watering belch. "I'm going to shoot straight with you, friend. You seem like a good sort—the kind of person I might be willing to vouch for, if you decided you want to join our informal club here." He absently gestured toward the training facility.

"There are lots of perks that come with membership. You get a class change for one, which means you gain access to the Thief Kit skill tree, with an option to specialize later. You also get lodging here at the Broken

Dagger whenever you need it, discounts on items, plus training, and access to class-specific quests." He paused, staring at me intently. "You interested?"

I mulled it over for a long while, but eventually shook my head. "I really appreciate the offer, Cutter, and I appreciate all you've done for me, but I just don't think this is a good fit for me."

He sighed, fingers restlessly tapping against the tabletop. "Can't say I'm surprised—I figured you were bound for a different path. Knew it the moment you helped that old Murk Elf instead of scalping her like any normal person would do. You're just too warm blooded for this line of work. Thought I'd offer, though, because you could be a great thief if you could get over that soft heart of yours."

He paused, rubbing at his chin while he seesawed his head left then right, left then right. "I still feel like I owe you," he finally said, "and I like to pay my debts. So, how's about I put you up in a room here for the week, and then, tomorrow morning, I'll train you up. Get you prepared for the big bad world out there, before sending you on your way. Sound alright?"

I couldn't argue with that.

Cutter led me back into the bustling tavern front— still rocking and rolling with folks—up a set of creaky wooden stairs, then to a cramped room. There was a twin bed, a nightstand, and a chipped porcelain washbasin with a pitcher of water on a nearby stool; not glamorous, exactly, but not much worse than my IRL apartment. Poverty lends perspective, I suppose. I headed in and dropped onto the bed with a sigh of exhaustion, and I found I really was tired. Weary all the way down to the bone as though I'd just worked a double shift then hit the gym for a couple of hours. As with the hunger, I hadn't expected this aspect to feel quite so real.

It was almost too lifelike.

"You need anything else?" Cutter asked, lingering at the door. "'Cause if not, I have a very concerned waitress, named Stephanie, who I need to see as soon as possible. Urgent business." He offered me a sly wink.

"Mind if I ask a personal question before you go?"

He shrugged, nodded. "No skin off my back one way or the other. Just make it quick—Stephanie won't wait forever."

For a long second I thought about asking him whether he was an NPC or an actual player. So far, he was the only person I'd had extended contact with since entering V.G.O., and I honestly couldn't tell if he was a part of the game. It was uncanny. Creepy. I'd played a lot of MMORPGs, but I'd never seen an NPC that could do what he did. I'd never seen an NPC that had his range of emotion or conversational prowess. I had IRL coworkers that seemed less human than Cutter.

"Never mind," I finally said with a shake of my head.

I wasn't sure how to ask the question without offending him, and part of me didn't really want to know the answer anyway. If Cutter was an NPC, that meant he was nothing more than a string of digits existing on some server somewhere. But in another couple of days my body was going to die, and if I survived the process, *I* was going to be nothing more than a string of digits existing on a server. So, what did that say about my future? If he wasn't real, did that mean in another couple of days, I wouldn't be real either?

That was a frightening thought I didn't much care to dwell on. Besides, I was simply too tired for an existential crisis.

"Alright," he said, tapping the doorframe, "well, you get some rest. I'll see you in the morning." He turned and pulled the door shut behind him with a soft *thud*.

Alone at last, I kicked off my leather boots and lay back on the mattress, which was surprisingly comfortable despite the fact that it *looked* to be made of straw. If I didn't know any better, I'd say the bed was actually memory foam, regardless of its physical appearance. I knew I needed sleep, but first I needed a distraction from my thoughts. This was the first real break I'd had since entering the game, so it seemed like an appropriate time to check out my character stats and see if I'd missed any other updates since I'd turned notifications off during combat.

With a thought, I pulled up my character menu, then toggled from my inventory to my main menu. A semitranslucent, vertical options menu popped up in the right side of my vision: Inventory, Spellcraft, Skills, Class Abilities, Character, Party, Quests, Map, Message Log, Notifications, Achievements, Auction House. I whistled softly. That was a lot of content to explore. Assuming I survived the integration process, though, I'd have a lot of time to delve into those other features. What I really wanted to see, however, was my character stats, so I selected "Character" from the menu. An extensive table immediately popped up:

J. A. Hunter

V.G.O. Character Overview					
Name:	Jack	Race:	Dokkalfar	Gender:	Male
Level:	3	Class:	Unassigned	Alignment:	Unassigned
Renown:	0	Carry Capacity:	260	Undistributed Attribute Points:	10

Health:	140	Spirit:	180	Stamina:	130
H-Regen/sec:	1.15	S-Regen/sec:	2.25	S-Regen/sec:	1.43

Attributes:		Offense:		Defense:	
Strength:	10	Base Melee Weapon Damage:	10	Base Armor:	13
Vitality:	11	Base Ranged Weapon Damage:	0	Armor Rating:	21
Constitution:	10	Attack Strength (AS):	19	Block Amount:	25
Dexterity:	10	Ranged Attack Strength (RAS):	16	Block Chance (%):	0
Intelligence:	10	Spell Strength (SS):	15	Evade Chance (%):	1
Spirit:	15	Critical Hit Chance:	5%	Fire Resist (%):	0.2
Luck:	5	Critical Hit Damage:	150%	Cold Resist (%):	0.2
				Lightning Resist (%):	0.2
				Shadow Resist (%):	0.2
				Holy Resist (%):	0.2
Current XP:	100			Poison Resist (%):	20.2
Next Level.:	1440			Disease Resist (%):	20.2

I lay there for a while, eyeing everything. Most of the stats looked pretty similar to the other MMORPGs I'd played in the past. Still, it didn't pay to make assumptions, so I pulled up the game wiki to see if I could find anything. Although I hadn't had much luck with the wiki so far, I was happily surprised to see information was starting to trickle in on a host of different topics. A variety of users were posting their initial experiences with the game, and one thing was immediately clear.

The startup sequence was different for everyone. Drastically so.

Some people started in holding cells like I had—though no one mentioned a character named Cutter, which led me to believe he was a unique NPC—while others woke up at taverns, in forests, and even, occasionally, in the heat of an ongoing battle. The variety was truly fascinating, but I didn't want to get bogged down, so I forced myself to close out of the general forum and pulled up a search bar instead. It only took me a handful of seconds to find a whole glut of information on basic character stats, most of it from players, but some of it straight from Osmark Technologies.

By and large, the primary attributes seemed pretty straightforward:

- Strength: increases Attack Strength (AS) and overall Armor Rating.
- Vitality: increases overall Hit Points (HP) and Health Regeneration.
- Constitution: increases Stamina, Stamina Regeneration, and carrying capacity.
- Dexterity: improves reflexes, including chance to evade and chance to block, while also affecting Ranged Attack Strength (RAS) and Attack Strength (AS) for certain classes.
- Intelligence: increases overall Spell Strength (SS) and adds 0.1% to all resistances per point.
- Spirit: increases the maximum Spirit and Spirit Regeneration.

<<<>>>

The last stat, Luck, didn't actually seem to affect any tangible character skills; there was some speculation that Luck influenced dropped items—gold amount or item rarity—but no one seemed to know anything for sure. The material provided by Osmark didn't offer much clarity, either. There was one thing everyone agreed on, though; luck was a locked attribute, at least for the time being.

At level three, I'd earned 10 points to distribute however I wanted, but since I wasn't sure what class I'd be taking, I decided not to invest them yet. In every RPG I'd ever played, maximizing your points based on your class and build was key to having a powerhouse character at higher levels. I closed out of the "Character" screen and saw I had a new notification. Apparently I had a PM in my player inbox. It was from a friend of mine, Abby—the game developer who worked for Osmark Technologies. The same developer that'd hooked me up with my NexGenVR capsule in the first place.

Personal Message:

Jack,

I wasn't sure you were going to take the leap or not, but I'm glad to see you're in here. Look, I've got a sensitive, ultra-rare quest. It's sort of a hidden feature created by some of the Devs at Osmark, but I need someone I can trust on this. I need *you* on this. I don't want to say too much, but this is big. Could be a game changer for us. I've attached a scroll of teleport to this message. Just activate it and it'll bring you right to the quest location. Please meet me tomorrow afternoon, 2 PM in-game time. This is a time sensitive mission, so please don't be late.

—Abby

    I fell asleep staring at the PM, wondering about what kind of game-changing quest Abby could've stumbled across.

ELEVEN

TRAINING

A N ALARM BLARED INSIDE MY EAR. *Brrp, brrp, brrp, brrp.* I shot up in bed, staring around wild-eyed, my hands groping at the straw mattress. *Where was I?* I blinked bleary eyes, squinting against the feeble sunlight trickling in through a dull, semiopaque window. I frantically searched for the alarm clock—that blaring was driving me up a wall—but as my vision adjusted, I couldn't find the source of the noise. Nothing looked familiar to me. I'd expected to wake up on my worn couch after a long night of gaming, but instead I was in some sort of Ren-Fest-themed hotel.

And I still couldn't find that alarm. *Brrp, brrp, brrp, brrp.*

I swung my legs over the edge of the bed and stared in shock. I was wearing crude leggings, leather armor, and my skin was a muted gray. My. Skin. Was. *Gray.* This had to be a nightmare. *Did I go out for drinks last night and overdo it? Maybe someone laced my drink with something?* I reached up, grinding the palms of my hands into my temples, trying to block out the noise so I could think. That only made it worse, though. It was like the alarm was actually going off *inside* my head, clanging like a pair of cymbals over and over again. "Someone turn that alarm off," I hollered.

And just like that, the noise died. "Alarm dismissed," came Sophia's comforting voice, also resounding inside my skull. "The current time in Eldgard is 7:15 AM. You have been asleep for approximately ten real-world hours. You have an automated message from the Osmark Technologies Customer Support Team. Would you like to play it?"

I continued to rub at my head, which pulsed with a dull pain, but agreed to listen to the recording.

"Welcome, traveler," said a friendly male voice, "my name is Matthew and I'm your customer support representative. Our system records indicate you've spent your first full night in Viridian Gate Online. Congratulations! Many fellow travelers have reported severe disorientation and head pain after their first night of In-game rest; these symptoms are common and are not a cause for concern. The confusion will pass in a few minutes, and a hearty meal at your nearest inn or tavern will help with any head pain or other lingering aftereffects. Thank you for playing." The message cut off, leaving me in early morning silence.

I sat there for a few more minutes, disoriented and unsure. Slowly, *slowly*, it came back to me.

V.G.O. The asteroid. The end of the world. The potential death sentence hanging over my head like the Sword of Damocles.

I shuddered involuntarily as a crushing wave of depression washed over me—all I wanted to do was lie back down and close my eyes until this was all over. Fall asleep until either the world died or I did.

But then I remembered my training appointment with Cutter at 8 AM, and despite how awful I felt, I certainly didn't want to miss that. So, reluctantly, I pulled myself from the bed with a profound groan, splashed a little digital water onto my face from the washbasin, then headed down to the tavern below for breakfast. The bartender—the same rotund, balding man from the night before—served me a bowl of warm mush that tasted like honeyed oatmeal. He tried to make small talk, but my grunted, monosyllabic replies quickly drove him away in search of more friendly patrons.

Matthew, from customer support, had been dead right about the food though. By the time Cutter strutted in like a garish peacock, my headache was gone, my attitude had improved significantly, and I mostly felt like myself again.

"Sleep alright?" he asked as he guided me back behind the tavern front and into the training room.

"Yeah, slept fine," I replied with a nod, "but I woke up feeling like someone beat my head in with a brick."

He nodded. "I've heard rumors," he whispered conspiratorially, "that some travelers experience such symptoms for the first few days here in Eldgard. Something to do with migrating from one realm to another. Some travelers, they don't adjust well to Eldgard. For whatever reason, they're incompatible with our world. Assuming your head doesn't explode in the next three days," he said, cocking a finger and pointing it at my skull, "the sickness will pass and you'll be fine. A permanent citizen, like me. Well, almost like me—just uglier. Uglier and less skilled.

"Now, let's try to make you slightly less terrible at life, shall we?" He winked as he shepherded me into a currently unoccupied room with lots of arrow slits, which let in sporadic spears of brilliant sunlight. The rest of the room, however, was coated in deep shadow. Those shadows, thick as a blanket, seemed to wither and crawl, to reach for me like a forest of dark hands. Something uncomfortable and cold stirred inside my chest, unfurling icy tendrils through my limbs, reminding me of the black handprint branded onto my forearm. Reminding me of the Shadow-Spark ability the dying Maa-Tál Shaman had unlocked within me.

"Welcome to the shadow room," Cutter said, breaking the tenuous spell as he swept out an arm. "This, Grim Jack, is where we teach rookies like you the fine art of Stealth." He shuffled through a shaft of light and into a pool of shadow—in a blink he was gone. Disappeared. "Impressive, eh?" he asked, still invisible. "You'll never be as good as me, obviously, but with a little work, you can probably Stealth your way past a blind guard."

We spent the next two hours slinking about the room, stealing from one pool of black to the next.

He showed me several different methods to improve my meager abilities. First, he walked me through how to *fade*, which involved using camouflage and cover to blend into the surroundings and seem innocuous. Then, he showed me how to roll silently and even how to perform quick Stealth dashes, meant to close in on an enemy while their backs were turned. The work was grueling. My thighs and calves burned from the low-squat walking and my shoulders ached from rolling and falling, which were apparently important qualities for someone who wanted to be sneaky.

Cutter was a great teacher, though, and his work paid off.

By the time we were finished, my Stealth ability had increased to level 6, which meant my chance to successfully hide from enemies climbed from 7% to 17%. Not exactly a ninja warrior, but not half bad either. On top of that, I gained a new character level, which brought me up to level four, and gave me an extra 5 points to distribute. Just after 10 AM, Cutter called it quits on the Stealth practice and led me over to a new area—a padded sparring ground with a few straw practice dummies. He removed a knife from the sheath at his side, holding it up in the light, examining its gleaming blade closely.

"Now, I can't teach you anything about that ridiculous, barbaric club of yours"—he nodded toward the heavy-headed warhammer hanging at my side—"but maybe I can still teach you *something*. Sure, knife work has its own principles, but the basics of a good scrap are often the same, regardless of the weapons. Now, take out that glorified carpenter's tool and have at me."

I pulled out the weapon, hands flexing around the haft, feeling its comforting weight in my grip. Then I charged him, raising the hammer up high and barreling forward with a roar. I swung down in a wicked arc, only to find Cutter tap-dancing away with a little fancy footwork. My attack whiffed completely, and the weight of the hammer carried me forward and off balance—a sharp pain like a red-hot fire poker slipped into my back, near my kidney. I gasped, choked, and stumbled to the ground, dropping my weapon as I clumsily reached for my back.

The pain made me want to vomit.

"Most of the brawlers you're going to fight out there," Cutter said, circling to my front, "are gonna be stronger than you. They're gonna have better weapons. Tougher armor. And even if you end up as a tank, the truth is there's always someone bigger, faster, stronger. So, you need to be smarter. Misdirection and a well-placed blow can fell even the most imposing warriors. Now, back on your feet."

For the next two hours we went over basic fighting techniques, first covering a variety of stances, then launching into guards, defenses, and attacks. As tough as the Stealth session had been, the fighting lesson proved to be even more difficult. Certainly more challenging than any MMO I'd ever experienced. In most games, attacks consisted of a few key strokes or the right combination of buttons. Not here. Here I had to actually perform the maneuvers, know the techniques, watch for the openings, and respond with the correct block or counter.

I did seem to be learning the techniques much faster than I would have IRL—it almost felt like remembering something I'd once forgotten, even though I'd never done anything even remotely like this in my life. The fact that Cutter constantly stabbed me when I did things wrong may have also contributed to the speedy learning curve. Once again, though, Cutter's grueling regimen paid off, earning me another level up, while also unlocking a new skill:

Skill: Blunt Weapons

Blunt weapons, such as maces, hammers, and clubs, can cause massive damage to foes. Blunt weapons are especially effective against undead creatures and heavily armored opponents. This skill is always in effect and costs no stamina to use.

Skill Type/Level: Passive / Level 1

Cost: None

Effect: Increases blunt weapon damage by 5%.

We finished up our training session around noon, then beelined for the tavern—lunch time at long last— which Cutter assured me would help with the aches and pains from our practice.

We grabbed a table in the corner, well away from the few other patrons loitering around, and ate some meaty stew with thick gravy and freshly baked bread, warm and fluffy. I was more than happy to admit that Cutter had been right. Just like this morning, the food set me straight in no time, easing my sore muscles as effectively as a great night's sleep with a couple of painkillers thrown in for good measure. I still had a couple of hours to kill before I was supposed to rendezvous with Abby, but I decided heading over early wouldn't be a terrible idea.

I could always wander around and grind out some EXP.

"Cutter, you have any plans for today?" I asked off the cuff, eyeing him over the edge of a hefty beer stein.

He shrugged noncommittally and ripped off a chunk of flaky bread. "Nothing official," he replied, smacking loudly as he chewed. "Why, you got something in mind?"

"A job," I said curtly. "One from a friend of mine."

He swallowed, took a gulp of mead, then wiped his face with his sleeve and belched. A real smooth operator. "If it's lucrative enough, you might be able to twist my arm. What do you have?"

I filled him in on the scant details and watched as his smile grew wider and wider with every sentence.

TWELVE

THE GRIND

AT JUST AFTER 12:30, CUTTER AND I TELEPORTED into a wide, grassy clearing, ringed by trees on every side. Warm sunlight washed down from above, warming my exposed skin as a cool wind rustled my hair. I turned in a circle, staring at the wildflowers dotting the field, taking in the distant mountain vistas; I halted as the fallen ruins at the northern end of the clearing came into view. A circle of drunkenly leaning stones, remarkably similar to Stonehenge, butted up against the tree line. In the center of the stone ring was a yawning pit with a set of crude stairs leading down toward an elaborately wrought door.

My first real dungeon.

I pulled up my player map to see where exactly this ruin was located. The map came up fine and detailed my surroundings, but it refused to show my in-world location at all, which was odd in the extreme. I could've been ten minutes outside Rowanheath or on the other side of the world. "Cutter," I said, turning toward the Thief, "do you know where we are? My map won't display the world location."

"What do you mean the map won't display the world location?" he replied with an eyeroll. "You're probably just reading it wrong, because you're a moron. Give me a second." His face went strangely blank for a long beat. He stood unnaturally still with his head slightly canted for a full minute before finally snapping out of it and offering a soft whistle. "Bollocks. You're right. I can't pull up world location info, which means this is supposed to be a restricted area." He gleefully rubbed his hands together. "We're not supposed to be here." He sounded excited by the prospect.

And for once, I shared his delinquent enthusiasm. My inner gamer was practically doing backflips at the thought of getting the first crack at a new, restricted zone. Maybe Abby really had discovered something game-changing.

"We've got a couple hours before my friend shows up," I said. "Any chance you wanna go out and hunt down some mobs with me? Get a little extra experience before we tackle those ruins?"

He pressed his lips into a tight line and gave me a *you-must-be-crazy* look. "Yeah, no." He flopped down into the lush grass and lounged back, lacing his hands behind his head and staring up at the clouds. "As thrilling as hunting down generic forest critters for mediocre loot sounds—and trust me, it sounds *great*—I think I'll just camp out here and wait for the real action to start. Keep myself fresh. You understand." He closed his eyes and smiled, basking in the sunlight.

"Fine," I replied. "But I'm going on record here— you're the worst teammate on the planet."

"You'll change your tune when we're in the thick of things, I think," he said, never bothering to look at me. "Now run along."

I turned away from the sunbathing Thief and headed east into the forest, grumbling the whole time about how worthless he was. When I finally made it to the tree line, I took a moment to open my limited map, set up a personal quest marker, then set an alarm for 1:30 so I'd have plenty of time to get back to the clearing. With that done, I took off, weaving my way haphazardly through the forest until the ruins vanished completely behind me.

It didn't take long before I heard something big and heavy rustle through the brush ahead of me.

I pulled my warhammer from the leather frog at my belt and quickly dropped into Stealth, creeping from tree to tree, clinging to the shadows. After a few heartbeats of tense stalking, I glanced around the trunk of a leafy birch and saw the source of the commotion: a pair of shambling creatures, [Corrupt Valdgeist], composed of discarded branches, rotten greenery, goopy black mud, and odd bits of stone or bone. They were bigger than me, broad across the shoulders, and oddly lopsided.

They also looked about as slow as a couple of three-toed sloths, which was good news for me since running was still high on my defensive strategy list.

The pair milled around listlessly and didn't seem particularly alert. Should be easy game, perfect for a little leveling. Still, a tight bead of fear sat in my belly, spurred on by the memory of Cutter's painful knife jabs during our training session. I didn't really know what these things were or what they were capable of, and there was a good chance they'd hurt me. Badly. *You've got to suck it up and get over the fear*, I scolded myself. This was my new life now, and yes, getting injured was unpleasant, but it was also the only path to success.

I steeled myself, resolve sharpening to a knife's edge, and pushed on, moving forward with only a whisper of sound.

I circled around until I was behind the creatures, then slipped into the open, bringing up my hammer for a brutal killing blow. I lunged into the swing, putting the full weight of my upper body into the strike. The first creature's head exploded in a shower of forest debris, its legs crumpling as its body dropped to the floor. *Critical Hit! Stealth Attack Damage!* The words flashed over the corpse, but I paid them no mind, turning my attention to the second Corrupt Valdgeist. I spun just in time to see a huge fist, capped with a wrecking ball of stone, sail toward me.

I saw it, but I wasn't quick enough to avoid it.

I shuffled back, bringing up my hammer in an awkward block, which diverted the strike. Instead of pulverizing my face, the creature's rock fist slipped down, colliding into my chest. The sledgehammer hit knocked me back into a nearby pine tree and ate up a fifth of my HP, despite being a glancing blow. I reeled from the vicious thump and lost my footing, hitting the ground with a *thud*. With a grimace, I clutched at my battered chest and tried to gain my feet, but couldn't. Something was holding me down.

Roots. Brown snarls of foliage had emerged from the ground, twining around my ankles and thighs, wrapping tight and pulling me into the dirt.

A message flashed in front of me:

Debuff Added

Rooted: You have been entangled and are unable to move; duration, 30 seconds.

I beat and clawed at the brown and green tangles of vegetation ensnaring me, but it was no use, and before I knew it, the bulky, slow moving creature loomed over me. A crude, earthen fist cannonballed into my mouth, knocking my head back and conjuring a gout of bloody saliva, which trickled down the back of my throat. I wasn't sure if I could lose teeth in this game, but I was going to find out. My life bar flashed: less than 10% of my HP remained. That last strike had been a monster.

I frantically fought to bring up both my warhammer and the crude wooden buckler strapped to my left arm—anything to stop or divert another attack long enough for the "root" debuff to vanish.

The Corrupt Valdgeist swatted away my weapon with a lazy backhand, leaving me rooted to the ground, completely defenseless, with next to no HP left to my name. In my gut, I knew I was dead. The creature raised its clubbed fist again, ready to deliver the killing blow. To bludgeon me into a bloody smear.

Cold rage boiled inside me at the thought of dying like this. At the indignity of it. I flatly rejected the idea of having my head caved in by some mindless, muddy shambler in some forgotten backwoods while Cutter sunbathed in a meadow twenty minutes away. Especially since I didn't actually know how respawns worked here—would I end up back in the meadow or all the way back in Rowanheath? Would it be instantaneous or would it take several hours? I didn't have a clue, but I absolutely *refused* to find those answers like this.

A familiar chill radiated out from the blackened handprint on my forearm, roaring through my body, fueled by the sudden flash of anger. The creature's fist descended, slicing through the air.

"No!" I yelled, throwing one hand forward in a final act of desperation, hoping to somehow halt the attack—

My mouth fell open in shocked surprise as a bolt of angry, withering shadow erupted from my palm, slamming into the creature's neck like a dull machete.

The creature staggered from the impact, shuffling stupidly, before its head finally tumbled from its lopsided shoulders and to the forest floor. Its body shortly followed suit, collapsing into a heap of sticks and rock and mud. I sat there, staring at my hand, totally flabbergasted.

What did I just do?

Several status windows popped up, one right after the other:

x1 Level Up!

You have (25) undistributed stat points

You have (5) unassigned proficiency points

Quest Update: Plight of the Maa-Tál

In an act of desperation, you've tapped into your inborn Shadow-Spark ability, drawing on the dark power of the Umbra. In doing so, you have spent (1) Proficiency Point of the Spell Umbra Bolt and initiated the specialized path of the Shadowmancer. In order to unlock the

Shadowmancer class kit, speak to Chief Kolle of the Ak-Hani clan in the Storme Marshes and complete the Maa-Tál initiation ordeal.

Quest Class: Rare, Class-Based

Quest Difficulty: Hard

Success: Report to Chief Kolle and survive the Maa-Tál initiation ordeal.

Failure: Die during the Maa-Tál initiation ordeal

Reward: Class Change: Dark Templar, Shadowmancer Kit

Skill: Umbra Bolt

Launch a fierce bolt of shadow energy that causes damage and also temporarily blinds the target. As your proficiency with Umbra Bolt increases, both damage and the duration of blindness increase. At higher levels, Umbra Bolt also has a chance of causing confusion—your target may become panicked and start to randomly attack friendly forces.

Skill Type/Level: Spell/Initiate

Cost: 75 Spirit

Range: 100 Meters (Sight)

Cast Time: 1.5 seconds

Cooldown: N/A

Effect: Shadow Damage (160% SS)

Effect 2: Blindness, duration 5 seconds

Restriction: Due to current class restrictions, you may only use Umbra Bolt when your health drops below 15%. To remove this restriction, you must change your class to Dark Templar.

Wow. There was so much awesome I didn't even know where to begin.

First, I'd reached level five as a result of my training with Cutter, and the last I'd checked, I'd needed almost 3,000 experience points to hit level six. To level up off of two forest mobs was huge. They must've been packing some serious EXP, which meant I was in the right place at the right time for some solid grinding.

Second, wow again, I'd just blasted a bolt of deathly shadow from my hand!

Awesome hardly began to cover it. Yes, the Umbra Bolt skill was badly restricted since I didn't have the proper class yet, but it was still incredibly, wickedly cool. Not to mention, I now had the option to gain the Dark Templar class. I instantly pulled up my wiki, hoping to gather some intel on what type of skills Shadowmancers had, but frowned in disappointment. The wiki was currently unavailable due to my restricted in-game location. Probably the same reason my in-world map hadn't been working properly earlier on—the Devs didn't want any information about this particular location leaking to the general public.

Finally, I gained my feet, brushed my clothes free from dirt and dead leaves, and retrieved my warhammer from the forest floor. I took a minute to loot the Corrupt Valdgeist. Each carried 5 gold—but nothing else. Not a huge surprise, considering the creatures were basically trees. Still, 10 gold from two mobs was nothing to scoff at. Part of me wanted to play it safe and go back to the clearing, but the gamer in me screamed that this was way too good an opportunity to pass up. After all, if this was a restricted area of the game, it meant no other players were farming here. Which meant great EXP and decent loot—all good.

So, yielding to the jabbering voice of my inner greedy gamer, I made my way further into the forest.

THIRTEEN

THE HAMADRYAD

I WOUND MY WAY DEEPER AND DEEPER INTO THE forest, stealing from one copse of trees to another, encountering larger and more aggressive groups of Corrupt Valdgeist as I progressed. The battles continued to be intense and grueling, but after the first five or six, I started to notice certain predictable patterns in the way they moved and fought. A big haymaker was almost always followed by a short jab and a lunging kick, which offered a narrow opening I could exploit. And exploit it I did: sidestep right, avoid the kick, plant my warhammer into an exposed chest cavity with devastating results.

But those openings and gaffs evolved and changed.

Apparently, I wasn't the only one learning. No, the Corrupt Valdgeist picked up on my strategy almost as quickly as I picked up on theirs, and they adapted accordingly. Just when I found myself falling into complacency, one of the tree creatures would change tactics, lashing out with a surprise uppercut or catching me off guard with a wild blow that'd knock me from my feet. Smart. Dangerous. And even more troubling, the deeper I went, the faster the creatures became, quickly eliminating one of my major advantages. It made things more difficult overall, but also more interesting.

Grinding often got mind-numbingly boring because it was so repetitive, but this was never that. I was never quite sure how things would play out.

It'd been nearly an hour—and about twenty Corrupt Valdgeist later—when I heard the guttural rumble of an inhuman voice coming from a small clearing up ahead. I pulled up my in-game clock and checked the time: 1:25 PM. I frowned. I really needed to turn around and head back if I wanted to meet Abby on time, but my curiosity got the better of me. I crept forward, wrapped in Stealth, cloaked in shadow, feet silent in the undergrowth, and pressed my body up against a tree, stealing a gander around the side of the trunk.

The breath caught in my throat …

I counted thirteen or fourteen Corrupt Valdgeist wandering around in a lopsided meadow—a few shuffled listlessly, a few more were curled into hollowed-out burrows of mud and stone. Fast asleep. Some were even eating, stuffing their misshapen jaws with clumps of dried dirt or munching on handfuls of rotten leaves. This was some sort of den. Strangest of all, though, was the large, gnarled birch tree in the center of the clearing, surrounded by a fairy ring of brown-capped mushrooms.

The tree, labeled as a [Hamadryad], had a face on it.

And not just some crude picture carved into the bark. No, an actual face protruded from the white bark: a bulbous nose of knotted wood, deep-set chestnut-brown eyes, a thin gash of a mouth framed by mossy facial hair. "You make me sick, all of you," the tree bellowed in an earthy voice. "Why can't you leave my forest in peace!" His mossy beard fluttered as he hollered. "You come in here and spread your rot around, corrupt my brothers with your presence. A pox on you, on all of you."

The Corrupt Valdgeist ignored the tree's accusatory rant, carrying on about their business as though they were alone in the world. None of them went near the tree man though; they avoided the toadstone fairy ring as though it carried a deadly poison. The tree continued his ineffectual muttering, offering up colorful curses, occasionally taking a break to complain about how bad the Corrupt Valdgeist reeked or fondly reminisce about better times, back before the infection in the forest.

It was a strange, surreal scene, and I couldn't help but think of Courage the Cowardly Dog, screaming and buggy-eyed as he confronted a talking tree. That was *my* life now. I was Courage the Cowardly Dog.

I didn't really know what to do here. The RPGer in me screamed there was a quest to be had, but the realist in me said there was no way I could take on that many Corrupt Valdgeist and walk away. I was simply outmatched and too low level. Especially without the benefit of having a class yet.

I pulled up my map and marked the spot with a personal quest marker, then jotted down a note: *weird tree-face creature in mushroom fairy ring*. I closed out of the map and turned away, ready to hustle back toward the ruined temple, and my alarm went off—the one I'd set for myself as a reminder to wrap things up. The *brrp, brrp, brrp* was only audible inside my head, but that didn't keep it from startling the heck out of me. I jumped at the sound, irrationally afraid the Corrupt Valdgeist would somehow hear it.

I managed to dismiss the alarm, but in all my reckless commotion, I'd broken out of Stealth mode.

A fact which was plainly obvious since the host of Corrupt Valdgeist immediately streamed toward me, warbling cries of hate ripping through the air as their lanky limbs ate up the distance between us. Looked like I was going to fight these things after all. The first one lunged for me from the trees, weathered root arms straining to spill my blood onto the forest floor. I ducked beneath the attack and dove into a roll, which carried me just outside its effective attack range. I popped back up onto my feet a moment later, pivoting, spinning, bringing the warhammer around in a vicious swing.

I caught the creature in the back of its neck, dropping it in a single, critical hit blow. I didn't have time to celebrate my lucky break, though, because three more of the creatures were circling around me, hemming me in. I didn't have much in the way of hit points, unfortunately, so I really couldn't afford to take a beating, tank-style. I needed space to maneuver. I feinted left, then shot right, catching one of the Valdgeist in the knee with the spiked tip of my weapon. The creature wobbled, suddenly unstable, so I charged into it, shouldering it aside and bursting into the meadow beyond.

Now in the clear, I sprinted straight for the fairy ring surrounding the strange talking tree.

Another of the root creatures barreled in as I neared the ring, throwing its body forward in an awkward dive. I leapt, feet passing above the outstretched creature—a running back clearing the offensive line for a TD—barely avoiding the tangle of limbs. I landed hard, stumbled, then wheeled around and smashed my hammer into the creature's exposed head, ending its existence. Finally, I hurled my body inside the protection of the fairy ring, safe at last. At least I *hoped* my hunch was correct and that the ring would offer some protection.

If I was wrong, my little excursion was going to quickly end with a painful game over.

I waited, shoulders tense, muscles flexed, as the horde of remaining Corrupt Valdgeist circled back around, pressing in toward the ring of mushrooms. One creature, partially composed of rock, twigs and old deer bones, charged my position—only to rebound from an unseen force field surrounding the strange tree. I let out a shuddering sigh of relief.

"Smart thinking, boy," came a booming voice from behind me. I leapt in shock and spun, hammer raised, though careful to stay inside the ring. "No need for that," the tree said, gesturing toward my hammer with bushy green eyebrows. "Me thinks we're on the same side. The real question now is, how do you plan to escape?"

I lowered the hammer and turned back to survey the scene. The tree man had a point. I was safe for the time being, but I was also trapped. Trapped and surrounded on every side. I'd have to leave eventually, but there wasn't a good way to go about that.

"You see the problem," the tree boomed sagely. "Not only are we on the same side, we are in the same boat. Exactly the same boat. You see, I erected the fairy ring barrier to keep their infection out"—he nodded toward the Valdgeist, his trunk groaning from the movement— "but, as a result, my influence is confined to this damned circle. A stopgap measure ensuring my safety, but a sure-fire loser in the long run."

Suddenly a wave of exhaustion hit me and I dropped to my butt, letting my weapon fall to the leaf-strewn ground beside me. Heading for the fairy ring had seemed like such a good idea in the moment. I let out a long, tired sigh and leaned back on my hands. I could jump in and out of the protection of the toadstool circle—try to take them out one at a time—but if even one of them caught me in a root spell, I'd be trapped and dead. Not a lot of good choices.

"It seems to me," the tree said after several moments of quiet, disturbed only by the restless shuffling of the Corrupt Valdgeist, "that we might be able to help each other."

"I'm listening," I replied, glancing over one shoulder at the tree.

"Excellent. Excellent. It might be that I could break this fairy ring and exert my considerable influence to see you safely from this clearing, but in return, I'll need you to do a somewhat significant favor for me. You see, once I break the fairy ring, I'll be exposed to the infection plaguing this forest. In time, it will kill me. Or worse, transform me into a [Greater Corrupt Valdgeist]. But if you destroy the evil tainting the forest, it will undo these vile abominations and restore the balance of this land. I help you, you help me. Tit for tat. And if you succeed in this quest, I'll even grant you the blessing of the forest." He paused, wooden lips puckered. "So? What say you, boy?"

A new quest alert popped up:

Quest Alert: Cleanse the Taint

A powerful Hamadryad has requested your assistance in cleansing an evil presence that is tainting the forest, creating a host of Corrupt Valdgeist. Venture to the fallen ruins not far to the west, and destroy the source of the dark taint.

Quest Class: Rare

Quest Difficulty: Hard

Success: Destroy the source of the dark taint within (24) in-game hours.

Failure: Fail to destroy the source of the dark taint within (24) in-game hours.

Reward: 10,000 EXP; Blessing of the Forest: Your relationship with forest-aligned factions will improve from *Neutral* to *Friendly.* If you fail, you will receive Curse of the Forest: Your relationship with forest-aligned factions will decrease from *Neutral* to *Unfriendly.*

Accept: Yes/No?

I stared at the screen, reading over the quest once, twice, three times, then checking and double-checking the reward. What were the chances the ruins this tree-guy wanted me to clear were the very same ruins I was already on my way to clear? Pretty good. And though the quest difficulty was listed as hard, turning down a rare quest at this stage in the game—or any stage, really—was stupid. Besides, what other option did I have? If I didn't accept, the tree wouldn't help me escape, which was a certain death sentence.

"Okay," I said somewhat halfheartedly, selecting accept.

FOURTEEN

SKILL BUMP

"ONE ... TWO ... THREE!" THE HAMADRYAD shouted, his voice nearly deafening up close.

Sweat dotted my brow and a nervous energy caused my warhammer to tremble in anticipation as I stared down the horde of Corrupt Valdgeist barring my path. Even accounting for the three I'd managed to kill, there were still over ten of them. Ten. This seemed like a dumb idea, but I was already committed, so when the tree hit *three,* I bolted straight out, dismissing the pang of worry nestled in my gut. The root-monsters came for me the second I cleared the toadstool ring, clawed hands extended.

I met their advance with my hammer.

Clocking one in the face with a glancing blow, sending it stumbling away in shock, then smashing a forearm and jabbing the weapon up at an angle into another's jaw. The damage wasn't sufficient to put down the Corrupt Valdgeist for keeps, but it did clear a path.

More streamed in from the left and right, though, so unless the Hamadryad came through for me, they were going to shortly converge on me and rip me limb from limb. I tried not to think about that, and instead hunched forward, dropping my head, and kept charging right on ahead. Just as the creatures entered my peripheries, a gigantic *snap-boom* reverberated in the air as huge tree roots, big as jungle pythons, ripped their way free from the ground, dusty earth raining down.

The tree roots writhed and stretched, curling around the encroaching Corrupt Valdgeist like giant hands, crushing frail bodies and holding them firmly in place. A mega version of the root spell that'd ensnared me earlier. Pretty cool, actually.

For a moment I kept running, eager to leave the clearing behind, but then I came to a stuttering halt. I turned and quickly assessed the scene. The tree-man had managed to snare all of the Corrupt Valdgeist, and although I didn't know how long his spell would last, for the time being, they were completely defenseless. Helpless. I'd come out here to grind some EXP, and those were basically free points if I had the guts to take them.

I rushed back in with a warbling war cry and went to town, caving in heads with brutal efficiency. They couldn't move, couldn't fight back. It was easier than smashing a piñata without a blindfold. The whole process took less than a minute—the Hamadryad enthusiastically spurred me on with hoots of approval the whole while—and before I knew it, I'd killed every creature and cleared a ton more EXP.

I looted the bodies with practiced efficiency and, after another quick "goodbye and good-luck" from the tree-man, headed back toward the ruins and my appointed meeting with Abby. I pulled up my menu as I walked, deciding a little multitasking would save me from the tedium of a long, boring return trip.

First, I checked my new quest and was pleased to find the evil presence tainting the forest was, indeed, located at the ruins I was already scheduled to raid. Two birds with one stone. Next, I toggled over to my "Character" screen, eager to examine the gains I'd made in this little restricted slice of the world.

x8 Level Up!

You have (65) undistributed stat points

You have (12) unassigned proficiency points

So far, I'd managed to push myself to level fourteen—not bad the way I figured things. True, there were probably players out there at much higher levels, but I still had some big quests remaining to my name, and those quests came with some hefty EXP bonuses. The biggest problem I had at the moment wasn't my level, it was my lack of class. Even knowing the Shadowmancer kit likely lay in my future wasn't much help, since I couldn't access a wiki or pull up a class description. Without that, I really had no idea what major stats to invest my finite stash of points into.

Annoying, but there was nothing I could do about it right now.

As soon as I wrapped up this business with Abby, though, I was jumping headlong into the quest provided by that Murk Elf Shaman. Satisfied with my progress, I dismissed my character screen and pulled up my inventory. I'd accumulated over a hundred gold coins and almost double that in silver, which was quite the haul, and I'd also managed to get a few item drops to boot.

Though most of the Corrupt Valdgeist only dropped coins, one had dropped a short sword with a +1 to Strength, and another had given me a set of black braided leather leggings with a +1 Constitution bonus and an extra 2% resistance to fire. Despite the sword's extra stat bonus, I decided to stick with my warhammer—it just felt *right* in my hands. Besides, during my short grind session, I'd already managed to raise my Blunt Weapons skill to level 4, which added an extra 11% damage to all blunt weapon attacks; it'd be a shame to start over after all of that.

The new leggings, though, were a heck of a lot better than the (shoddy) rough trousers I was currently sporting, so I swapped those in a heartbeat.

With that done, I decided to finally check out my Skills section. After unwittingly spending a point on the Umbra Bolt spell, I had 12 unassigned Proficiency Points remaining, and I wasn't even sure what they did. When I pulled up the Skills menu, a huge screen spread out before me, with a variety of different Skill Trees splayed out in the air: Blunt Weapons, Bladed Weapons, Archery, Unarmed, Forging, Crafting, Enchanting, Merchant-craft, Heavy Armor, Medium Armor, Light Armor, Stealth, Lock Pick, Mage-craft, Animist, and Healer.

Wow, there was almost too much information to take in. Each Skill had its own unique branch with specialty abilities, which could be invested in by allocating Proficiency Points. Since I was reasonably sure I was going to stick with the warhammer, regardless of which class I ultimately ended up with, I selected the Blunt Weapons Tree to see what kind of cool abilities I could unlock.

At my relatively low level with Blunt Weapons, there weren't many options available. At the higher levels, however, I could unlock skills like Skull Bash—a special power attack capable of stunning enemies while also ignoring 50% of an opponent's base armor rating—or the Crush Armor ability, which came with a 250% attack bonus against opponents in heavy plate. Powerful stuff.

Even at my paltry level 4, however, there were a few cool things I could do. First, I invested one point into Savage Blow, an attack that cost 20 stamina, increased damage by 25%, and raised Critical Hit by 15%. I also picked Parry, increasing my chance of blocking without a shield while additionally giving me a 10% chance to counterattack with a 125% movement bonus. That dropped me down to 10 points to invest, but I felt happy with my choice.

I was getting ready to check out what the Stealth Tree had to offer when I broke from the tree line and into the meadow I'd left Cutter cooling his heels in. I paused mid-step and dismissed the menu hovering in front of me. There was a broad-shouldered Risi warrior wearing heavy, black-coated plate mail, and he had Cutter pinned in front of him—a wicked blade held tight against the Thief's throat.

FIFTEEN

ABBY INTRIGUE

"**D**ON'T TAKE ANOTHER STEP," THE RISI warrior growled, fangs barred in a rictus. "Not unless you'd care to see what the inside of your friend's throat looks like."

"How did you let him sneak up on you?" I hissed at Cutter, trying to decide what to do. "You're supposed to be a super ninja thief. That guy doesn't look all that stealthy."

"I fell asleep," Cutter replied through gritted teeth. "Now please do what the smelly thug says, since I'm a huge fan of not dying. My kind doesn't respawn like you travelers—death is sort of a big, permanent deal for us."

"So this Thief really is with you," came a female voice off to the right. In my peripheral vision, a swath of tree line rippled, distorted, then changed, revealing a short, curvy woman with an intricate pile of brown curls. She wore an elegant blood-red robe, studded with shimmering jewels, and carried a sleek dark wood staff carved with ember-red script and topped by a fat crimson ruby the size of a pigeon's egg.

"Is that you, Abby?" I asked, squinting at her. Abby and I went back all the way to our college days. We'd stayed in touch through a variety of MMOs, but I hadn't actually seen her IRL in years. The woman over there could've been Abby, though. She had the same dark skin, the same frame and build, the same hair, though everything was refined and dusted with the sheen of over-perfect VR.

She nodded and offered me a soft smile, dimples blooming in her cheeks. Those dimples were certainly the same. "It' good to see you, Jack. Otto"—she turned toward the armor-clad warrior—"you can let him go." The warrior grunted noncommittally, then removed his blade and gave Cutter a little shove, opening up some distance between the two. "Otto, why don't you and the thief—"

"Name's Cutter, not *thief*," Cutter interjected.

Abby offered him a tightlipped smile. "Okay. Otto, why don't you and *Cutter* get to know each other while Jack and I have a word. Just catch up a bit, then we'll all be on our way."

"Of course," the gruff warrior, Otto, replied, before promptly grabbing Cutter by one arm and dragging him away. "This way, *thief*."

Abby came over and pulled me into a tight hug. "It's so good to see you," she said, pulling back and regarding me from arm's length.

"You too, Abby. You too. I can't believe this place," I said as an awkward ice breaker. "V.G.O. is seriously incredible—I've never seen anything like it."

"Oh, it's definitely incredible," she replied, though she didn't look nearly as happy as I would've imagined. If I'd helped to create something as awesome and groundbreaking as V.G.O—even in a small way—I would've been through-the-roof ecstatic. "Will you walk with me a bit?" she asked.

I nodded and offered her my arm, a small grin pulling up one corner of my mouth. Back in college, we used to walk between classes like that, linked arm in arm. Those were the days when I thought we might turn into something; though, for whatever reason—timing, romantic complications, geography, career paths—that had never panned out.

"You look good," I mentioned offhandedly. "Are you a human?"

She nodded. "A Wode. I wanted to actually look like myself, and the human races were the only ones that offered my natural skin tone." We kept walking, but she gave me a quick once-over from the corner of her eye. "Personally, I'm sort of surprised you went with a Murk Elf. Not that I mind, exactly—you just look so different. I sort of expected you to be human, too."

"The Murk Elves had some cool racial bonuses," I offered. We trotted on in uncomfortable silence, feet carving a path through the vibrant green grass. "So, how's stuff been back IRL? I mean aside from the world ending," I added weakly. *Moron.* What kind of question was that? Who would want to talk about real life, what with real life teetering on the verge of total destruction?

She offered me a halfhearted smile and punched me lightly in the shoulder. "Good to see you haven't changed too much. Still the same old, awkward Jack I remember." She paused, glancing down, shuffling along. "Truthfully, I'm tired. It's been a long year for me. A tough year. I lost my dad about six months ago. Large cell lung cancer. Ugly stuff. And with the schedule

Osmark had us on, I didn't even get time off for the funeral."

"Wow, Abby, I'm so sorry to hear about your dad."

She shrugged and waved off my comment. "It's the end of the world, Jack, everyone's going to lose loved ones. Everyone. But, to really top things off, despite my best efforts, my mom won't make the leap to Viridian. She says she's too old to start over, even though she's only sixty-five. So, I guess it's been a pretty shitty year, all things considered. How 'bout you?"

"Yep. Pretty much the same," I said, red rising into my cheeks. "By the way, I never properly thanked you for the capsule. But, you know, thank you—you saved my life, after all."

"You're welcome," she replied, "but maybe you should wait to thank me until you've fully transitioned. I've seen what happens to people who don't live through the process, and it's worse than watching someone die from cancer. I know from personal experience."

Well, that was certainly off-putting and terrifying. I puckered my lips, trying to think of anything I could say that might salvage this train-wreck of a conversation. I floundered completely. How could I possibly follow up with anything appropriate after a downer like "it's worse than watching someone die from cancer"? Tough to recover from that. "So, what's the deal with the tank?" I finally asked just to break the terrible silence, jerking a thumb toward the retreating Risi.

"Otto? Oh, he's my starting NPC," she said dismissively, "the one who walked me through my intro to the world. A lot of players end up forming pretty strong bonds with their paired NPC. Is Cutter your starting NPC?"

"Well, he was in prison with me, if that's what you mean." I faltered. "Wait, so are you saying everyone starts with their own NPC?"

She nodded, her gaze averted, still deep in thought. "Every player has a completely unique starting scenario with a custom NPC to lead them into the world of V.G.O. The seven Master AI controllers—the Overminds—analyze each user based on that specific user's internet profile and personal history. Then, the Overminds create a starting NPC guide and a specialized initialization sequence which acts as a sort of hyper-advanced Myers-Briggs Type Indicator. The way each player reacts during the sequence and interacts with their NPC tells the Overmind what type of character class they'll most likely meld well with."

"Wow," I replied, feeling dumb. "That's incredible. Intense. But it's also kind of creepy. How does Osmark Tech get away with profiling people like that? Seems like a massive invasion of privacy—aren't there laws against that kind of thing?"

"Oh, it's definitely a breach of privacy"—she stole a look at me and bobbed her head—"and yeah, there are *totally* laws against it, but Osmark Tech gets away with it because players sign an information release in the user agreement. Naturally, the release is written in legalese so dense a team of Harvard lawyers couldn't figure it out, and then it's tucked away in print so fine, you'd need an electron microscope to find it. But it's there, and when you agree to play, you accept Osmark's terms of service, profiling and all."

"Man, if players found out, they'd be *pissed*. Why even go through the hassle anyway?" I asked. "Seems like it'd be a lot easier to just let players choose their class like in every other MMO in the world."

She shook her head and shrugged. "That's not my area of expertise, but if I had to guess, I'd say it's because the VR game play is so intense and personal, that if you played a class outside of your personality tolerance it could have adverse side effects. Or"—she paused, arching an eyebrow—"it could be a marketing gimmick. I don't know. But then, there's a lot I don't know about V.G.O."

"Hey, out of curiosity, do you know if the NPCs are actually self-aware or not?" I voiced the question since it'd been lingering on my mind ever since meeting Cutter in prison. "If I didn't know any better, I'd say my starting NPC's a real person. Sort of a jerk, but a fully fleshed out jerk. He certainly seems to think he's real—but it's weird, because from what I've gathered, he also genuinely believes V.G.O. isn't a game. It's really tripping me out, actually."

"Honestly …" She frowned, hesitated. Trying to decide what to tell me. "Honestly, I'm not sure. No one is. We rushed the testing to get the game online, so I can't give you a straight answer one way or the other. The NPCs are procedurally generated by drawing on information from all over the internet—history, Facebook profiles, fiction novels, movies, games— which gives them their uncanny realism. I've never met an NPC that failed to pass the Turing Test, but whether they're *actually* aware?" She shrugged one shoulder. "Time will tell I guess."

Once more, we lapsed into tense quiet as we edged nearer and nearer the ruins. The more and more I learned about V.G.O., the more I began to wonder what exactly I'd gotten myself into. It was too late to second-guess myself at this point, but it was still disconcerting. Maybe Abby was feeling the same way—it'd certainly explain her attitude. "Well, would you like to tell me about this big secret mission you've got for us?" I asked, trying to find any topic that would be a little less *heavy*. A little less depressing.

She stopped, pulled her arm from mine, and took a step away as she folded her arms across her chest. "Jack, maybe you should just go. It might've been a mistake to drag you into this mess." A tear leaked from her eye and ran down her cheek. She reached up and swiped at it with the back of her hand.

"Abby, what in the hell is going on?" I reached out and placed a reassuring hand on her shoulder. "You're not a weepy damsel in distress. I've never seen you cry, not in all the years I've know you. So why don't you tell me what's eating at you? Just get it off your chest."

"It's bad, Jack," she said with a slight sniffle. "Bad for everyone. Maybe as bad as the asteroid. Even telling you could land you in a lot of trouble." She paused, chewing on her lip. "Are you sure you want to know?"

"Abby, tell me," I replied, much more confidently than I felt. What could possibly be as bad as the asteroid?

SIXTEEN

BAD TO WORSE

ABBY AND I SAT ON A TOPPLED LOG TWENTY OR thirty feet from the ruins. "Tell me what's going on," I prompted her again.

"It's hard to know where to even begin," she said, looking away. "Jack, there's just so much crazy shit going on. Like mind-blowing, world shaking, secret conspiracy, Illuminati shit. Tin-foil hat shit. And I haven't shared this with anyone else because I don't know who'd believe me or who I could trust. Most of my 'friends'"—she used air quotes—"work for Osmark Tech, and I sure don't trust anyone there. Not anymore.

"It all started a few months ago," she continued. "It was a typical day—I was checking a line of code when I ran across an oddity. Someone had added an unauthorized, locked quest, accessible only by special players. There'd been all kinds of other crazy stuff leading up to this, so when this popped up, I decided to take a peek. Thought it might offer some clue about what in the hell was going on around the company. That's when I discovered there were *hundreds* of these locked areas scattered all around V.G.O., inserted by Robert Osmark's inner circle."

"Are they supposed to be some kind of content for future patches or expansions?" I asked, trying to think of the most reasonable explanation.

"At first, I thought so too, but I kept looking. Digging. Hacking." She shook her head, her gaze distant. "These areas were never meant for the general player population. These areas were built into the game as rewards for some of the big financial backers of V.G.O.—people with lots of money and lots of power. Here's the thing, Osmark Tech knew about the asteroid long before the general public ever did. The government didn't release the info to the masses because they didn't want to cause premature panic, but my boss, Robert Osmark, *knew*. I'm sure of it.

"He didn't tell us peons, obviously, but in hindsight it's clear. He had us working around the clock, paying out overtime through the nose, rushing through beta trials to get things up and running ahead of schedule. And then his inner circle started adding in all of these extra features last minute. To top things off, a few weeks before the media started to carry the story about the asteroid, Osmark himself dropped the news on us worker bees—sort of an extra *work-your-asses-off* incentive.

"Now, based on a series of hacked emails I uncovered," she continued, "I think he had these special areas installed in order to help certain individuals game the system. I personally believe Osmark realized that V.G.O. wasn't just a video game—not with that asteroid inbound. He realized V.G.O. was the birth of a new world. A new dimension. Initially, the game was set up to put all starting players at the same disadvantages, to level the playing field for *everyone*. But the mega-wealthy, the politicians, the banksters, people in organized crime, they don't want a level playing field. They want an edge.

"And all of these new areas were expressly added to give those people that edge. In a couple of weeks, after the asteroid hits and it's too late for anyone IRL to do anything about it, V.G.O is going to turn into a new feudal dark age, and everyone is going to be scrambling to carve out a piece of this empire for themselves. And the little guys, people like us, are going to get crushed in the mix. People like us are going to end up being the serfs, Jack. The unwashed masses for uber players to lord over. Unless … Unless we fight dirty."

She fell silent for a time, the distant thrum of birdcalls warbling through the air. I certainly didn't know what to say.

"This zone right here"—she gestured toward the meadow—"has already been bought and paid for by a South American dictator named Aleixo Carrera. I don't know what's buried in these ruins, but I know Carrera paid twenty million for it. *Twenty million*, Jack. That's a lot of money for a few strings of digital code, so I've got to think whatever's here is powerful. These entitled assholes are going to have an advantage none of us regular folk get, and in the long run it's going to turn ugly. And all the chaos coming down the pipeline only accounts for the *human* elements.

"The AI controllers running this system are cutting-edge beyond belief. None of the Overminds are really conscious, thinking beings—they're more like forces of nature that maintain the world's integrity, spawn creatures, create quests—but they're still dangerous. Really dangerous. I mean, the Overmind responsible for overseeing Serth-Rog and his personal army is run by a *repurposed* military AI unit. Osmark acquired it from the Chinese military last minute to save time with development. Who knows what that thing might do?" She shook her head.

"Wait," I said, rubbing at my temples as I mentally waded through the tsunami of info I'd heard so far. "Okay, I can believe Osmark Tech might have the ethics code of a Banana Republic Dictatorship, but here's what I don't get. Why sell off V.G.O. real estate for IRL money in the first place? The world's going to end in less than nine days. So, what's the point?"

"Well, Carrera didn't actually pay cash," she replied urgently, almost fervently. Needing for me to believe her. "Nope, maybe six months before news of the asteroid broke, Carrera selflessly "donated" twenty million worth of essential tech components to help get V.G.O. operational in time. He supplied Osmark Tech with colossal amounts of refined indium, gold, silver, copper, platinum, palladium—all essential components in the physical machinery powering V.G.O. He also supplied cheap labor to help at the NextGenVR capsule facility, churning out capsules at a crazy rate. And Carrera's not the only one, either.

"US politicians railroaded laws allowing Osmark Tech to bypass testing requirements, they rubber-stamped the import of dangerous and restricted materials, plus about a hundred other illegal things. Osmark even got help from NASA to launch his satellite into orbit. And that repurposed AI I told you about? Another 'donation' from Chinese military leaders. The amount of supplies and materials to get V.G.O. up and running ahead of schedule were *staggering*, I'm sure.

And I bet my completely worthless life savings there were people lining up around the block, willing to help in return for future kickbacks.

"I think he's repaying favors to the powerful people who made V.G.O. possible. Now, I want to give my boss the benefit of the doubt and assume he isn't actually a monstrous asshole—I like to believe he was just doing what he needed to do to save a lot of people, but he made some really shady deals to do it. And even if he isn't a monster, I can't imagine people like Carrera or the CIA or the KGB are going to be beneficent masters. They're going to amass power for themselves and be colossal dick heads just like they were in the real world, except there's not going to be a Constitution or police force to keep them in check."

"But why go through the quest system?" I asked, turning the information over and over in my mind, examining it from every conceivable angle. "Why not just turn these players into in-world gods right out of the gate? Just program it into the system?"

"It's complicated," she said, glancing around nervously as though someone might be listening. "After we brought all of the Overminds on line," she whispered, an edge of fear in her voice, "they closed the system to major changes—they're calling the shots now. The Devs can only tweak things that're already consistent with the Overmind directives. Hence using the quest system as a back door."

I was stunned into silence for a long while, my stomach churning with uncertainty. I bent over, leaning against my thighs as I hyperventilated. Abby had been right, this was some mind-blowing, world shaking, secret conspiracy, Illuminati shit. I knew transitioning into V.G.O. was going to be a humongous, life-altering challenge, but I'd never expected anything like this. I was a thirty-two-year-old EMT from the west coast. I lived in a crappy apartment and made less than the typical burger flipper. I wasn't the kind of person embroiled in international politics or multi-million-dollar conspiracies, which was *definitionally* what we were talking about here.

"You okay?" she asked, rubbing a hand along my back.

"Nope, not even a little," I replied, still hyperventilating a little. "V.G.O. was supposed to be a safe haven," I said finally, "but if this is true, dying back on Earth might actually be the better option."

She didn't answer—probably because she knew I was right. Instead, she sat there, tracing a hand along my shoulders until I could breathe normally again.

"So what are you suggesting?" I asked eventually, pushing myself upright. "We're nobodies, Abby. We don't have money or connections or powerful friends. What exactly do you think we can do about this?"

Her face hardened with resolve—gone was the weepy damsel from a few moments ago. "We *aren't* nobodies, Jack. We know MMOs better than most of the assholes entering this world, and knowledge is power, too. What I'm suggesting is that we get ahead of this shitstorm while we still can. What I'm suggesting is you and I form our own clan—one that actually has a chance of standing up against the rising powers in this new world. One that can give people like us hope. And we start by stealing whatever's inside this restricted zone. Whatever Carrera paid twenty million to get his hands on."

I stood with a groan and headed over to the standing stones; Abby trailed behind me, giving me some distance. I halted at the edge of the earthen pit, staring at the stairs that would take us into the dungeon. Or not. I could walk away. Just pretend I hadn't heard any of this—write Abby off as a nut job. As a loony conspiracy theorist. I almost wish she *were* just some crackpot psycho.

But I didn't *believe* that.

I opened my mouth to speak, but she raised a hand, cutting off my question.

"Before you say anything, before you answer, I just need to tell you that if we do this, there's no going back. You need to know that. We're going to buck the system in a big way and potentially make some very powerful enemies with connections and deep pockets. And they'll come for us. Sooner or later, they'll come." She paused and turned toward me, concern etched into the lines of her face. She was afraid I was going to turn her down and walk away. "Now, what were you going to say?"

"I want to know, why me? This is my life you're asking me to put on the line," I said, "and I don't want to be manipulated into being someone's fall guy. You could've picked anyone, but you came to me with this. So I want to know why."

She stole another glance at me, teeth working at her bottom lip. She sighed. "Because I trust you, Jack. And because I like you. And because you're the kind of guy who plays a Cleric instead of a glory-seeking warrior or a flashy mage."

"Wait. What?" I asked, lips screwing up. "You picked me because I usually play a Cleric? I don't understand, not even a little."

"Clerics aren't about glitz, glamor, flash, or glory. They're a support class. They end up in the background, and they worry about the success of the team instead of their personal achievement. I thought about reaching out to some of the other guys from the Crimson Alliance"— our gaming group—"but in my gut, I wasn't sure I could really trust any of them with something this big. At least, not in the beginning. But you're a good guy, Jack, one who's always wanted to make a difference. That's why I worked my magic to ensure you got a capsule well before the news about the asteroid hit. Because I wanted you on my team even then." She turned on me, pinning me in place with an unwavering gaze. "So, what do you say?"

I looked away, regarding the mountains cutting across the horizon in the distance. "Alright," I said with a nod, "I'm in."

SEVENTEEN

INTO THE HOLE

WE CREPT ALONG A MUSTY, DOWNWARD-sloping passageway, the stone slabs worn smooth from age, the ground damp and soft from accumulated water. Abby's NPC pal, Otto, took the lead—only natural since he was a hard-hitting melee fighter and a born tank. I padded along in the middle of the column, warhammer out and ready as a backup line of defense, while Abby trailed behind. She was a sorceress, already creeping up toward level thirty, and kitted out as a Firebrand—a type of flame-centered spellcaster—with some cool offensive and team-buff skills.

But, she was also a total glass cannon: one good hit from an enemy was liable to wipe her out completely.

Cutter wasn't anywhere to be seen. He was scouting ahead, ghosting through the shadows, using his abilities to disarm any potential traps well before we got there, while also keeping an eye out for potential opposition.

The hallway, which dove solidly for thirty or forty feet, eventually leveled out and opened into a wide room with a vaulted ceiling, which might've been a grand entry hall at some point in the far distant past. The place was all stone walls, massive earthen columns, and partially dilapidated statues marching along either side of the room. For all its former glory, though, time had really done a number here. Moss clung to most surfaces, creeping tree roots dangled from the ceiling in spots, and piles of rubble and debris littered the floor.

Despite the decrepitude, however, I could tell the place was currently inhabited.

Weak firelight, obscured by a hulking column in the center of the room, illuminated the far end of the chamber. A second later, Cutter stepped from a pocket of shadow, urging us all to silence with a finger raised across his lips. "Unfriendlies, up ahead," he whispered as everyone pulled in close to hear him. "I disarmed several very nasty traps on the way in—spring-loaded spikes, a plate-triggered flame wall, a ceiling mounted buzz saw big as a horse. Someone definitely does *not* want visitors."

"What about the unfriendlies?" I asked, still searching the room for any signs of movement.

"Tough. Not your typical brainless cave dwellers. These are real guards. Mercs. They're sitting around the fire gabbing and eating, but they look dangerous." He knelt down and began to trace a rough map into the dirt with a finger. "There's a trio of plate-armored warriors, nearest to us"—he made three quick Xs in a rough semicircle—"a Ranger with a mean looking bow, on the left." A hasty circle marked the Ranger's position. "Plus two spellcasters, one might be a priest or a Warlock of some kind, here and here." Two triangles, tucked away behind the Xs, entered the fray. He paused, turning his eyes on Abby. "What's the plan, flame-lady?"

Otto turned, sharing a brief look with Abby, then nodded even though no words were spoken. "We're going to play this one straight and simple. You and you"—he pointed to me and Cutter—"will Stealth out. Thief, you target the sorcerer. Grim Jack, you take the Ranger. I'll give you both a fifteen count to get into position, then I'll blunder out and draw their focus. Once the fighting begins, Abby will lay down wholesale suppressive firepower. Straight, simple, easy." His speech was delivered coolly, practically, like a well-seasoned field general with a thousand engagements under his belt. "Well, don't just stand there, move," he barked.

Otto's sheer confidence was more than enough to convince me, so I nodded and dropped into Stealth mode.

Cutter broke right and vanished, while I went left, slipping from broken statue to statue, maneuvering ever closer to the other end of the chamber. It didn't take me long before I spotted the hostile party for the first time: Cutter hadn't been joking, these guys looked tough as old boot leather. Two of the three melee fighters were hulking, muscle-laden Risi warriors in heavy plates that gleamed like polished onyx. The third, similarly attired, was a stocky female Dwarf with a blunt-faced mace at her side. A Templar or a Paladin of some kind, if I had to guess.

The sorcerer was garbed in fine battle robes of heavy blue silk. Flares of fanciful silver scrollwork ran over the outfit in elaborate swirls. The priest, a Dawn Elf, wore plain brown robes, but the heavily worked staff he carried suggested he wasn't a lightweight either. Last was the archer, decked out in muted black leather armor; she was the only one not crowded around the fire. Instead, the vigilant huntress leaned against the far wall, a pair of large brown wings folded up behind her, her hawkish eyes roving ceaselessly over the terrain.

I gulped. She was my mark.

Truthfully, the thought of merking these guys made me salivate—I bet they had some phenomenal loot. Only part of me felt that way, though. The other part of me felt terrified, because even a casual glance at the party told me they were way out of our league.

I fidgeted with my warhammer, adjusting and readjusting my grip as I stalked my victim, carefully placing every foot, checking every step so I wouldn't alert anyone prematurely. If Cutter and I lost the element of surprise and the backstab bonus that came with it, we didn't have any shot at all. At one point, just a few feet away from the archer, I put a foot down on a piece of stone which made a barely audible *clack*. I froze, because as soft as the sound had been, the Ranger's eyes locked on my position like an owl spotting a field mouse.

For a long, tense beat I stood there, unmoving, unbreathing, sweat rolling down my face and slicking my palms.

Then her gaze softened and shifted as a noise came from the front of the cave—the clomp of heavy footfalls on damp earth. Otto. Thank god.

The group of NPCs mobilized in a heartbeat, standing from their spots around the fire and moving almost as one toward the center of the chamber. The winged Ranger glided past me, her eerie yellow eyes fixed dead ahead, the tip of one wing almost close enough to graze me. I wheeled about, bringing up my hammer, preparing for my strike, but stopped just shy as Otto came into view.

Curiously, the hostile NPCs didn't attack. Rather, the priest in the burlap-looking robes shouldered his way to the front of the party, his head canted to the side, his face screwed up in a picture of puzzlement. "Who are you?" he asked at last, his voice a resonant baritone. "How did you get here? You don't have the seal of Lord Carrera, yet here you are in an area reserved for him. Explain yourselves or perish."

I held my hammer in upraised hands, trembling with indecision. *What's going on here? What should I do? Strike or hold?*

Abby stepped forward from the entryway tunnel, her heavy cowl obscuring her face completely. "We are servants of Lord Carrera, the owner of this reserved area," she replied smoothly, confidently. I knew Abby well enough to hear the bluff in her voice, but it was still a convincing performance. "I wasn't told to expect your party," she continued, hands carefully smoothing out her robes, "so can *you* please explain what you are doing here? What is the role and function of your group?"

"We're the mercenaries," the priest replied, eyes narrowing in suspicion. "Mercenaries hired to lead Lord Aleixo Carrera through this dungeon, to help him and his party power-level and claim the treasure at the dungeon's end. That is the nature of our contract. If you are Lord Carrera's servants, why aren't you aware of these details?" On some unspoken cue, the mercenary warriors pulled free their weapons, the rasp of steel on leather hanging in the air. "Unless, of course, you are schemers and connivers." The words oozed scorn like venom. "Give me the pass code. Now."

The priest's tone said no nonsense or further delays would be tolerated.

Abby hesitated for a second longer, her body tight with indecision. Otto solved the problem for everyone by charging forward with a bellowing roar, his meaty sword flying from its sheath as he moved. The Ranger drew an ebony recurve bow and sighted in—

It was now or never, I knew. So I leapt, bringing my warhammer down before she could unleash a volley of arrows at Otto and Abby.

EIGHTEEN

FIRESTORM

I DROVE THE NASTY SPIKE OF MY WEAPON INTO THE Ranger's back, aiming for one of her feathered shoulder joints. And I triggered my Savage Blow skill as I did it, increasing both my critical hit chance while adding a whopping 25% increased damage to the attack. Her bowstring snapped as she unleashed an arrow, but the shot went wide as she fell under my hammer, shrieking from the pain of my surprise attack. The spike punctured feather, skin, and muscle with ease, and the sheer force of the strike snapped the base of her wing bone with a sharp report that almost sounded like gunfire.

Her HP bar dropped below 50%—a critical hit combined with the added damage of a Stealth attack and my special blunt weapon move. A brutal combination.

I yanked my weapon free as she wheeled toward me, slinging her bow in one practiced movement, then drawing a wickedly sharp knife. She lunged at me with an enraged shriek, lashing out with a lightning quick thrust. I dropped back, raising my dinky wooden shield in a sloppy attempt to block, which I knew from the get-go wasn't going to do me a lick of good. And I was right. She was far too quick, shifting her weight as she moved, sidestepping right, then hooking the blade past my guard. The razor slid into my gut as though I were wearing a silk nightshirt instead of leather armor.

I staggered under the terrible blow, the pain a hot poker wriggling inside me, making it hard to think. I sputtered, red burbling from between my lips and dribbling down my chin. She pulled the knife free with a grunt, my blood gleaming along the edge, and jabbed upward with a merciless heave, the tip aimed at my neck. With a desperate jerk, I batted away the incoming blade with the shaft of my hammer, diverting the potentially deadly thrust. She didn't seem to mind, though; she simply spun, catching me in the jaw with an elbow, before dropping low and slashing her blade across my exposed thigh.

Totally outclassed.

I went down like a sack of concrete, my bleeding leg refusing to support my weight, while my health bar flashed like an angry strobe light. With gritted teeth I pushed away from her, using my elbows to scramble back, to gain some extra distance. She moved forward with a feral sneer, her blade upraised—a mountain lion, preparing to maul some weak, injured deer. I fought to bring up my buckler, knowing it wouldn't do any good against an opponent like this, but doing it anyway. I wasn't going down without a fight. I flinched as she lunged, steeling myself for the agony of a killing blow—

A wall of super-hot air thumped into me like a giant unseen hand as an explosion ripped through the chamber. A deafening *boom*, which sent rocks scattering as great gouts of fire snaked and twisted around me.

The sheer force of the detonation slammed me back, my head slapping up against a piece of rough stone. With all that said, the brilliant wave of flame didn't actually do any damage to my HP meter, which meant Abby had to be the caster. When I finally mustered the strength to lift my head, the Ranger was no longer looming over me. Instead, she was rolling on the ground a few feet away, trying desperately to extinguish the hungry red flames crawling over her body, chewing mercilessly at her skin and hair. Her feathered wings were completely gone, now, replaced by blackened nubs jutting from her shoulder blades.

It was an awful scene to witness, game or not. The medic in me demanded I check her breathing, get some pressure dressings on those horrendous shoulder wounds, and slap some WaterJel on the burns for pain relief. Every instinct in my body said that's what I needed to do. Instead, I accessed my inventory, drained a health potion, then hastily gained my feet as the elixir went to work, knitting my torn flesh back together.

Mustering as much speed as I could, I padded over to the dying bird-woman and brought my hammer down on her throat with a sickening *thud*.

For a long moment I just stood there, staring down at the body, staring at the woman's crushed trachea, fighting the terrible urge to vomit onto the floor. This was the first human I'd killed since entering V.G.O., and it was awful. Why would someone design a game like this? A game that'd force office workers, schoolteachers, and retail clerks into situations where they'd be forced to murder people in gory detail?

Another brilliant lance of flame streaked across my vision, jarring me from my own thoughts.

On instinct, I pulled my hammer away and took a quick survey of the room: the spellcaster was already dead by Cutter's hand, and one of the melee warriors was down as well, his head nearly cleaved off by Otto's vicious sword blade. That left the priest and two other fighters. Abby was going to town with her magic—slinging powerful and flashy spells at the enemy swordsman—while Otto and Cutter fought the beefy Templar woman head-on. Otto drew aggro as Cutter danced around her in a whirl of steel, his blades flashing out in streaks of silver, drawing blood with every swipe.

That left the priest, who was currently in the back, chanting some sort of divine spell.

A chanting priest was too dangerous to ignore.

I tried to slip back into Stealth, but failed. My stamina was too badly depleted from my scuffle with the Ranger.

So instead, I broke into a sprint—low-grade panic spurring me on—ducking past the brawlers before throwing myself at the priest. I sailed through the air like a cruise missile and hit him around the waist, driving a shoulder into his gut. We both went to the ground in a tangle of limbs. He landed with a muffled curse, dust mushrooming up around him in a puff, while I ended up on top of him. A relieved smile broke across my face—I'd managed to interrupt his spell, even if my tactic hadn't been elegant or graceful.

The priest awkwardly flailed at me with his staff, but without distance and leverage, the attacks were merely a nuisance instead of actually being harmful. Unfortunately, the same thing applied to me. Straddling the guy didn't offer me much opportunity to use my hammer. I let the weapon clatter to the floor and promptly laid into him with my fists, working over his face and torso until he finally stopped struggling. Not dead—his health bar still had over 25%—but stunned. Even after he stopped resisting, though, I kept hitting until someone finally dragged me off the bloody priest.

"You're good, Grim Jack," Cutter murmured, his arms wrapped around my chest, restraining me.

"But he's still breathing," I snarled, straining toward my hammer, ready to kill the priest. To finish him for good.

"We know," Abby said, strutting over and kneeling next to the downed man. "And that's a good thing. Hard to get a dead prisoner to talk, and I've got a feeling this guy has a few more things to tell us before his usefulness is exhausted." She ran her hands over the priest's downed form, palms a few inches above his body, while she chanted in some archaic language. Tendrils of fire, most as thin as my pinky, spread over him, wrapping him in a tight, brilliant cocoon of flame. Suddenly he lurched upright, lifted from the ground by Abby's magic, though he was still unresponsive.

"Flame of Holding," she said, glancing at me over one shoulder. "This'll keep him immobile while we question him." Next, she stood and pulled a red vial from her bag, identical to the one I'd chugged a few moments before. She regarded the glass bottle, before uncorking it and dumping the liquid into the priest's slack mouth. After a long moment, the Dawn Elf sputtered and coughed, his body shuddering and shivering as he opened swollen eyes.

"Good work, Jack," she said, patting me reassuringly on the forearm. "Now we don't have much time—Aleixo Carrera and his thugs could show up any moment—so

Otto and I are going to interrogate our friend here. See if we can't get a heads-up about what we're going into. In the meantime, you and Cutter loot these bodies. Sound like a plan? Oh, and you can keep whatever you find."

She didn't even wait for me to respond. Instead she offered me a dimple-cheeked smile and dragged the priest off with Otto's help.

Cutter finally let me go, offered me a hearty slap on the back, then swaggered over to the body of the mage he'd killed and began searching the bloody corpse. Happy as a kid on Christmas morning. I shuffled from foot to foot as I eyed the brutalized and smoldering Ranger. The last thing I wanted to do was go and pick over her charred and battered body, but loot was loot. Still, it felt dirty. Wrong. But, loot *was* the goal of these kinds of games, I reminded myself. Cheap loot meant money in the bank. And good loot meant *life.* Good loot meant power. Influence. Status.

Good loot reduced the chance of being killed or feeling the pain of this place.

With a sigh, I headed over, squatted down, then began checking her person.

Thankfully, like with the Corrupt Valdgeist, I didn't actually have to search her pockets or rip the armor from her body. An inventory menu popped up in front of me, displaying my spoils. I whistled. Very impressive. The boots were standard leather, though of "superior" quality, which meant they were a heck of a lot better than what I was currently sporting. I slipped them on without a qualm, then turned my sights on her armor, which was truly a cut above:

Night Blessed Armor.

Dark black leather covered in swatches of ebony ring mail in the most vulnerable places—like along the shoulders, across the stomach, and down the spinal column. It was medium armor, instead of the light armor I'd used up to this point, which offered better defense, though slightly reduced speed, movement, and evade bonuses.

Night Blessed Armor

Armor Type: Medium; Modified Leather

Class: Rare

Base Defense: 62

Primary Effects:

- +5 to Constitution
- 15% Resistance to Piercing Damage
- 15% Resistance to Slashing Damage
- 10% Resistance to all Elemental and Arcane-Based Damage

I threw the armor on and instantly felt stronger, more resilient, less tired. Lastly, I snatched up a beautiful recurve bow with a +10 Dexterity boost and a 10% increased chance to evade, worth a staggering 150 gold, and also pocketed a small bag of silver coins.

I moved on to the next body, one of the warriors Otto had killed, and began the process all over again. This time rummaging through the belongings of a butchered NPC didn't bother me quite so much, which was a little troubling in itself.

In the end, I walked away with another 225 in gold, a Ring of Slaying—+5 to Strength—and Heavy Firesteel Gauntlets, worth another cool 75 gold. I hadn't been to a proper store yet, but I imagined these kinds of weapons and armor weren't the types of gear lowbies were supposed to get. I wasn't sure what else awaited us inside this dungeon, but if these were the *door prizes*, it had to be something epically awesome.

NINETEEN

THE LONG ROAD DOWN

WE MOVED FROM THE ENTRY CHAMBER INTO A circular stairway that drilled into the earth. The steps were slick stone; vines and strands of moss hung down from ancient archways, constantly brushing up against me as I moved. Once more, Cutter was gone—scouting—and Otto was out in front, treading carefully, searching for anything our resident Thief might've missed. This time, though, we had a new member to our party: the burlap-robe wearing prisoner, who turned out to be a mercenary Warlock, not a priest.

That'd be the same burlap-robe wearing Warlock I'd almost bludgeoned to death. He was still bound by the Flame of Holding, and he floated along between Abby and me—carried by a simple levitation spell.

So far, we'd made our way through passageway after passageway, always winding deeper into the heart of these old ruins. We'd run across tons of deadly rigged traps in just about every variety and flavor, but so far Cutter had proven to be as good a thief as he kept claiming. And he claimed to be the absolute best in Eldgard often and loudly. We'd also tangled with a near-endless horde of Corrupt Valdgeist, though no more

NPCs, which I was silently grateful for. Surprisingly, the Corrupt Valdgeist were pushovers one and all.

Superficially, the creatures looked identical to the beasts I'd tangled with in the forest beyond the ruins, but that's where the similarities ended.

These things moped about aimlessly, only attacking when you were in spitting distance, and even then a strong breeze would knock them over. Pitiful, really. The strangest thing of all, however, was the amount of EXP each one had: easily 8,000 apiece, which was larger than some low-level bosses. Yes, we had to split the EXP between four, but that was still 2,000 points per head, and we must've killed sixty or seventy of the things. Since we were in an almost constant state of combat, I didn't take the time to pull up my character stats or check my skill notifications, but I was sure once I finally had some time to look them over, I was going to be as pleased as a cat with a ball of yarn.

The Corrupt Valdgeist didn't drop much by way of gear, just like their counterparts topside, but they practically exploded with gold. Each kill netted us 50 gold—50 gold *each*. Most also carried a potion or two, which were certainly a nice bonus.

"So this is some kind of quick and easy grind for the uber rich, huh," I mused out loud after collecting my share from yet another group of shambling mobs. At this point, I wasn't really worried about making noise since the resistance here was basically nonexistent.

"Yeah," Abby said from behind me, a slight note of scorn in her voice. "Doesn't seem fair, does it? Everyone has to start off fresh in a new world, but guys like Carrera still find a way to game the system in their favor. It's incredible." She shook her head. "Really pisses me off, you know?"

"But you're benefiting," our hostage Warlock replied, "and you don't seem to be complaining." Other than the terse answers he'd provided during the interrogation, he'd been silent up until now. "If you were really so noble," he said, "you'd leave this place untouched. Just turn around and walk away. The fact that you're continuing onward suggests you don't mind the benefit so long as it's directed at you." He sounded smug all the way down to his toes. The worst part was, he was sort of right. I shared an uneasy look with Abby.

Are we really doing the right thing here?

"It's different with us," she replied, a bit unconvincingly. "We're doing what we need to in order to make it in Eldgard, and we're going to help other people. To benefit the people who couldn't afford to pay to cheat their way to the upper echelons in this new society."

"Ahh," the mercenary said with a slick grin, "so you're an ends-justify-the-means kind of lady."

"No. You're twisting my words and skewing the situation out of context," she protested. "All I'm saying is this stuff *is* here, and that means someone is going to get it—and I'm just saying it's definitely better for people like us to get it than some cocaine-financed dictator."

"Yeah," I said, nodding in agreement, working to convince myself. "Besides, what's it to you anyway?" I asked the merc, my brow furrowed in annoyance. "You're a mercenary who works for the highest bidder— I don't think you're in a position to judge us on issues of ethics."

"No judgement," he replied with a tight shrug, made awkward by the bands of fire encircling him. "You're right, I'm a mercenary. Personally, I think your logic is flawless, but then I regularly do questionable things for money. I only bring it up because I think there might be an opportunity for us to work together in the very near future, supposing you all can get past your veneer of self-righteous hypocrisy."

"What are you talking about?" I asked.

"You'll see soon enough," he replied, once more overflowing with smugness.

Abby gave him a hard look, her lips puckered into a tight line, and suddenly the priest had a gag of flickering fire in his mouth. It didn't seem to hurt him, but it certainly prevented him from speaking further. "That's enough out of you," she mumbled, gaze downcast. She looked guilty. Maybe the mercenary's accusations had gotten under her skin.

They'd certainly gotten under mine.

After a time, the hallway morphed into a natural underground cavern with jagged walls and a small burbling stream, studded with large boulders, that zigzagged its way through soft black earth. Bioluminescent moss clung to the ceiling overhead, shedding a pale green light that reminded me of a toxic waste spill. We walked on in silence for a bit longer, following the stream.

"I wonder why they didn't give the mobs here even more EXP?" I asked idly, just trying to break the thoughtful quiet. "Not that eight thousand a pop is bad," I said, "but if cheap leveling is the name of the game, it seems like the Devs should've just dumped a bunch of

Corrupt Valdgeist with like, I dunno, a hundred thousand points apiece or something crazy like that."

"I'm sure they would if they could," Abby replied, the sound carrying over the muted clomping of our feet and the burble of the water. "Trust me on that. But the Devs only have so much control. Early on maybe they could've done something like that, but not now. Now, the Overminds are the real power in V.G.O., and once they were up and running, we could only tweak relatively insignificant things. Really, the Overminds do all the heavy lifting—they generate content, creatures, quests, everything—they're basically in-game gods.

"Each Overmind has an underpinning of base directives that govern their 'character'—keeps them from going completely rogue, but it's like holding a lion in check with a leash made of bacon." She paused and fidgeted with her robes, smoothing out fabric that didn't need it. "Anyway, one of those essential directives is to prevent hackers and game modders from tinkering around in unsanctioned ways. Cheating the game, specifically. And this"—she swept a hand around the cavern—"*almost* qualifies."

The cavern ended at a small cliff, the water from the stream cascading over the side and disappearing into a cavernous black pit without end. There was, however, a rocky slope that led to a dirt path running along the base of the cliff. Otto surveyed it for a moment, but since there was no sign of Cutter or any enemies, he quickly began picking his way down the rocky slope and to the path below.

"So to get around the rules and the Overmind screening protocols," Abby continued as she followed Otto down, "I think the Devs probably created these restricted areas with a carefully balanced ratio of EXP, loot drops, and mob difficulty. I'll bet a thousand gold the algorithm they came up with skirts just below what the Overminds will flag as unsanctioned modding. It's still cheating, obviously, but it's really smart cheating. The kind of cheating only insiders could come up with."

After a little maneuvering, we made it to the bottom of the treacherous slope, passed behind the cascading waterfall, and started trekking along the path, which led into another natural cavern. One littered with torches, burning merrily on the walls. "We've got something strange up here," Cutter called, his voice echoing and bouncing from ahead, oddly distorted by the stone walls. We all picked up the pace a bit, following a natural bend in the cavern, only to stop suddenly in our tracks. Cutter was dead ahead, squat down on his haunches, one hand rubbing at his chin while he regarded a colossal set of double doors at the end of the earthen chamber.

They were huge wooden things, studded with bronze fastenings and carved with complex runic symbols. I'd played enough MMOs to know we'd finally arrived at the boss's lair. No doubt in my mind.

"Can you ungag him?" I said, hooking a thumb toward the Warlock.

Abby nodded and complied.

"I've got a question for you—what were you and your team doing here?" I asked, sudden worry tugging at my mind. "Anybody could work their way through this dungeon without the help of a mercenary team," I said, "so why were you put here?"

The Warlock smiled, a malicious glint in his eye. "We were specifically contracted to help with the thing beyond that door. Before this mission, my team and I were briefed about this dungeon. And your friend is right, this is a very special place. Drastically underpowered mobs scattered throughout—easy kills for weak players, granting significant EXP—but the tradeoff is a dangerously overpowered Guardian. One so powerful it raised the difficulty level of the dungeon as a whole." He paused and offered a sly sneer.

"And I happen to know that without me, you don't stand a chance of getting into that room"—he nodded toward the door—"and even if you do *somehow* manage to find a way in, you'll never get out alive. But, as I mentioned earlier, I might be willing to help, assuming of course you can find it in your hearts to work with someone like me. And assuming you're willing to pay my price…"

TWENTY

BOSS BATTLE

"E VERYONE READY?" THE MERCENARY
Warlock called out.
I took a deep, calming breath and stole one last final look around me. Cutter was invisible, as was I—both of us cloaked in Stealth. Abby was at my back, Otto my front, with a slew of conjured creatures flanking him on either side: a few walking skeletons with worn swords and basic long bows; a spattering of earth and flame elementals; plus, one very angry-looking demonic lord with blackened, heavy-plate armor and glowing red eyes. Minions, summoned by our Warlock friend, and future cannon fodder for whatever boss lurked in the next room.

"We are as ready as we will ever be, mercenary," Otto replied tersely. "One thing though," he added, turning and glowering at our former prisoner. "If you betray us as you betrayed your former master, I will find you. And I will end you. One way or another, I will end you."

"Keep me well supplied with gold," the mercenary Warlock said, "and we won't find ourselves at cross purposes." He paused, offering the Risi warrior a tight, feral smile. "Now, shall we?" He swept one arm out, muttering some strange spell, a ball of glowing blue light forming around his hand.

The massive door—which boasted a complex and unpickable lock—swung open on silent hinges. The Warlock hadn't exaggerated in his claims; we literally couldn't have gotten into the boss's chamber without his help. Apparently, the Devs for this area had fitted the dungeon's door with one final safeguard, ensuring that only the right person got through. And that safeguard was a custom key, soulbound to the mercenary leader. It was a stroke of blind luck that I hadn't killed him, or I would've doomed this operation before it ever got off the ground.

We were luckier still, because it turned out the Warlock was willing to sell his loyalty, along with the key, for gold. A bunch of gold. A small mountain of gold. But that was one thing we weren't in short supply of thanks to the easily dispatched Corrupt Valdgeist.

The doors finished opening with a resounding *boom*, which echoed around us like a warning siren. Otto bowed his head and muttered a quick prayer before heading in, accompanied by the Warlock's conjured minions. As soon as they were through the grand entryway, I forged ahead, skirting around a flame elemental and a skeleton, stealing up the left, positioning myself so I could sneak attack when the moment was right. The door let out into another natural cavern—this one dotted with ancient stalactites and stalagmites so large they were nearly columns—which quickly gave way to the ruins of some sort of temple:

A massive circular chamber of roughhewn stone blocks liberally carved with runic symbols and horrifying pictographs, most of them involving human torture and dismemberment in one form or fashion. Bones, yellowed with age, littered the floor like trash on a highway. Weak sunlight streamed in from a jagged opening in the ceiling that revealed a glimmer of blue sky. Below, in the center of the temple ruins, illuminated by a single shaft of sunlight, lurked a twisted tree. A bent, bone-white thing like an arthritic finger, its stunted branches devoid of leaves or life of any kind.

At the base of the tree, surrounded by knobby roots, sat a heavy wooden chest heavily tooled with gold and bronze script.

Whatever was in the box was the real reward we'd come for, but the question was, where was the chest's guardian? Where was the uber boss?

I moved further into the room, creeping slowly, continually scanning the space, looking for some telltale sign of our opponent. The room didn't have any nooks or crannies a hulking super-guardian could secret away in. As I crept closer, I caught sight of a crude stairway at the back of the temple proper, jutting from the stone, winding its way up to a partially hidden tunnel high in the temple wall. The stairs were partially outlined in purple, meaning my Keen-Sight skill had kicked in.

I was pretty sure that passageway would, almost impossibly, connect back to the beginning of this dungeon. That, or let out directly into the wider world of Eldgard. The game Devs for this kind of RPG knew how tedious it was to backtrack all the way through an already completed dungeon, so they often built in a secret exit for player convenience.

I caught a brief flash of movement over by the right wall—Cutter, positioning himself just to the side of a toppled column. Still, though, I saw nothing else. So I crept closer and closer, moving toward the stairs. By now, Otto and the minion squad were almost to the treasure chest, their movements marked by nervous anxiety.

"Where's the boss?" Otto demanded, glancing over one shoulder at the Warlock. "I told you betrayal would be met with swift violence, sellsword."

The Warlock shrugged. "Just because I was hired for this quest doesn't mean I know what we're up against here. Not the specifics, anyway."

"The chest, Otto," Abby called. "Open the chest and I'll bet we flush this thing out."

The Risi warrior offered a grunt and a curt nod, turning back toward the tree. "Everyone take your positions," he ordered.

Cutter and I were already in place, but the minions reacted as one, spreading out in a loose arc. The bow-wielding skeletons moved back a few paces so they'd be able to sink in a volley of arrows. The flame elementals, also ranged attackers, took up positions near the left and right walls, giving them a clear line of fire for whatever might appear. The conjured demon and the earth elementals—hulking things of stone and mud with gleaming obsidian spikes protruding from their backs, shoulders, and arms—made a tight circle around the tree.

They were the frontline defense.

Otto surveyed the scene with a practiced eye, grunted his approval, and edged past the demon and the earth-hulks. He knelt in front of the chest, rubbed his hands together, then extended one trembling limb toward the box. The second his thick fingers touched the clasp, the room exploded with movement: the ground trembled, the walls rattled, small baseball-sized stones clattered down from above, while that bone-white tree began to sway and surge upward in herky-jerk lurches.

Earth and dirt fell away in a shower as a massive *something* pulled its way from the ground of the temple.

The stunted tree rose into the air, directly attached to a bulbous, misshapen head covered in maggot-white flesh, which was larger than a gas-guzzling SUV. The creature, a Greater Corrupt Valdgeist, sported a single bulging eye, milky and dead, situated above a monstrous maw riddled with jagged fangs. Its misshapen head sat perched atop a host of octopus-like tree root limbs covered in thorns the size of meat hooks, while more fat tentacles whipped and writhed in the air, sprouting from every free patch of skin.

Whatever Dev had designed this thing deserved both an award for horrific creativity and also a year-long voucher for psychiatric treatment.

Everyone stared for a tense moment, held captive in fascinated horror. That uneasy truce ended abruptly as the creature spread its massive jaws and issued a defiant roar, which rocked Otto back on his heels and sent a tremor running through the floor and up into my teeth. Then the creature surged forward, lashing out with a massive limb, smashing Otto in his breastplate. The Risi warrior let out a rumble of pain as he popped up into the air, cartwheeling head over heels before finally landing in a heap ten feet away.

"Attack," Abby screamed, a thread of fear weaving through the words.

The Warlock's minions responded to the command.

In an instant, everything was pure chaos—all manic motion and whipping tentacles, intermixed with the ring of steel on stone and the blaze of magical power. The Warlock's hard-hitting melee minions threw themselves at the creature: skeletons unleashed a hail of arrows, flame elementals hurled fire balls, earth elementals charged the thing with spiked fists upraised, while the demon laid into the freakish beast with its massive two-handed sword. The fury of the Warlock's summoned help was truly impressive, but the Greater Corrupt Valdgeist seemed to shrug off most of their attacks without sustaining much damage.

A tornado of flame engulfed Abby, swirling around her as she chanted, arms upraised. A vortex of red, orange, and blue light radiated waves of heat as she blasted out continuous balls of flame, which lit up the room like a shower of falling stars. I just stood there, unsure what to do, how to act. Despite my increasing proficiency with the warhammer, I wasn't a brawler—one hit from those tentacles would likely put me out of the game. The only thing I really had going for me was my Stealth attack bonus, and pragmatically that was a one-off ability, so I needed to deploy it wisely.

Still invisible, I hustled left, behind a fire elemental, then scurried up the winding stairs at the rear of the temple.

Otto was back in the fight, hurling himself into the fray, a whirling tornado of steel, his sword flashing out faster than my eye could follow, shearing through a forest of the smaller tentacles with a lazy ease. The Warlock also began launching a direct assault, planting his feet shoulder width apart and machine-gunning his arms like a boxer working a heavy bag, bolts of angry-green light flying from his palms. The tentacle beast staggered from the blasts, but fought on, finally turning the earth elementals into rubble piles.

I was halfway up the staircase—a solid ten feet above the hulking monstrosity—when I caught sight of Cutter sailing through the air, materializing as he slammed into the side of the Greater Corrupt Valdgeist's head, plunging his blade into the beast's single eye. A gout of sickly green gore spewed from the puncture wound like projectile vomit, showering down onto Otto and the summoned demon. Cutter's Stealth attack achieved a critical hit and nearly halved the boss's health points, dropping him below 60%, but the Thief wasn't done yet.

As he dangled from the creature's eye, he pulled a second dagger free and slammed it in next to the first, a snarl on his face.

The boss reared back, shrieking in pain and defiance, violently shaking its head, flinging Cutter away like a dog shedding water. The Thief tumbled through the air, slamming up against a toppled column with a terrible *crack.* He wasn't on the ground for more than a heartbeat before a host of wriggling white roots erupted from the floor, ensnaring the combatants below. The creature bellowed again, but this time, the bone-shaking noise was accompanied by a creeping green cloud. An area effect spell. A combat notification popped up in the corner of my eye:

Debuffs Added

Rooted: Your party has been rooted and is unable to move; duration, 1 minute.

Toxic Cloud: Your party is poisoned: 10 points of stamina damage/10 secs; 20 points health damage/10 secs; duration, 2 minutes.

Death Cloud: Instantly kill all summoned creatures.

My jaw fell open in shock. *Yep, we were dead. So, so dead.*

The Warlock's remaining creatures keeled over, dropping to the ground, each dissolving into a pile of harmless dust. The rest of my teammates were on the floor downing potions to fight off the Toxic Cloud's effects, battling to stay alive. I, however, wasn't affected. My elevation above the fight kept me clear of the deathly green fog and the ensnaring tree roots. That was a huge break, but it also meant this fight was now firmly on my shoulders—if I didn't do something, my party was toast.

But what could I do against a thing like that? If I headed down into the thick of things, I'd likely be poisoned, rooted, and killed. And, since I couldn't access my Umbra Bolt skill, I didn't have any kind of range attack to employ.

I wrestled with what to do for a beat longer, knowing every second I wasted could mean the difference between life and death for someone below. Then it occurred to me—there was one thing I could do. One reckless move that might pay dividends …

I threw myself from the edge of the stairs without a second thought, falling like a stone, slamming the spike of my hammer into the boss's skull as I landed on top of its head with a wet *thwack.* I threw my whole body into the strike and unleashed my Savage Blow attack. That, combined with the added damage from the Stealth Attack, dropped the creature's HP to 35%. Once more, the Greater Corrupt Valdgeist began shaking its head, whipping back and forth, trying to buck me to the floor where it could crush me underfoot.

Try as I might, I couldn't keep my feet and before I knew it, I landed on my belly, clinging desperately to the warhammer still lodged into the creature's skull, using it like a climbing pick. The beast bellowed again, bucking up, then slamming down, but I refused to let go. Refused to be shaken. To fall. To fail.

The chaotic bucking seemed to last forever, my body flopping like a rag doll, and just as I thought my grip was going to give out, the beast settled back down, returning his attention to my teammates as his "root" spell wore off. Otto and Cutter were still down and chugging potions, but Abby was somehow back on her feet, throwing fireball after fireball, shaving off points with every hit. With the creature's focus once more elsewhere, I clumsily crawled to my knees and pried my weapon free with a jerk. Fetid gore, dark and viscous, oozed from the wound.

Then, while the creature swayed and fought, I started hammering at the withered tree trunk protruding from its skull. Pounding over and over again with the face of my hammer. *Thud. Thud. Thud.* Each blow, though clumsy and ungainly, knocked off a noticeable chunk of its hit points.

Finally, a weak spot.

All bosses had a weak spot, and usually it was in the most annoyingly difficult place to reach. Like a gnarled tree on *top* of the boss's head. I sunk my hammer home one more time, twisting my torso, throwing all my weight into the blow—a *crack* reverberated in the air as the trunk shattered and tumbled. The creature bucked below me one last time as its HP bar hit zero, before pitching forward like a felled tree.

Unfortunately, despite my victory, there was no graceful way off the boss's back.

The fall flung me into the air, my arms flailing as I flew, the ground rushing toward me at an incredible rate.

"Don't worry, friend," Cutter called out, stepping into view, a devilish grin plastered all over his face. "I've got you." He thrust out his arms as though to catch me, then, at the last moment, stepped aside. I face-planted into dusty earth, stars exploding in my eyes as a "stunned" debuff flared in front of me. Ouch, did that hurt. My head ached, my ribs were tender from top to bottom, and generally it felt like someone had pushed me down the side of a steep mountain.

I coughed, rolled over, and grimaced as Cutter offered me a hand. "What I meant," Cutter said, "is let me help you up."

"Thanks, jerk," I muttered, reluctantly accepting his hand, letting him pull me to my feet.

He clapped me on the shoulder, grin widening. "You'll be fine, Grim Jack. Besides, what do I look like, that meathead over there?" He motioned toward Otto, just now pulling himself from the dirt and rubble. "Me? I don't catch falling damsels in distress," he said, "I rob them and sell their jewelry to the highest bidder. On an unrelated note, good work with the boss." He clapped me on the shoulder again. "You're not as completely worthless and incompetent as you look, which is truly the *highest* praise I can give someone."

"Wow, Jack!" Abby ran up to me and hit me with a fierce bear hug that hurt my already tender ribs. "That was incredible. Seriously. How did you ever think of that?"

"Lucky guess?" I offered, carefully prying her arms off my torso.

"Well"—she beamed at me like a ray of sunshine— "I don't care how you did it, that was a brilliant move. Seriously epic." She leaned in and pecked me on the cheek. "I knew I picked the right guy for this. Now, let's go see what's worth twenty million dollars."

Our party—bruised, battered, but alive—headed over to explore the vanquished boss. I was dismayed to find he didn't have anything on him except a tarnished gold key, which I assumed went with the chest. I was sure whatever was in the chest was totally worth all this trouble, but I still felt a little disappointed; bosses were supposed to drop the best loot. That's just the way it worked. Anything else was an abject failure in the system.

Abby held the key in trembling fingers, her eyes fixed on the piece of metal like it was the Holy Grail of gaming. After a moment, though, she sighed and turned toward me, extending the slip of gold. "Why don't you do the honors," she said with a sad smile.

"You sure?" I asked.

She paused, twitched her nose, then nodded halfheartedly. "I think it's for the best. Besides, you deserve first crack at the goodies—you did save the day this time around."

I shook my head, finally clearing the "stunned" debuff from my fall, then accepted the key and meandered over to the chest, excitement filling my belly. I brushed past Otto and dropped to a knee, sliding the key home, then gave the thing a jiggle and a tug. The lock dropped away and the chest creaked open, an inventory screen popping into view before my eyes as it did. I heard a chorus of whistles echo all around me— apparently, the whole group was seeing this same screen.

And they had good reason to celebrate. There was something for everyone, and it was all *Ancient Artifact* gear.

TWENTY-ONE

FACTION SEAL

T HE LOOT ENDED UP BEING FAIRLY EASY TO distribute, since most of the items were class-restricted. Staff of the Enchantress and the Ring of Insight for Abby. Blade of the Ancients and the Amulet of Bloodletting for Otto. Cloak of the Nightborn and the Ice Prick—a sleek deadly dagger that radiated unnatural cold—for Cutter. Even the Warlock got something: a legendary, scalable helm called Frightful Visage. My gear wasn't class specific, a good thing since I currently lacked a class, but somehow the AI seemed to read me like a book and provided just what I needed.

First came my new and improved weapon, the Gavel of Shadows, a wicked looking warhammer of black forged steel with shadowy runes of violet power crawling up the haft of the weapon and twirling around its blunt face. A cruel hooked spike, serrated on one side for sawing, extended from the back, while a second, smaller spike jutted from the top of the weapon like a pointing finger. The thing seemed to radiate dark energy, to pull at the shadows around me and draw them in tight. To harness them.

And the stats were as impressive as its formidable appearance.

Gavel of Shadows

Weapon Type: Blunt; Warhammer

Class: Ancient Artifact, Two-handed

Base Damage: 47

Primary Effects:

- 50 pts Shadow Damage + (.5 x Character Level)
- +10% Damage to all Blunt Weapon attacks
- Strength Bonus = .25 x Character Level
- Spirit Bonus = .5 x Character Level

Secondary Effects:

- +250 EXP per kill
- +29% Extra gold dropped
- Increases all Blunt Level Skills by 1 while equipped

Can be used with a small buckler (5% reduced weapon speed)

I also snagged the Ruby Ring of Foxfen, which offered me a 12% increased chance to receive a magical item drop, +8% critical hit chance, +10 to all primary attributes (minus Luck), and +1 to Luck. These prizes were a truly huge find, certainly the kind of thing only the highest-level players were likely to stumble upon, and then only after murdering a major level boss. Still, as great as all of the loot and easy EXP was, it hardly seemed like the kind of gear that'd run someone twenty *million* real world dollars. Which meant the EXP and loot had to be the frills.

Bonuses to sweeten the pot, but *not* the major ticket item.

The only other thing in the chest, though, was a worn gold talisman the size of an antique CD with the image of a noble-faced man in profile on one side and a huge tree on the other. The metal trinket was inscribed around the edge with the Latin phrase *Imperatorius Factio Signum* on the top and *Domini est Terra* on the bottom. The dual phrases appeared on both the front and back. Otto succinctly informed us the words meant Imperial Faction Seal and Lord of the Land; the only problem was no one knew what it was for. The NPCs had never heard of the thing, and Abby, an actual game Dev, had never seen the feature either.

A true mystery, only bolstered by the fact that the item came with exactly no description whatsoever. Despite that, it was clear the strange talisman was the real prize, since that was the only item no one could place.

The mood of the party was equal parts excited and subdued as we made our way up the stairs and through a long, boring stone passage, which dumped us back at the dungeon's entry, via a "secret" door panel. Typical. We headed up topside, everyone letting out a collective sigh of relief as fading rays of warmth washed over us and a cool breeze lapped at exposed skin. We'd only been in the dungeon for a little over four hours, but it felt much longer. A short lifetime. Being out in the rolling expanse—with the sky stretching endlessly above and the mountains cutting across the horizon—I felt free. Safe.

"Well," Abby said, shuffling over to me, eyes downcast, hands clasped in front of her. She glanced up at me, the ghost of a smile lingering on her lips. "I think it might be time for us to part ways for a bit."

"Wait. What?" I asked, genuinely taken aback. "Why would we do that? We worked great together as a team. Jack and Abby all the way," I said, with a smile and a fist pump. "We rocked it down there."

"I know." She nodded, before reaching up and tucking a loose strand of hair behind her ear. "And this isn't over. But right now, I think it's best if we divide and conquer. Otto and I, we need to go see some people. Ask around about that weird disk we found. See if we can find out what its purpose is." She rooted around in her bag for a moment before fishing out a curled scroll, bound shut with a loop of red silk. "A portal scroll to get you home," she offered. "This'll take you to your bind point, wherever that happens to be."

I slowly accepted the proffered paper, then opened my inventory bag and removed the golden disk. I turned it over in my hand, studying both sides of the strange talisman before holding it out to her.

She grimaced and shook her head. "Better not," she replied. "I think it's safer with you for the time being. I stumbled on this info by snooping around in company records that, *strictly speaking*, I wasn't supposed to have access to. By which I totally mean I hacked them. So, when Aleixo Carrera shows up here and finds this place empty, he's going to start asking questions over at Osmark Technologies, and those questions will likely point to me. It'll take a while before they find out about you, though."

Her reasoning made perfect, logical sense, but there was something off about this whole thing. The way she stood, back slightly bent, hesitant to meet my eye. Abby was a tough woman—you had to be to make it as an IRL girl in a lot of gaming circles—and this didn't seem like her at all. She seemed sad.

"I hear what you're saying, Abby, and I believe you. I do. But there's something you're not telling me. Some piece of the puzzle you're purposely leaving out."

She paused, chewing at her lip, then nodded. "I'm coming up on my third day, Jack. Just a few hours away, now. That's why I needed you here so quickly. Statistically, one in six die during the transition, which means in another five or six hours, I could be dead. Gone"—she snapped her fingers—"just like that.

"I don't want to put you through that, Jack. I know it probably doesn't make much sense, but if it's my time to go, I want to be alone. So, I'm going to head back to Harrowick, get a good, hot meal, and go to sleep. If I wake up"—she shrugged narrow shoulders—"then I guess I survived and I'll PM you. If not ... well, know that I wish the absolute best for you."

I wanted to hug her, to tell her not to worry, that things would be okay. They *had* to be okay. I couldn't, though, because they might not be. She was right after all: one in six died. Statistically, there was a decent chance we would *both* be dead in another two days. So instead of offering her meaningless platitudes, I tucked the disk back into my inventory and asked her what I should do in the meantime.

"You need to get a little rest," she replied, "and then you need to acquire a class, Jack. As is, if you weren't reasonably smart and passably good-looking, you'd be entirely useless to the party. So, while I do the legwork and turn up leads about what that trinket does, you find out what kind of character you're going to be and start maximizing your stats. I have a feeling things will get really intense around here before long."

She smiled again, a small sweet thing, and turned to go. She faltered a step away, spun back, and pulled me into a tight hug. "I know we didn't work out in college," she whispered into my chest, "but if we both live through this, survive the next few days, maybe we can do things differently this time around."

She tilted her head up and drew me into a soft kiss, her lips warm against mine. "In case this is our final goodbye," she murmured as she pulled away. She patted me on the cheek, wheeled around, and left.

Otto, the taciturn warrior, offered us a grim nod before stalking off after her, leaving me alone with Cutter and the mercenary Warlock. A second later there was a flare of brilliant light—a portal—which fizzled and faded. Vanished.

It was distinctly possible I'd never see her again.

"Unless you plan on killing me," the mercenary Warlock pitched in a second later, "I, too, shall depart. Time to spend a little of this hard-earned money." He tapped a fat coin purse at his side, the *clink* of gold carrying in the air.

"We're not going to kill you," I replied halfheartedly, still thinking about Abby. "You were good on your word, and we really couldn't have done it without you. Thanks. I mean it."

The Warlock seemed to struggle with something for a moment, uncertainty playing out across his rough features. "You and your friends aren't so bad, either," he said, "for being hypocrites, obviously." He faltered, fingers restlessly drumming on his coin purse. "Listen, if you ever need the hand of an experienced mercenary, you can find me at a tavern in East Harrowick—a place called the Drunken Donkey. Ask for Morgan, and you'll find me. I don't work out of the goodness of my heart, mind you, so make sure you bring gold."

Recruit Follower

You can now recruit Morgan Sellsword as an in-game follower. You can find Morgan at the Drunken Donkey in East Harrowick, and hire him as a loyal companion for (5) gold a day.

He didn't linger long after that.

"What about you?" I asked, turning to Cutter. "You gonna take off, too?"

"Pffff." He folded his arms across his chest. "You must be positively mental if you think I'm going anywhere. First you helped me break free from that hellhole of a prison, and now, after one mission, I've pocketed more gold than I'd normally see in ten years. You're my lucky charm, Jack." He shot me a wink. "You'll literally have to beat me away with a stick if you want me gone. Otherwise, I'm gonna follow you around and scoop up the loot you leave in your wake until I can retire fat and happy on a mountain of gold, surrounded by beautiful women."

"How altruistic of you," I noted, face deadpan.

"You know, that's what everyone is always telling me—'Cutter,' they say, 'you are one of the shining jewels of humanity.' True story."

"Yeah, I bet," I replied with an eyeroll.

He grinned. "So, where to now, lucky charm?"

"I've got a quest to turn in," I replied.

TWENTY-TWO

DOWNTIME

CUTTER AND I THREADED OUR WAY THROUGH THE forest, backtracking along the path I'd taken earlier in the day, making light conversation as we went. I filled him in on the *Cleanse the Taint* quest details, then fell silent as he prattled on about beer and gambling, telling me all about how his father had taught him knucklebones before he was old enough to walk. Once more I was dumbstruck by the depth of Cutter's character: his memories, his mannerisms, his humor. He seemed more alive, more real, than the majority of my real-world friends.

I listened more than talked, constantly scanning the forest for any sign that the Corrupt Valdgeist I'd killed earlier had respawned. With the Greater Corrupt Valdgeist dead deep in the heart of the ruins behind us, however, the forest seemed to be free from the twisted taint. After twenty minutes of hard trekking, we broke into the clearing with the Hamadryad that'd offered me the temple clearing quest.

"The hero of the hour," the old tree boomed, mossy mustache fluttering as he spoke. "I had my doubts about you, boy. Even felt guilty sending a whelp such as you out to contend with an evil as powerful as that which dwelt in those accursed ruins, yet here you are. Returned a conqueror." He smiled big and wide, revealing a mouthful of acorn teeth. A laugh followed, a hearty thing that sounded like a clap of distant thunder.

"I can already feel the difference," the tree continued. "The goodness in the land returns. The earth cries out in joy, the trees shiver in relief. Even the air tastes cleaner as it rushes through my leaves. A genuinely great day for the forest. A great day for me and my kind." He laughed again, stirring up a chorus of happy birdsong all around us. "Now, I know you're likely eager to get along. You mortals are always rushing about—sprinting from place to place—so quick to move on to what is next, to what is new. So, let me see you properly rewarded before you go."

I cast a glance at Cutter, letting him know to stay back, then edged closer to the towering tree. On the ground, directly in front of the Hamadryad, a green shoot sprouted from the ground, curling up and out, reaching and yearning for the fading sunlight; vibrant green leaves and barbed thorns bloomed along the stalk. I dropped to one knee, admiring the magical sight, watching raptly as a petite bulb blossomed into a rose so blue it was nearly black, its petals unfurling in triple speed time.

Absolutely stunning.

When the flower finally opened all the way, I saw the gleam of metal within: a silver cloak brooch in the shape of an intricately worked warhammer with a fat emerald the size of a dime at the center. The tree nodded at me, *take it, take it.* Tentatively, almost uncertainly, I reached out and plucked the brooch free—the little trophy came away with ease, but an unseen thorn bit into my finger. I hissed as a bead of blood welled at the tip of my digit then dripped, *splat*, onto the flower below. The plant trembled in pleasure, pulsing with an eerie light before promptly withering—decaying as fast as it'd been born. After a moment, nothing remained of the strange flower but a withered pile of mulch.

Quest Alert: Cleanse the Taint

You have vanquished the evil presence tainting the forest and earned the thanks of a powerful Hamadryad. In return, as your reward, you have received 10,000 EXP and the Blessing of the Forest, which instantly improves your relationship with forest-aligned factions from *Neutral* to *Friendly*. You have also been awarded 100 renown—in-world fame—for completing this quest. Greater renown elevates you within the ranks of Eldgard and can affect merchant prices when selling or buying.

The tree sighed, content. "Thank you again, traveler," he said. "We trees are a close-knit group, and I will spread the word of your help. Even the lesser tree-folk, those who cannot speak, will treat you as a friend."

The brooch, called *Blessing of the Forest*, didn't seem to have any stat bonuses besides improving my relationship with forest-aligned factions, but interestingly it was also a *soulbound* item, meaning I couldn't drop it. Not even if I wanted to. I nodded my thanks as I pinned the metal brooch in place, then wished the tree a final goodbye and activated the scroll Abby had provided for our return.

The portal dropped Cutter and me off in the alley outside the Broken Dagger. Guess that was my bind point—must've been some kind of automatic feature, since I certainly hadn't set it there.

It was full dark in Rowanheath, the moon was a ghostly sliver in the sky overhead, and a chilly breeze cut through the narrow alley, sending a shiver up my spine. At this point, all I wanted to do was sleep for the next few days straight, but first, I needed food. My belly felt like an empty hole and now that I wasn't preoccupied with other things—like not being murdered—the shooting pangs of hunger were almost unbearable. Curious, I pulled up my character screen and accessed a menu that listed any current active effects. Aside from all the active buffs granted by my gear, I also had a small list of status debuffs:

Current Debuffs

Tired (Level 3): Skills improve 15% slower; Carry Capacity -25lbs; Attack Damage -10%; Spell Strength reduced by 25%

Thirsty (Level 2): Health, Stamina, and Spirit Regeneration reduced by 25%

Hungry (Level 3): Carry Capacity -50lbs; Health and Stamina Regeneration reduced by 30%; Stealth 25% more difficult

Unwashed (Level 1): Goods and services cost 5% more; Merchant-craft skills reduced by (1) level

I grumbled in mild annoyance. What kind of demented person would've thought to add in those types

of features—to actually penalize characters that didn't eat or sleep enough?

Cutter pushed his way into the tavern; music, laughter, and the warmth from the roaring fireplace washed over us like a soothing balm. Cutter was apparently suffering the same negative debuffs as me, because he immediately sauntered over to the bar and ordered us food and a round of drinks, then promptly acquired us a table near the stage performer—tonight it was a fresh-faced bard wearing a puffy-sleeved jacket. The bard chanted a story, going on and on about some long-forgotten battle while a quartet of colorful balls twirled and spun through the air.

I gratefully took my seat and remained quiet, lost in the bard's performance, waiting for our food, which came a few minutes later. A hearty meat pie filled with tender lamb chunks and bits of roasted vegetables, all slathered in thick gravy. Sensing my subdued mood, Cutter kept quiet for a change, eating in peace, though occasionally chuckling at the performer or clapping his approval between heaping mouthfuls of stew. It only took me a handful of minutes to devour the food and down a few pints of the Broken Dagger mead, which wiped out the *Thirsty* and *Hungry* debuffs, leaving me in slightly better spirits.

Still, I felt tired to the bone. Not to mention, depressed.

So far, it'd been easy to forget about the relatively high mortality rate for people transitioning into V.G.O. permanently, but knowing Abby could be dead in a few hours was an uncomfortable and sobering thought.

What I really needed right now was to be alone and to get a little sleep. So, with a few quick words, I excused myself from the table and headed up to my room.

"Hey, Grim Jack," Cutter called over the music as I made for the stairs. I turned back toward him, and was shocked to see something that might've been concern in his face. "Everything's gonna be alright," he said. "You're gonna get through this, one way or the other. And tomorrow, I'll head out with you, help you find a class that'll fit you like a glove. Considering your disposition, I'm thinking servant girl might be a good place to start"—he flashed me a toothy, asshole grin—"but we can talk it over in the morning."

I nodded and smiled back, in spite of my disheartened mood. When you got past his rough edges, Cutter was okay. I caught a whiff of myself on the way up the stairs—a pungent mixture of sour sweat and dirt—but decided I could figure out how to bathe in the morning. I'd done enough for one day.

My room was empty, the bed freshly made, the pitcher filled with clear water, a clean length of towel lying beside the basin. I shut the door with a kick, beelined for the basin, and splashed my face, rubbing wet hands over my cheeks then down onto the back of my neck. It did nothing to the *Unwashed* debuff, but boy did it feel good. With that done, I headed over to the bed, shrugged out of my boots and armor, and stripped all the way down to a pair of woven undershorts. The only gear I left on was my pieces of jewelry. I flopped back onto the bed, letting the mattress pull me in as I sprawled, stretching my back with a groan.

God, what an amazing bed. Whatever evils the Devs had done, this bed almost made up for all of them. *Almost.*

Following my ritual from the night before, I decided to take a few minutes to look over my stats and notifications, even if to just clear things out. With another groan, I laced my hands behind my head and called out into the air, "Sophia, please bring up my user interface."

"Of course, Jack," came the comforting voice of my digital assistant.

The semi-translucent screen popped up in front of me. "Notifications," I mumbled. The menu interface was promptly replaced by a long list of boxes:

x7 Level Up!

You have (100) undistributed stat points

You have (17) unassigned proficiency points

<<<>>>

Skill: Stealth

Skill Type/Level: Active / Level 9

Cost: 15 Stamina

Effect: Stealth 23% chance to hide from enemies.

<<<>>>

Skill: Backstab

Skill Type/Level: Active / Level 5

Cost: 20 Stamina

Effect: A brutal backstab attack can be activated while an adventurer is in Stealth. 6x normal damage with a knife; 4x normal damage with all other weapons.

Effect 2: 7% increased chance of critical hit while backstabbing.

<<<>>>

Skill: Blunt Weapons

Skill Type/Level: Active / Level 8

Cost: None

Effect: Increases blunt weapon damage by 19%.

<<<>>>

Skill: Medium Armor

Though medium armor doesn't offer the same defensive benefits of heavy plate, it is far less bulky and heavy, granting the wearer decent protection while simultaneously offering a greater range of speed, dexterity, and maneuverability. Perfect for classes that rely on speed and brutal surprise, but also aren't afraid to fight close in—at least for short periods of time.

Skill Type/Level: Passive / Level 2

Cost: None

Effect: 10% increased base armor rating while wearing Medium Armor.

<<<>>>

I read over the various boxes, spending a few extra minutes on the "medium armor" section, then closed out of my notifications. As tired as I was, now that I finally had access to the game's wiki again, I really wanted to look for information on my future class. "Sophia"—I stifled a yawn—"please search for any information on Dark Templars or Shadowmancers," I muttered, both too lazy and too comfortable to switch over to it manually. The screen blinked and changed without a word of reply.

A long list of forum topics populated, but it was the page entitled "Dark Templar Class Kits," that immediately caught my eye. Bingo. I pulled up the screen and began scanning the information, courtesy of an Osmark Tech Admin by the handle of JACOBPAIGE:

Lore

The mysterious Dark Templars, also called the Maa-Tál in the Dokkalfar tongue, serve as the enforcers of the Shadow Pantheon—the native gods and goddesses of Eldgard. Like the Holy Templars of the Viridian Empire, the Dark Templars are often defenders of the downtrodden, fighting against injustice and upholding the traditions of Eldgard's natives with both dark magic and cold steel. Unlike Viridian's Templars, however, Dark Templars rely not on the power of holy light but on the sinister and pervasive strength of shadow.

Game Play

Dark Templars are a hybrid class available to Wodes, Dokkalfar (Murk Elves), and Accipiter. Essentially, any natural enemy of the Viridian Empire is eligible to receive this class. Unlike many other classes, players seeking the path of the Dark Templar must locate a Shadow Pantheon trainer and undergo an initiation ordeal to be accepted into the ranks. If they fail the ordeal, the class becomes *permanently* blocked.

If selected, there are five class kit specializations—Shadow Knight, Plague Bringer, Umbra Shaman, Necromancer, and Shadowmancer—which allow Dark Templars to fulfill a variety of roles, depending on the chosen kit. Becoming a Dark Templar instantly grants the player a "dark" alignment, which is not the same things as an "evil" alignment; possessing a "dark" alignment does, however, instantly lower the player's relationship with all Viridian-aligned factions to Unfriendly. In return, all Dark Templars receive a 10% damage bonus against "light"-aligned players and NPCs, making them valuable assets within the Eldgard Rebellion.

Hmm, very interesting. Sort of like a Paladin class, then, but with a "dark" alignment. Next I pulled up the page on the Shadowmancer kit in particular, since that seemed to be the path I was headed for:

Shadowmancer Kit Specialization

Though all Dark Templars have a certain affinity for shadowmancy—the magical manipulation of void and shadow energies—Shadowmancers specialize and thrive in this arena. Like other Dark Templars, Shadowmancers can have powerful melee abilities, but unlike other Dark Templars, Shadowmancers cannot wear heavy plate armor, which can make this kit particularly tricky to play. Because of kit restrictions, Shadowmancers don't make good tanks, relying instead on speed and stealth in physical combat; they also possess a wide variety of spells that can inflict medium to high single-target damage. Additionally, spells such as Umbra Bog, Plague Burst, and Night Cyclone offer Shadowmancers some formidable crowd control capabilities.

- **Advantages**:
  - +5% faster movement rate (+1% per 4 Character Levels (C.L.))
  - +10% Stealth (+1% per 5 C.L.)
  - Immune to Morale Failure
  - +10% damage bonus against "light"-aligned players and NPCs
  - +20% resistance to shadow damage
  - Access to Dark Templar and Shadowmancer Restricted Skills
- **Disadvantages**:
  - Race Restricted (Wodes, Dokkalfar, Accipiter)
  - "Dark" alignment
  - Can use all weapons; can only specialize in Blunt Weapons skills
  - Cannot wear Heavy Armor
  - Shadowmancer spells have a high Spirit cost
  - Weak against Holy Damage
- **Typical Skill Allotment:**
  - Dexterity: Attack Strength is calculated as a "Rogue" class

o Intelligence: Increases Spell Strength

Spirit: Increases Spirit supply

I felt extremely optimistic after reading through the limited information I could get my hands on, and it was good to finally have some kind of idea where I should start sinking my attribute points. I quickly pulled up my Character stats and decided to allocate the bulk of my undistributed points. I dropped 5 points each into Strength, Vitality, and Constitution—just so I wouldn't have a completely lopsided character—then 25 points into Dexterity, 25 into Spirit, and 20 into Intelligence. That left me 20 points in reserve, just in case I needed to tweak things after I finally meet with Chief Kolle, who I assumed was my Shadow Pantheon trainer.

I took a look at my character stats with my new skill allocations:

V.G.O. Character Overview					
Name:	Jack	Race:	Dokkalfar	Gender:	Male
Level:	21	Class:	Unassigned	Alignment:	Unassigned
Renown:	100	Carry Capacity:	455	Undistributed Attribute Points:	17

Health:	470	Spirit:	815	Stamina:	520
H-Regen/sec:	9.55	S-Regen/sec:	11.1875	S-Regen: 1.10/sec	5.72

Attributes:		Offense:		Defense:	
Strength:	35.25	Base Melee Weapon Damage:	47	Base Armor:	68.2
Vitality:	26	Base Ranged Weapon Damage:	0	Armor Rating:	96.4
Constitution:	31	Attack Strength (AS):	268.75	Block Amount:	25
Dexterity:	45	Ranged Attack Strength (RAS):	147.25	Block Chance (%):	21
Intelligence:	40	Spell Strength (SS):	60	Evade Chance (%):	11.1
Spirit:	60.5	Critical Hit Chance:	13%	Fire Resist (%):	17
Luck:	6	Critical Hit Damage:	150%	Cold Resist (%):	15
				Lightning Resist (%):	15
				Shadow Resist (%):	15
				Holy Resist (%):	15
Current XP:	19,180			Poison Resist (%):	35
Next Level.:	25,200			Disease Resist (%):	35

I closed out the screen and brought up my Skill section. Until I found Chief Kolle, I couldn't access my specialized class skills and abilities, but there was still plenty I could do in the general skills department. Although I already knew most of the areas—Heavy Armor or Bladed Weapons, for instance—weren't going to factor into my character build, I decided to look through each and every tree, just so I'd have a solid idea of what kind of skills and abilities other players might have. After spending more than an hour reading through everything, I realized there would never be a "standard" build—there were just far too many skill and general

177

specializations to choose from for that to ever be the case.

Finally, I homed in on the skills that seemed pertinent to the Shadowmancer.

First, I focused on Blunt Weapons, adding another point to Savage Blow, which had been a lifesaver more than once, and one more to Parry. Since I'd reached level 8 in Blunt Weapons, there were now several new skills available to me as well. I dropped one point into a passive ability called Trauma, which allowed all Blunt Weapon attacks to ignore 15% of an enemy's armor. I also put a point into a skill called Featherweight, which increased attack speed by 10% and critical hit by 2.5%.

Unfortunately, Medium Armor didn't offer anything until I hit level 3, so I headed over to the Stealth skill tree instead. I was a little reluctant to invest too many proficiency points into this tree without first acquiring my main class, but since the Shadowmancer class came with a +10% bump to Stealth, I figured Stealth was going to be an important part of my overall game strategy, which meant my points wouldn't be wasted. And besides, at level 9, there were lots of cool extras to pick from.

I immediately dropped two points into a passive ability called Whisper Step, which reduced the noise I made by 30%, making me much harder to detect while in Stealth. One point went into an active technique called Camouflage, giving me a 20% better chance to blend into my surroundings—even in bright lighting conditions—and one more went into Deadly Grace, reducing the weight of my armor, allowing me to be lighter and quicker on my feet.

By the time I was done, I had to fight to keep my eyes open, so I finally dismissed my player interface, offered a silent prayer for Abby—hoping I would wake up tomorrow morning with a PM from her, knowing I might not—and closed my eyes. I let the weight of my exhaustion draw me down, down, down into a restless sleep filled with horrific half-seen visions of Abby screaming, convulsing, dying as fiery slabs of space rock peppered the Earth.

TWENTY-THREE

RISE AND SHINE

B*RRP, BRRP, BRRP, BRRP.* THE SHRILL ALARM exploded in my ears, clanging like a gong magnified by a bullhorn.

I shot up and instantly began rubbing at my temples, trying to beat back the skull-splitting headache—it felt like Donkey Kong was trapped inside my head, desperately trying to smash his way free. I swung my legs off the bed and hunched forward, dropping my elbows onto my thighs as sweat cascaded down my face and my heart pounded sporadically in my chest. Everything was oddly blurry and my lips and hands felt dull, numb. I wheezed, sucking in giant lungfuls of air, frantically trying to control my labored breathing.

"Sophia … turn the … alarm off …" I forced the words out between strained gasps.

"Alarm dismissed," Sophia replied calmly, unmoved by the fact that I was *dying*. "The current time in Eldgard is 7:15 AM," she droned. "You have been asleep for approximately nine real-world hours. You have an automated message from the Osmark Technologies Customer Support Team. Would you like to play it?"

"In a … minute," I slurred, which wasn't a good sign. The confusion and disorientation weren't nearly as profound as the day before, but the physical symptoms were a hundred times worse. If I'd been back IRL, I would've called for an ambulance already. Currently, I was experiencing physical symptoms that related to both a heart attack *and* a stroke. But this was V.G.O., and I was well beyond the help of ambulance techs or modern medical treatment.

Maybe I should try to find a priest or healer?

No, I dismissed the thought.

My HP bar wasn't affected by whatever was happening, which meant I was likely experiencing *actual* pain from my *actual* body. Theoretically, I had another day before my transition would be complete—either that or I'd die—but this sure seemed like dying. I sat that way, bent over, struggling to breathe for a minute, then two, then five, before the sensations finally began to recede. "Sophia, play the message," I finally barked as my heart rate dropped to something sort of resembling normal.

"Good morning, traveler," came an overly perky voice. "This is Matthew, your customer support representative, and our system records indicate you've successfully spent your second full night in Viridian Gate Online. Congratulations! Since you're hearing this, I have some great news for you: your overall chance of surviving the transition has increased from approximately eighty-three percent to nearly ninety percent. With that said, you're likely feeling *extreme* physical discomfort, but those symptoms are to be expected and should not be a cause for concern. Make sure you stop by your nearest inn or tavern and eat a hearty meal. Thank you for playing."

The message faded, died.

I grumbled. Stupid Matthew. Intellectually, I knew poor Matthew was probably just some underpaid worker bee reading from a script, per Osmark Tech's instructions, but his naturally perky and energetic nature really made me want to punch him. I'm not a violent guy by nature, but just then I wanted to show him some *extreme* physical discomfort.

Muttering disgruntled curses under my breath, I crawled from the bed, tossed on my armor and gear, then hit up the washbasin, splashing water across my face, trying to clear away a few of the cobwebs clogging up my brain. I grabbed the towel and patted at my eyes, which is when I remembered Abby. Frantically, I dropped the bit of damp cloth into the wash water, not caring, and pulled up my player interface.

"Woo," I shouted with a fist pump, startling a fat pigeon sitting on the ledge outside my window. "Hell yeah," I yelled again, doing a victory jig, boots click-clacking on the wooden floors. I had a message from Abby—the subject head simply read: I'M ALIVE!!!!!

I pulled up the message, a giant grin running from ear to ear.

Personal Message:

Jack,

I made it! I'm alive! I'd kiss you if you were here. Honestly, I feel awful—it's like someone dipped my insides in fire ants. No joking, this is the worst experience of my life, but I got a message from a Customer Service Rep saying that's normal and that their systems indicate I've transitioned! I'm supposed to stay off my feet for the next couple of hours, but then Otto and I are off to the Grand Archive in Alaunhylles (it's basically a giant library over on the West Viridian side of the continent). If anyone's going to know about that seal we found, it'll be one of the Loremasters at the Archive. But I'm temporarily going dark—no wiki, no PMs, no in-game connectivity—since it'll be harder for Carrera and Osmark Tech to track me down. It'll be a couple of days until you hear from me again, but in the meantime, you get a class, and grind out some more levels.

Best,

—Abby

With a sigh of relief, I pulled open the door and headed out. Cutter was waiting for me at the bottom of the stairs, leaning casually against the wall, his arms folded, his head back. He looked relaxed, at ease, but something was subtly off about him.

"Morning. Care to have breakfast with me?" I asked.

"Naw," he said with a shrug, "busy day today. Lots to do. I think it'd be best if we picked up something from the street vendors. Just about no better place to get questionable street food than Rowanheath. A little fried rat on a stick is exactly what you need to set you straight this morning."

I paused and frowned, brow wrinkled. *Fried rat? Was he being serious?* After a second, I decided it wasn't a good idea to ask questions I didn't actually want answers to.

He slung an arm around my shoulders when I reached the bottom of the staircase and gently guided me toward the exit. He smiled the whole time, trying to play it cool, but even in the short time that I'd known Cutter, I knew this wasn't normal. If I didn't know any better, I'd say Cutter was nervous—except Cutter wasn't the kind of guy to get nervous. Greedy? Yes, obviously. Sneaky? Without a question. Cocky? Probably his middle name. But not anxious.

Despite my achy muscles and awful headache, I put on an easygoing grin as we walked. Didn't want to draw any extra attention in case something was up.

We made it out of the Broken Dagger without being accosted, but the second we cleared the door, Cutter picked up his pace, quickly heading onto a busy thoroughfare, then weaving through a bustling crowd. "What's wrong?" I hissed at him, before glancing over my shoulder, expecting to see someone following us.

Except no one was.

"In a minute," he replied, dragging me past a rolling wagon and into a pool of deep shadow. He paused, tense, regarding the roadway, before urging me into motion. We moved with speed and purpose, though not so quickly as to draw unwanted attention. Ten minutes and fifteen switchbacks later, he finally slowed his manic pace, leading me over to a rickety wooden cart near an open fire pit with skewers of meat lazily spinning above the flames, greasy juices dripping down into the dancing fire. With a few muttered words, Cutter snagged us five or six spits of meat-on-a-stick.

"Sorry for the cloak-and-dagger shite," he said, handing me a too-hot skewer.

I regarded the seared meat—it *did* look an awful lot like rat.

At this point, though, I was so hungry I didn't even care. I took a disgruntled bite, thinking about the honey porridge I could be eating at the Broken Dagger, but quickly revised my opinion. A buff popped up, alerting me that the [Rat Skewer] was restoring 50 HP over 35 seconds, but it hardly mattered because the meat was *delicious*. A little spicy, with the smoky flavor you only get when cooking over an open flame. Even better, my headache vanished almost at once, a wave of sweet relief cascading through my body.

I finished the first skewer in a few wolfish bites, and immediately started in on a second one. I began to eat a third as I walked, trailing Cutter down a wide cobblestone street bordered mostly by narrow plaster-faced houses instead of shops. A residential section of the city, by the look of it.

"So?" I prompted around a mouthful of rat meat. "Care to tell me what that was all about?"

The Thief regarded me out of the corner of his eye. "There's something wrong with Gentleman Georgie," he said at last.

"What do you mean, there's something wrong with him? I thought he was gone on business or something?"

"I'm getting there if you'd give me a chance," he replied with an eyeroll. "Apparently, Georgie's been gone for almost a week, but he turned up early this morning. Naturally, I sought him out. Wanted to tell him about the incident with Serth-Rog's acolyte, but there was something wrong with him, Jack. He looked like Georgie—identical down to the last detail, at least physically—but that man *wasn't* Georgie." He paused, running a hand through his blond hair, then rubbed at the back of his neck. "I'm sure of it."

"In what way?" I asked, before taking another mouthful of rat meat.

"It was just little things, I suppose," he replied. "His mannerisms were slightly off. His eyes were hazy, distant. It's hard to put my finger on exactly. But in my gut, I know he's not the same. Georgie took me in after my father passed, taught me most of what I know about thieving and killing. The man was like family to me, and whoever I met today?" He shook his head, worry lingering in his eyes. "It wasn't him."

I nodded, trying to be supportive.

We hooked a left onto another cobblestone boulevard, this one filled with robe-wearing Viridians and armor-clad travelers in a variety of stripes and races. This road held stone-fronted shops edged with intricately carved wood and studded with large, shiny windows. I hadn't been here before and I immediately felt out of place. These stores seemed far swankier than anything I'd seen so far, and the customers looked like the kind of people who could afford the finer things in life. Despite the few awesome items I'd acquired, I still sort of looked like a down-and-out drifter.

"So, what's the plan, exactly?" I asked, finally done with my rat skewers. "Do we kidnap fake-Georgie? Try to dig some answers out of him, maybe?"

Cutter shook his head, once more looking worried, frayed around the edges. "Honestly, I'm not sure what to do. If it were anyone else, I'd go to Georgie with my suspicions, but who can I go to about Georgie himself? He's at the top of the food chain—no one's going to believe me over him, and even if they do, no one would dare make any kind of overt move against him. That's a surefire way to end up in a ditch with your throat slit.

"And kidnapping him?" he continued. "No, he's surrounded by covert bodyguards thick as flies in a shitter. Worse, I think *not*-Georgie might be on to me. Until I can come up with some kind of plan, I don't think it's safe to head back to the Broken Dagger. Thought I might stick around with you for the time being, help you find a class while I think through things. Try to come up with some options. Assuming it's all the same to you, of course."

A quest box popped up:

Quest Alert: Imposter Georgie

Cutter suspects that something is wrong with Gentleman Georgie, the unofficial head of the Thieves' Guild in Rowanheath. Help Cutter get to the bottom of the mystery.

Quest Class: Unique, Personal

Quest Difficulty: Hard

Success: Help Cutter get to the bottom of the mystery surrounding Gentleman Georgie's sudden personality change.

Failure: Refuse to help Cutter or allow him to die before the mission is complete.

Reward: ?

Accept: Yes/No?

<<<>>>

"How could I say no to you?" I asked, sarcasm oozing through my teeth as I accepted the quest he'd just provided to me.

"Precisely," he replied with a grin. "My charm is rather irresistible. Besides, let's face it, you wouldn't survive a day without me. But still, thanks all the same," he mumbled weakly, refusing to meet my eye. We walked for a few more minutes in relative silence. "Ahh, here we are," he said eventually, stopping and sweeping an arm toward a thickly carved wooden door. A sign above the building read *Trajan's Emporium*.

TWENTY-FOUR

THE EMPORIUM

I STARED AT CUTTER, THE QUESTION EVIDENT ON MY face, then shifted my gaze to the storefront.

"If we're going to do any more strenuous adventuring," he said, "it's time you properly equipped yourself. Sell off all that junk loading you down and pick up some nifty trinkets that might keep you breathing. This place"—he nodded toward the shop—"is a bit pricey, but, assuming you can afford it, it's a one-stop shop for just about everything you'll need. Weapons. Armor. Potions. Spells. Whatever." Without further comment, he shoved his way in, a tiny brass bell ringing out, announcing us to the shopkeeper.

I followed, not sure what to expect.

The inside of the emporium looked like a cross between a posh antique store, a new-age bookstore, and a medieval armory.

Expensive rugs and fanciful tapestries littered the floors and walls. Rows of bookshelves, laden with old tomes and rolled scrolls, lined the right wall. Dark wood tables, polished until they shone, were loaded down with glass vials and a hundred different types of herbal ingredients, presumably used for potion creation or alchemy. A huge array of weapons and armor crowded the left-hand side of the shop. There were polearms, axes, swords, and maces: some cheap and plain, but most covered with silver and gold runes or studded with precious stones.

The armor was equally diverse and abundant. Black plate mail hung on training dummies while intricately tooled leather armor dangled from the walls. Helmets with horns or horsehair crests decorated more tables, while boots sat neatly lined on the floor below the tables. And there were lots of other knickknacks too—like sturdy utility belts, studded with pockets and pouches, or boot-sheathes made to conceal an extra dagger.

A ridiculously short man with phenomenally broad shoulders and a long, wispy beard waddled out of a storage room and toward a service counter near the back of the shop. He looked like a squat cube of muscle, and his steps were slow and plodding: a man built for power, not speed. A Dwarf, then, his features weathered with age, his skin wrinkled like dried leather. He slipped behind the counter, only his head visible for a moment, before he clambered up onto something—maybe a stool or a chair—allowing him a clear view of the shop.

"Welcome to Trajan's Emporium," he grumbled, his voice gruff, a perfect match for his homely face, "the finest importer and exporter of all your adventuring needs." He paused and squinted at us, lips transforming into a hard, thin sneer. "Cutter." He said the name like a curse. "You know I don't buy your pinched goods, *thief*. Go to that fence of yours—Jorgen, Jensen, Jabsor, whatever the hell her name is—you're not welcome here, you uncouth miscreant."

"Trajan," Cutter said with a smile and a clap of his hands. "Is that any way to greet an old friend, eh?"

"You, sir, are no friend of mine. You're a barbaric, foul-mouthed hoodlum, and you'll leave before I summon the guards and have you clapped in irons."

Cutter waved off the Dwarf's protests and pulled me over to the counter.

"Allow me to introduce a friend of mine, Grim Jack." He stepped aside and waved at me with a flourish and a bow. "He's a traveler, new to our lands."

"Then take him over to Poor John's and see him outfitted there," the Dwarf glowered, folding beefy arms across his chest in disapproval.

"Nonsense," Cutter said, "my friend is practically royalty." His hand flashed beneath his leather armor, and in a blink, gold appeared in his hand. Cutter dropped the pile of glittering coin onto the glowing wooden countertop with a subtle *clink-clink-clink.* The Dwarf's eyes bulged, staring at the gold with hungry greed. "And that's only the tip of the iceberg, Trajan," Cutter said, one eyebrow cocked.

The Dwarf leaned in. "How much gold are we talking about, you unwashed filth?" he whispered, though not so quietly that I couldn't hear him.

"His nickname on the street is Grim Jack Money-Bags," Cutter replied with a shifty wink in my direction.

Suddenly, the Dwarf was all smiles and bows, issuing a host of profound apologies and hasty welcomes. "Please, good sir, come and peruse my wares. I have the absolute finest goods in all of Rowanheath. The absolute finest."

Hesitantly, I meandered toward the Dwarf. A popup inventory window appeared before me as I drew up to the counter. The Dwarf's inventory floated on the left while mine floated on the right. I quickly scanned over the Dwarf's goods and nearly choked at the prices. Not because they were high, but because they seemed rather *low*. I'd made out pretty good yesterday—even after paying the mercenary Warlock, I'd walked away with a little over 2,200 in gold—and that wasn't counting the items I still had left to sell, which would probably bring in another 300 gold.

But even the most expensive items the Dwarf had to sell didn't cost more than a paltry 20 gold.

Mentally, I pulled up a game wiki, trying to figure out how much a gold coin could get you in V.G.O. It didn't take long before I found a page with a table laying out how V.G.O. coinage compared to real-world currency. Each copper coin corresponded to roughly one US dollar, and there were 10 coppers per silver and 10 silvers per gold, which meant each gold mark was roughly equivalent to a hundred IRL dollars. That meant after I finished selling off the items I'd acquired, I'd have damn near a quarter of a million in my account. That was more money than I'd ever *dreamed* of seeing back in my old life.

Suddenly I felt faint, my legs weak, my arms shaky. I was *rich*. Well, relatively speaking. But certainly *rich-ish*. Despite everything else that had happened, I found myself grinning like a maniac—time for something I'd never been able to do IRL: an impulsive shopping spree. First, though, I needed to get rid of all the junk weighing me down.

I pawned the Ranger's bow with its +10 to Dexterity and 10% increased chance to evade, netting me 175 gold.

The short sword with the +1 Strength modifier and the Heavy Firesteel Gauntlets brought in another 120. The other items, a crappy assortment of starter weapons and shoddy armor, brought in a small bagful of silver; more importantly, though, selling those items relieved me of some significant dead weight. With that done, I started combing through the Dwarf's wares. I already had a bunch of Health, Stamina, and Spirit Regen potions, so I focused instead on filling in my missing armor items.

Assuming Cutter was on the level, and the Dwarf's wares really were the best I could find at the moment, I still knew it was likely lowbie crap. Even though I was something of a casual gamer—at least compared to some of my hardcore friends—I knew you only got the really good drops from raids or off the player auctions. Still, I was in desperate need of gear, so this was better than nothing.

After a little strenuous haggling with the Dwarf, I picked up a pair of medium armor gauntlets (superior), a Belt of Agility—which granted me +7 to Dexterity and also allowed me seven quick access slots—and a Helm of the Owl, which increased my Night Eye ability by 15%. That ran me 11 gold and change, not even a drop in the bucket, though the Dwarf seemed pleased as punch, despite the fact that I'd talked him down by nearly half. My Night Blessed Armor and Gavel of Shadows were *way* better than anything the Dwarf had on display, but my little wooden buckler was desperately in need of an upgrade.

I sold it for a measly 2 silver, but quickly replaced it with a bronze buckler that increased Block Chance by 10% and doubled my total Block Amount from 25 points of damage to 50. Another 5 gold down the drain, which I considered a laughably small amount considering that shield might prevent someone from splitting my head in two.

I already had two rings equipped, but I still had six more ring slots available, not to mention two earring slots and two bracelet slots. Most of the jewelry was crap—generic +1 items not worth spending any money on—but I did find one ring, called the Scholar's Signet, with a +5 to Spirit and a +6 to Intelligence, which I snatched up in a heartbeat even though the Dwarf flatly *refused* to drop the price. The little band of iron practically screamed *Shadowmancer* at the top of its lungs, and somehow the Dwarf seemed to *know* I wasn't going to pass on the item. A real huckster, that one.

The rest of the gear was subpar, but there were still a few essentials I needed badly. I closed out of the Dwarf's gear menu and headed over to his arcane wares.

He had a variety of tomes and scrolls obviously designed for wizards and priests—Fireball, Ice-spike, Lesser binding, Power Word: Barrier—but nothing that catered to my end of the spectrum. Not that I actually expected to find anything. Since Dark Templar was one of the few classes requiring practitioners to actively seek out a trainer, I'd already come to terms with the fact that I wouldn't find anything in the normal stores. That was fine, though, because the Dwarf did have what I'd been looking for. At the bottom of his inventory, he had a Tome of Return: a permanent spell allowing the caster to teleport to their bind point, so long as they weren't in battle or surrounded by hostiles.

That would be the Broken Dagger, in my case. In light of Cutter's suspicions, however, I'd have to figure out how to get that changed. Truthfully, though, I couldn't really think of any other place that'd be better. Though I'd been playing the game for two solid days, I didn't really know much outside the Broken Dagger. Another worry to add to the list. Last, I headed over to the miscellaneous items and grabbed a "camp set"— which amounted to a small tent, a cook pot, and a fire-starter kit—then picked up some rations: water, bread, cheese, cold mutton.

By the time I was done, my coin supply had dropped by another 22 gold, leaving my fat coin purse virtually untouched. Assuming Aleixo Carrera or his cronies didn't disembowel me, I was really going to have to thank Abby again.

Business done, I closed out of the buy menu and took a moment to equip my new gear. I certainly didn't look all that heroic yet, but I *felt* much better. Then, before closing out of my interface, I toggled over to the Tome of Return and selected it.

Using this item will destroy it, permanently removing it from your inventory. Are you sure you would like to learn Tome of Return?

"Yes," I said to the empty air. There was a pop and a flash of light, a small tornado swirling around me in a rush of warm air.

Skill: Conjuration

Conjuration is one of the nine branches of magic: Abjuration, Enchantment, Divination (Divinus), Conjuration, Transmutation/Alchemy, Invocation, Illusion, Light, and Dark. Conjurers are masters at manipulating, distorting, and transforming the Astral Fabric; using their power, they may manifest Astral energies, summon creatures and other beings through the Aether, or rend the Astral Fabric in order to travel great distances in a single step.

Skill Type/Level: Passive / Level 1

Cost: None

Effect: Casting cost for spells in the Conjuration School are reduced by 2%

I shook my head, dismissing the notification.

Cutter was leaning on the counter, picking his fingernails with the tip of his knife. "Good?" he asked, cocking an eyebrow.

"Good as I'm gonna be. Now let's go see some swamp folks."

TWENTY-FIVE

STORME MARSHES

I STEPPED THROUGH A SHIMMERING PORTAL AND directly into a fetid puddle of ankle-deep water bordered by boggy, squishy marshland. The cloudy sludge, oddly warm, immediately rushed into my boots, swirling between my toes, bringing a grimace to my face.

"Eww," Cutter remarked as he followed me into the pool with a squishy *splat*. He paused, looking left, then right. "What an awful place," he grumbled, continuing his scan of the area.

So far, in my brief relationship with Cutter, there wasn't a lot I could agree wholeheartedly with him on—but for once we had common ground. Wet, squishy, disgusting common ground. At my core, I was a city boy, far more familiar with the backstreets of L.A. than the backwoods of *anywhere*, so this place put me well outside of my comfort zone. Something large, green, and covered with eyes buzzed by my face, before vanishing into a swatch of gnarled trees protruding from the water. Yuck.

I turned in a slow circle, *splat-squish-splat-squish*, surveying the thick warren of trees and waterways stretching off in every direction. We were in a mangrove swamp—a tangle of dense vegetation surrounded us on every side, a host of fat roots plunging into the water. The leafy canopy overhead blocked out the sunlight, casting everything in perpetual gloom and deep shadow. After filling Cutter in on my class quest, we'd headed over to *The Mystica Ordo*—V.G.O.'s version of a Wizards' guild—and I'd paid a sorcerer to port us to the edge of the Ak-Hani controlled territory in the Storme Marshes.

I'd expected to end up on the edge of a village or outside the gates of a Murk Elf city. I hadn't been planning on stepping into a gloomy bog with no sign of human habitation.

Anywhere.

"Perfect," Cutter uttered again. "This is exactly the way I wanted to spend my day. Tromping around in nature's version of a toilet. Yes, perfect."

I waved off his objection as I pulled up my user interface and checked my map. This place was obviously in the middle of nowhere, but thankfully a quest marker populated, giving me a rough idea of which way we needed to head. I turned, rotating slowly until I was facing the marker, then dismissed my interface. The section of swamp directly in front of me didn't look any different from the rest of the boggy wetlands, but that was our heading. "This way," I said, setting off, my pace drastically slowed by the treacherous mud sucking at my boots.

Every step was a tremendous effort.

I took the lead, checking my map every few minutes to keep my bearings, while Cutter trailed behind, grumbling disgruntledly with every single step. The walk was torturously sluggish, the endless minutes filled with sludgy goop and a never-ending swarm of biting insects, constantly circling my head like planets orbiting a sun. Their bites and stings didn't actually deplete my HP bar, but they were still irritatingly painful, and it seemed like no matter how many I swatted into bug paste, there were always replacements ready to fill the void.

After twenty or thirty minutes of hard trekking, we reached a little spit of land extending into the water. Finally, a small break. Not that moving onto land did anything about the awful bugs. If anything, the swarms intensified, a cloud of black, buzzing bodies so thick it was a challenge to see through. It came as an immense relief when the annoying critters finally thinned into a tolerable trickle ten or fifteen minutes later. The shift came as the marsh gave way to a more traditional forest full of twisted oaks, creeping ferns, and squat palm trees with broad-leafed fronds.

The ground here was still muddy, but a spattering of dead leaves and old, decaying vegetation made it a little easier going.

I checked my map again, once more readjusting my position—angling slightly left—then pushed on, deeper into the wood, Cutter following sullenly at my back. We saw our first signs of genuine habitation a few minutes later; unfortunately, it wasn't *human* habitation: thick swatches of silver webbing decorated tree branches and trailed down from the dense canopy above, snaring birds and fat, low-flying insects. Maybe there was a good reason the annoying swarms had let us be—this place looked like certain-death incarnate. The webbing even coated the ground in areas, huge patches of silver covering yawning holes gouged into the earth.

"You're sure this"—Cutter swept an arm toward the expanse of webs—"is the right way to go?"

I nodded and pulled out my warhammer, borrowing courage from the comforting weight of the weapon.

"Yes. Obviously. Of course it is," Cutter replied with a shake of his head while he drew dual daggers, giving each a nervous spin. "Well, let's just get it done, eh?"

I nodded again, resuming our trek.

At first, the forest was strangely silent—no chirping birds, no chittering squirrels, just the sound of our muted footfalls on damp earth, the occasional leaf crunching or twig snapping. As we got deeper, though, beyond the point where we could head back for the mangrove swamp, I heard a soft but persistent rustle. The sound of sandpaper sliding over a piece of fabric. The sound of a fall breeze stirring a pile of dead leaves. That noise put my teeth on edge, set the hairs lining my neck to stiff attention.

There was definitely something in here with us, and despite seeing nothing, it wasn't hard to guess what it was.

"Stealth?" I whispered over my shoulder to Cutter. "Maybe try to slip away while we still can and find a different way?"

"Yeah, Stealth," he replied, barely constrained fear creeping into his voice.

I immediately dropped into a crouch, subconsciously activating my Stealth. But instead of blurring into the shadows, a notification appeared:

<<<>>>

Stealth failed! You are being directly observed by hostile parties.

I gulped and shared an uneasy look with Cutter. "I failed. You?"

"Same," he said, uncharacteristically terse.

So much for that plan.

The rustling increased with every passing minute—at one point something flashed by on my right, a blur of movement too quick to follow. I spun, eyes flicking over the creepy, web-strewn forest, but whatever had been there was long gone, vanished back into the deep shadows cast by the canopy. I did notice, however, that the path we'd just come through was now crisscrossed by thick strands of silvery silk, barring our way back. I gulped, a nervous twitch running through my hand, but at this point we could only move forward.

"Why do you think they haven't attacked yet?" Cutter asked, his voice a low whisper, his eyes constantly roving.

"They're afraid, maybe?" I offered weakly, knowing that was pretty implausible.

"Keep telling yourself that," he replied, dropping into a low crouch, ready to move in any direction. "I've got a bad feeling about this, Grim Jack."

The rustling increased until it was an almost constant background drone, the noise scratching at my ears; and as the noise grew in intensity, so too did the flashes of movement. Just a half-seen glimpse of a long arachnoid leg, a bulbous belly, or the glint of a dark eye. We were being stalked and hunted, a truly unnerving sensation that left me increasingly on edge. The tension mounting in the air—the promise of swift and sudden violence to come—was worse by far than just having something leap out at me.

"Just attack us already," I finally yelled, my challenge bouncing off the trees, then dying, swallowed by the thick shrubbery.

Nothing responded. But that rustling almost sounded like laughter now. The spidery freaks were mocking us. That had to be it. Or maybe the paranoia was starting to get to me.

Eventually, we broke through the claustrophobic tangle of trees and webs, emerging only to find an enormous concave pit set into the forest floor. The colossal divot was as big around as a subway tunnel and covered with layer after layer of thick webbing. Towering trees—old, dark, twisted things—ringed the pit, and dangling from the mammoth branches high above were silken cocoons. Some the size of small forest animals, skunks or racoons, while others were easily as large as a full-grown man. The rustling seemed to build to a crescendo, the trees shaking and pulsating with the sound.

But I still couldn't *see* our enemies.

Quickly, I pulled up my area map and immediately felt my stomach sink: this was a marked location, similar to a dungeon. The marker read *Lowyth the Immortal Orbweaver of Hellweb Hollow*.

Which is why it didn't surprise me at all when the ground started to quiver beneath me as something giant dragged itself from the center of the pit. A pair of enormous legs came first, long black things with too many joints, covered in bristling red hairs. More legs joined the first two, followed in short order by an enormous head the size of a slugbug, with about a thousand gleaming eyes and a set of barbed fangs, more closely resembling swords than teeth. After a second, more legs broke into the air, clawing at the sky like monstrous fingers, before the rest of the body finally pulled free.

The creature flexed its legs and stood, its terrible head affixed to a ginormous black thorax tattooed with looping swirls of neon red, which pulsed with uneasy light.

As the massive [Spider Queen] finally emerged, the ceaseless rustling around us seemed to shift and strengthen as a flurry of brown forms appeared between the trees or rappelled from the canopy above on fat strands of silk.

"Well done, my children," the nightmarish uber-spider bellowed. Her voice was like the drone of an entire colony of wasps, though there was a decidedly feminine quality to it. "These two will make a fine hatchery for the new wave of young ones," she buzzed. The Spiderkin encircling us broke into jubilant celebration at her declaration, many raising their front-most limbs high into the air, while others rubbed their rear legs together—the source of that terrible rustling. Like crickets, only way, way bigger, and way, way grosser. "Catch them," the Queen buzzed. "String them up, but keep them alive—the younglings will need living flesh and hot blood to feast on when they hatch."

The spider jubilation continued for another moment, growing in fervent intensity, and then suddenly the first spider broke—charging us from the left with an inhuman and inarticulate screech. The rest followed, crashing toward us like a tsunami of legs and fangs and hair.

TWENTY-SIX

LEGS, LEGS, LEGS

O N INSTINCT, I TURNED TO RETREAT THE WAY we'd come—any direction away from the massive Spider Queen—but the passage was already blocked with both strands of heavy webbing and fat spider bodies. There was no going back—these things had herded Cutter and me into this hollow with the express intention of sacrificing us as an offering to their disgusting matriarch. They certainly had no intention of letting us slip away now. Cutter seemed to come to the same realization, his normal cocky smile gone, his jaw tight, his eyes filled with a claustrophobic terror.

"This way," he shouted, bolting right, heading for a small, undefended gap in the tree line—

A bloated spider, larger than a beefy Rottweiler, sensed Cutter's trajectory and scuttled to intercept while more of its hairy-legged kin pushed in around us. Cutter—always one for dramatics—leapt into the air like an acrobat, twisting and turning in a graceful flip, before landing on top of the spider's swollen thorax, sinking both of his daggers through chitinous flesh. Driving the blades down to the hilt. Green blood, sludgy and putrid, bubbled up as the spiderling reared back in pain, thrashing left and right in an attempt to throw the Thief.

With its front legs up and waving manically in the air, its soft underbelly was temporarily exposed.

An easy target I didn't want to squander.

I sprinted forward, canting my weapon to the side as I ran. I closed the distance in a few long strides and lashed out, driving the hammer face forward and up, battering into the spider's sensitive underside like a wrecking ball of steel. The blow smashed through the creature's brown flesh, sinking in with a spurt of green goo. The creature convulsed as I tore my weapon free; its belly ruptured under the sudden strain, a mass of glistening gray intestine spilling from the ugly wound and onto the ground.

The [Spiderkin] let out a final shriek of rage and pain before collapsing, dead.

Unfortunately, that creature was only the tip of a giant, horrific, many-legged iceberg.

"Cutter, keep going," I hollered, wheeling around to face the rest of the incoming Spiderkin. "Don't worry about me," I screamed as I lunged forward, thrusting my weapon upward at an angle, sinking the spiked top into an encroaching spider. "Just keep going." I didn't know if he was behind me or not, and I couldn't spare even a single second to check, but I sure hoped he'd taken my words to heart. Obviously, I wasn't too keen on experiencing death-by-spider—after all, spiders were well known for stringing their victims up before sucking them dry like a juice box—but, no matter how terrible the death, I would respawn.

Cutter wouldn't.

I shuffled back a few paces and turned my mind fully back to the brawl as three more spiders converged on me. I shifted right and brought up my buckler as a spider lunged in, curved fangs flashing out. I bashed the creature in the mouth with the tiny shield, absorbing the damage, before stepping through, swinging my hammer into the side of the creature's head. Its skull caved in, its eyes flashing momentarily before going dull and lifeless.

Unfortunately, the maneuver opened me up on the right, leaving my back partially exposed and vulnerable. Another of the Spiderkin seized the opportunity, charging me in an eyeblink. A heavy body slammed into my side, knocking me sideways as a pair of fangs, like butcher knives, sank into my chest. I screamed and thrashed, bringing a knee up into the Spiderkin's jaw, knocking it back a step as I twirled my warhammer, bringing it down on top of the spider's skull—using it like a sledgehammer to drive a stake into the ground.

I unleashed Savage Blow, and the spider's head exploded like a rotten pumpkin; shards of bone, strings of gristle, and gelatinous green blood splattered everywhere. I grimaced and backpedaled, clutching at the puncture wounds in my chest, which were making it terribly difficult to breathe. A combat notice flashed in my peripheral vision:

Debuffs Added

Punctured Lung: You have suffered a punctured lung; Stamina Regeneration reduced by 15% for 5 minutes.

Orbweaver Poison: You have been poisoned: 1 HP/sec; duration, 10 minutes or until cured.

Crap, that wasn't good. The DPS on the poison was relatively low—60 points a minute—but over ten minutes, that'd cost me 600 HP. Far more than I had even at full health, and I wasn't anywhere close to full health.

I stole a glance over my shoulder—the narrow opening in the trees was still clear, though Cutter was nowhere to be seen—and backtracked in a slow retreat, still clenching at the puncture wounds, feeling my life and strength leak away one ragged breath at a time. I wasn't optimistic about my chances. These Spiderkin were tough and vicious, and the few I'd managed to put down were hardly a drop in the bucket. I caught sudden movement on my left and wheeled just in time to get blasted with a stream of sticky webbing. Yet another debuff:

Debuff Added

Snared: You have been snared by Web Vomit, slowing your movement by 50%; duration, 3 minutes.

<<<>>>

I fought at the gossamer material binding my legs and clinging to my arms, working to tear my way free of the stuff even as I shuffled toward the tree line at a snail's pace. A loose ring of the Spiderkin were now arrayed before me in a horseshoe, but instead of charging me, they bided their time, waiting for something. A moment later, I found out what: one of the shifty, long-legged jerks had strung a trip line of spider silk directly behind me. My already tangled feet caught on the taut line and suddenly I was falling, arms flailing as I fought to keep upright.

A useless effort.

I hit with an *umphf* of expelled air, landing near the stinking corpse of the first spider Cutter and I had managed to take down. The horde of Spiderkin didn't waste a heartbeat, rushing in, jostling each other in order to get first crack at me. A particularly beefy sucker won the battle and scampered over me. I expected it to strike in an instant and send me for respawn, but instead, it repositioned its bloated belly and began to blast my feet with a thick stream of webbing. I began to panic, recalling the words of the Spider Queen: *"Catch them … string them up … keep them alive—the younglings will need living flesh and hot blood to feast on when they hatch."*

It was cocooning me, preparing me for later consumption. Oh my god, this game was awful. Osmark Technologies was lucky players were stuck in V.G.O. permanently, or they would've had a slew of lawsuits on their hands—filed by traumatized players who would never have a peaceful night's sleep again.

The creature's abdomen continued to pulse, swelling and contracting as it spewed ever more webbing onto my body, working its way up my legs. At this point, I was thinking the poison coursing through my veins was actually a blessing—if I didn't do anything to stop it, the poison would kill me, which was the *best* option.

Still, I couldn't just lie there, waiting to die, so I raised my hammer, preparing for a last-ditch assault.

Before I could strike out, however, the fat Spiderkin hovering above me reared back, issuing a horrendous shriek of angry disapproval. I glanced at my warhammer, trying to figure out what I'd just done and how, but then Cutter's face flashed in front of mine.

"Hang in there, Grim Jack," he said, prying his hands into my armpits and dragging me away from the howling spider and into the relative safety of the trees. He lifted my bulk with a grunt and gracelessly tossed me over his shoulder like a sack of potatoes so my torso dangled down his back. "I think we've overstayed our welcome," he yelled as he broke into a lurching run. The ride was far from pleasant—each step sent a lancing pain up through my stomach and into my punctured lung.

Another round of terrible spidery yowls brought my head up. We were being pursued, a small pack of the creatures scuttling through the foliage, leaping from tree to tree, closing the distance in a hurry. My health was still dropping by the second, but I hesitated to down one of the Health Regen potions at my belt. Quick as Cutter was moving, those things would overtake us in no time, unless I could find a way to slow them down …

"Faster, Cutter!" I hollered as I flopped up and down, gritting my teeth as his shoulder dug into my gut.

My health bar began flashing an angry, infected red as it dropped to 15%, but a sweet flood of arctic cold filled my limbs in an instant. With my life hanging in the balance, I had access to my otherwise restricted Umbra Bolt ability. I lifted my right hand, envisioning a burning ball of shadow forming in my palm. Something inside me moved, *shifted*, and suddenly the cold congregated to my outstretched limb, seeping from my skin, wreathing my hand in flickering shadow.

I grinned and willed the Umbra Bolt out.

Light erupted, streaking away, slamming into one of the pursuing arachnoids. The creature exploded in a ball of violet shadow, hissing and stumbling, both hurt and temporarily blinded. I pumped fistful after fistful of shadow power at the Spiderkin, keeping one eye on my health bar as I worked. This was a fine balance—I could only access the Umbra power with my health below 15%, but I didn't want to die either.

I clipped one of the creatures in mid-leap, swatting it from the air and amputating the majority of its legs in the process. Another went down for good as I scored a critical hit in its horrifying face, turning its eye-studded head into a disgusting spray of green mist. At 75 Spirit per shot, the barrage of Umbra Bolts quickly ate through my Spirit supply, but thankfully a purple potion at my belt restored me to 50%, giving me another four or five blasts. My health was still plummeting, but I didn't want to waste my limited opportunity to use Umbra Bolt.

I sent out a few sporadic shots, kicking up dirt, and felling a palm tree, hoping to slow our pursuers down. One particularly well-placed shot—by which I mean *lucky*—knocked a scurrying Spiderkin from the side of a tree; the creature fell directly into the path of several other arachnoids, tripping up one while being trampled by the other. With my Spirit once more low and my health hovering at around 5%, I finally pulled a health potion from one of my belt slots and downed the thing in a single pull, the taste of cherry-flavored medicine burning across my tongue and down my throat.

About as pleasant as real-world medicine, but it worked much, much faster. My health bar almost immediately jumped to 25%, saving my skin, but robbing me of my death-dealing Umbra Bolt spell, which was problematic—especially since even more spiders were scuttling out of the woodwork, joining the hunt. And they were close now, ten or fifteen feet away.

"Faster, Cutter, faster!"

"I'm moving as quick as I can go, fatty—you weigh a lot more than you look!" he shouted, huffing and puffing. We rounded a bend, slipping between several trees, and then we were temporarily airborne as Cutter leapt over a meandering stream three or four feet wide, landing on a narrow dirt trail on the other side. We didn't come down easy—the pain redoubled in my middle— and worse, the rough landing also cost us precious seconds. When I glanced back up, though, I could only stare in slack-jawed amazement; the spiders had stopped.

Just stopped.

They were lined up along the edge of the stream, staring at us with malicious, greedy eyes. But they made no move to cross the slow-moving water.

Why in the world would these things stop? They couldn't be scared of a shallow stream, could they?

That's when I caught sight of the totem. A crudely carved log jutted from the ground near the path. The wooden post was covered in harsh, angular script and topped by the yellowing skull of a spider, decorated in swirls of red paint. We must've entered some kind of safe zone, though a small part of me wondered what a horde of Spiderkin had to fear. That thought fled, however, as the ground gave out below Cutter and me, and we plummeted into a gaping hole, the bottom lined with jagged wooden spikes.

We'd carelessly run into a trap.

I flipped forward, head over tail, screaming as I braced for the impact to come. As I prepared to be impaled through the chest, stomach, neck, or face. That was a bad way to go, but still probably better than being cocooned alive as a late-night snack for a bunch of hungry spider babies. I smashed hard into the ground, landing on one shoulder; an assortment of dirt, twigs, leaves, and gravel chewed at my skin like sandpaper as I flipped and rolled.

I finally came to a jerky stop on my back, hurt, but surprisingly free of spikes. I pushed myself up onto my elbows and stole a look around. I'd landed on the edge of the pit—one of the only areas devoid of the angled wooden spears sticking up from the ground like rusty nails. Cutter hadn't fared so well. He lay just a few feet to my right, whimpering softly as he stared at a bloody spike piercing one thigh clean through. He slipped trembling fingers into a pouch at his belt and pulled free a health vial, uncorking it with his teeth, then taking a long gulp.

"Bollocks," he grunted at me through gritted teeth, his brow coated with sweat, his face stained with dirt. "This wazzock arsebadger right here"—he slapped at the gore-tipped spear in his leg—"is preventing me from recovering. It's gonna keep on sapping my health until I can get it out."

I pushed myself upright with a groan, downed another health potion myself—I wouldn't do Cutter any good dead—then wobbled over, took a knee, and began examining the wound with gentle fingers. The shaft was really lodged in there, and I couldn't see an easy way to get him free, which was probably the whole point of the trap: someone falls in and slowly bleeds to death no matter how many health potions they have in their inventory. There was only one thing I could do—I needed to break the shaft.

"This might hurt a little," I warned as I stood and spread my feet, hammer raised.

Cutter grimaced and nodded. "Do it."

He flinched as I laid into the crude spear. My hammer thudded into the wood a few inches above his leg, and he cried out in protest. All that vibration couldn't feel good, but this was the only way. Again and again I smashed at the wood, chips and chunks flying away as Cutter screamed. After a few minutes, the spike finally broke in two, which allowed me to wiggle his leg out, revealing a ragged hole the size of my fist running clean through his upper leg.

It was bad and graphic, but I'd seen worse IRL. Though not often.

With that done, I dragged him over to the side of the pit, away from the death spikes, wadded up an extra shirt from my pack, and applied pressure to the wound on instinct. Not sure if it made any difference—probably not—but between that and a few more health potions, Cutter was more or less back to normal in a few minutes. By that time, both of my spider-induced debuffs had also faded, meaning we were in the clear, healthwise. The only problem was, we were now stuck in a hole twenty-five feet deep, without a foreseeable way up, while the already gloomy forest was moving toward genuine night.

Far from an ideal situation.

I scooted back and flopped down, leaning against the sheer earthen wall behind me, sudden exhaustion starting to set in. I wasn't quite sure how the "Tired" debuff worked in V.G.O.—was it related simply to the sleep versus wake ratio, or were there other factors to consider, such as physical effort and injuries? I didn't have an answer, but I *was* tired and also hungry. I opened my pack, removed the campfire kit I'd picked up at Trajan's, and coaxed a little flame to life using some kindling and the split spear end I'd smashed to pieces.

Cutter watched me in silence.

Next, I dug into my pack and removed some of the food I'd picked up for this expedition—bread, cheese, mutton. The food appeared in my hands—the bread a little too hard, the mutton cold—but a few minutes over the fire warmed the meat right up. I distributed the meat once it was done, dripping hot grease to the ground.

"Don't suppose I ever told you how much I hate spiders, did I?" Cutter said around a mouthful of mutton, eyes watching the fire as the night grew damp and a smidge chilly.

I shook my head and tore off a chunk of pungent cheese.

"Well, then let me go on the record and say it. I royally hate spiders. Miserable bastards, the whole lot of them. They always turn up in the worst situations, too. One time—several years back this was—I'd fallen into a bit of a tough financial bind, so I agreed to clear a dungeon as part of a merc team. Picking up a little extra coin on the side to repay some outstanding debts I owed to an *unfriendly* fellow with a penchant for leg-breaking.

"At any rate"—he waved a hand through the air, the gesture saying the backstory wasn't important—"while scouting out traps, I stumbled into a room filled with the leggy buggers. Not quite so aggressive or *large* as these, but very unfriendly. They swarmed me in a blink and had me strung up before I knew what hit me. My team rescued me before the creepy-crawlies could turn me into a meal, but I haven't been able to stomach the sight of 'em since." He shivered at the memory.

"Speaking of," I said, suppressing a yawn with one hand, "thanks for coming back for me. With the spiders, I mean. I know I can respawn, but I sure wasn't looking forward to being lunch for the Queen."

His face grew dark. "I'm not what anyone might call a moral man, but I couldn't leave you to *that* fate, even if you'd eventually recover." He shook his head. "And, so you know, she wasn't going to eat you, Grim Jack. She was going to string you up, cut you open, then load you full of eggs. You'd live in total agony for a week or so, right up until those eggs hatched and the baby Spiderkin ate their way out of your body. Nasty as they come." He arched an eyebrow. "I suppose she might've ate what was left of you, though."

I sat in quiet horror for a spell.

Again, under normal circumstances, this game was a lawsuit waiting to happen. "Wow. That's total nightmare fuel," I said, leaning my head against the dirt wall. I closed my eyes for a moment, a giant yawn escaping my mouth. Then, despite the day's experience and the fact that I was dirty and in a pit, I somehow dozed off.

TWENTY-SEVEN

CAPTIVES

SOMEONE URGENTLY SHOOK MY SHOULDER, roughly jerking me back and forth. "Wake up, Jack," a vaguely familiar voice whispered at me.

I shrugged and tried to turn away. A bright flare of pain exploded in my cheek as an open-handed slap smashed into my face, knocking my head to one side. Begrudgingly, I cracked open my eyes: Cutter loomed over me, gaze swapping back and forth between me and something up on the edge of the pit. "Wake up, you moron," he fervently hissed again, jostling my shoulder. The fire had burned down to red embers, blanketed by a coat of gray ash, and the sky was still dark above. At most, a couple of hours had passed.

It took my eyes a handful of seconds to adjust to the dim light, but when they did, I easily spotted the quartet of strange specters regarding us from the top of the pit.

Lean, humanoid figures—two men, two women— with chalky white skin, decked out in crudely stitched armor, soft boots, and bracers lined with gleaming razors. The gear was studded with chunks of bone, ferocious teeth, and feathers in a myriad of colors, giving our onlookers a feral and dangerous appearance. I could tell they were watching us, but it was impossible to guess their thoughts or intentions since their faces were covered by horrifying masks, crafted from animal skulls decorated in a similar manner to the spider head I'd seen affixed to the totem marker by the river.

"These blokes don't look particularly friendly," Cutter said, glancing over his shoulder, "but if I had to bet, I'd say this is the lot we're here to find." He stood slowly, raising his hands skyward, showing he held no weapons.

"Hello there, friends," he said with a wave toward the figures. "Not sure if you understand me or not, but I'm hoping you do. Me and my friend here have come in search of Chief Kolle of the Ak-Hani clan. Don't suppose you fine folks would be willing to give us a hand out of this pit, then point us in the right direction, eh?"

The masked faces regarded us for a long minute, then disappeared, retreating from view.

"Good work, Cutter," I said, pushing myself upright, then brushing the flaky earth from the seat of my pants with one hand. "You scared them off."

"As long as they don't murder us," he replied, voice drawn and worried, "I'll consider that a win … Unfortunately, I don't think we're going to get that lucky," he finished as the masked faces appeared once more.

"Chief Kolle," one of them said, his voice deep and gruff, "where did you hear this name? Who told you to come to the lands of the Ak-Hani? And speak true, outsiders. If you lie, we will find out and you will suffer. Lie, and we will personally ferry you back across the stream and into the many arms of the *Mairng Mong*—the Spider Queen and her brood."

For a long stupid moment, I looked to Cutter, expecting him to take the lead and answer. Instead, he stole a glance at me and planted a sharp elbow into my ribs. "You're on, Grim Jack. These are your people, your quest, after all."

I gulped then reached a hand into my tunic, pulling the leather thong the dying Murk Elf had entrusted into my care—the mark of the Maa-Tál, embossed with a raven. "My friend and I"—I hooked a thumb toward Cutter—"were taken captive by a black priest of Serth-Rog," I began, then, as quickly as I could manage, I spooled out the tale, recounting our escape and my subsequent encounter with the dying Murk Elf. "So," I concluded, "she gave me this talisman as a sign of my trustworthiness, and charged me with bringing word of her death to the chief of the Ak-Hani."

They were silent for a moment. "I don't like it," a woman said, giving a shake of her head, the great horns of her mask swishing and swaying. "They are outsiders, Baymor, and he"—she nodded toward me—"is of the Lost Tribe. Everyone knows the Lost Ones cannot be trusted. How do we know they are not merely Viridian sympathizers? Sympathizers looking to curry favor by mapping our lands or assassinating Kolle? The human has a certain sneaky look to him. Is it so hard to believe he could be *Sicarii*?"

"And what of the talisman?" the man asked in return, more statement than question. "Does that not merit some small measure of trust?"

"No," she replied flatly. "It is unwise. What if they captured this missing Maa-Tál, tortured her to learn the name of our chief, then stole the talisman? It is not beyond belief, Baymor. The Viridians' shame and indecency know no bounds. Caution is better here, I think. Smarter. Let us kill them and wash our hands of this."

"Amara makes a good argument," said a different masked man. "These are evil days, after all. We'll give them quick, clean deaths, then hang their bones by the path as a deterrent against other interlopers. This is good, I think."

"Whoa boy, this is about to turn ugly," Cutter whispered sharply in my ear. "Do something. Anything. This is your show, Jack. You're the Murk Elf."

The four on the ridge spread out, and suddenly each held a short curved bow, carefully knocking arrow to string. Oh no. They were going to execute us on the spot.

"Wait," I shouted as a bout of inspiration struck. "The woman, the Maa-Tál who gave me the talisman, she gave me something else, too." I whipped open my inventory and hurriedly removed my leather bracers, then hastily rolled up my left sleeve. I held my forearm up like a shield, the black handprint standing out in sharp relief against my gunmetal gray skin. "She marked me with this."

For a long beat, nothing happened—which was both good and bad, considering the circumstances—but eventually, one by one, they lowered their raised bows. "He has the mark," the man, Baymor, said. "Is there some explanation for this, Amara?" he asked, tone slightly accusatory.

"No," the woman replied with a sigh. "No Maa-Tál would offer the mark unless the Shadow-Spark is present." She paused, slung her bow, then crossed her arms as she regarded us. "I suppose the truth of his story is for Kolle to decide. We could still kill the human, though," she offered with a shrug. "He has neither the talisman nor the mark. Truly an outsider. What say you, Lost One?" she shouted down to me. "Will you allow us to kill this traveling companion of yours to spare your life?"

Cutter stole an uneasy look at me, a nervous grin stretching across his face. "Don't hang me out to dry here, Jack. We're in this together, eh?"

I smiled, shook my head, and slid right, repositioning myself in front of Cutter. Using my body as a shield. "No," I replied to the Murk Elf woman above. "Either you offer us both safe passage, or you kill us both." I drew my warhammer from the frog at my belt. "But, word to the wise, we're not going to go easy." That wasn't true—if they decided to kill us, we'd fold like a bad hand, but maybe they wouldn't know that.

The four Ak-Hani suddenly broke into a chorus of chuckles and hoots. "Good answer," Amara replied. "Perhaps you have what it takes to be Maa-Tál, after all. We will take you and your friend to see Kolle, but be warned. If there is deceit in your heart, Kolle will know, and what he will do to you will be far worse than death by spider."

With the threat made, the four Ak-Hani quickly lowered down a pair of ropes and hauled Cutter and me out of the pit. It wasn't all hugs and high fives after that, though. No, in short order, they bound our hands behind our backs with chafing strips of rope, then fitted us both with metal collars affixed to chains so they could drag us along. The collars, aside from being positively frigid, offered a string of terrible penalties:

<<<>>>

Debuffs Added

Bound: Movement rate reduced by 10%; duration, indefinitely.

Drained: Health, Stamina, and Spirit Regeneration reduced by 30%; duration, indefinitely.

Inhibited: Carry Capacity -40lbs; Stealth is 50% more difficult; all spells have a 50% increased chance to fail; duration, indefinitely.

Assuming Cutter and I lived through this, I'd need to get my hands on a few of these collars—they'd sure come in handy against the enemies I'd made for myself over the past couple days.

"If you fail to keep up," the woman said, rounding on me, "I will sling you over my shoulder and carry you all the way to Yunnam like a mewling child. And you"—she gave the chain attached to Cutter's collar a stiff yank—"will keep up, or I will slit your throat and leave your remains for the crocodiles. Now move."

TWENTY-EIGHT

CHIEF KOLLE

I T TOOK TWO OR THREE HOURS OF HARD WALKING to get to the Murk Elf city, Yunnam. At first, the path was easy to follow, but the further into the forest we went, the more often the trail veered into thick tangles of swampy vegetation or hooked through shallow bogs, which made moving nearly impossible. Our guides, though, walked the route with the confidence of people who'd made the same trek a thousand times before. They seemed to know every pitfall, every stone, and their steps always found the stable rock in the mud or the dry patch of grass in the otherwise mushy marshlands.

Not that they shared any of that information with us. They were an abnormally tight-lipped group, and our time passed in silence, with the exception of the occasional muttered curse from Cutter.

Eventually, we started to see subtle signs of habitation: at first it was guard towers, built into the branches of spreading trees. The towers were nearly invisible, heavily camouflaged with mud, sticks, leaves, and vines, but my Keen-Sight ability quickly outlined the blurred edges of the structures. Then, after a time, I noticed the jungle had been cleared back in places to make room for the increasingly broad dirt path, which almost resembled a crude road. After even more walking, the dirt path finally morphed into a cobblestone street, made from dark worn river rock.

The stone walkway carved through the trees, twisting and winding this way and that, following the natural contours of the land. We rounded a corner, identical to a thousand others before it, and suddenly found ourselves at a wooden palisade with a rough gate, already open, waiting to receive us. The town beyond the gate was a far cry from what I'd experienced in Rowanheath. While the Wode city vaguely resembled a mix between medieval Europe and the ancient Roman Empire, this place didn't look like any city I'd ever seen—in real life or on the big screen.

The town was built among twisted, moss-covered trees, the urban sprawl taking great care to give the towering plants room to grow. The buildings were built from an amalgamation of wood, mud, and palm fronds, all joined together with odd bits of leather, tangles of luminescent green moss, and gobs of silvery spider silk. Not a lot of curb appeal—no cozy little townhomes I could see myself settling down in—and also, no actual curbs to speak of. All of the buildings towered high above the ground, raised up on dark wooden struts, giving the homes a strangely arachnoid appearance.

Considering we in a swamp that probably received a fair amount of rainfall—this area was likely called the *Storme Marshes* for a good reason—I guessed the elevation was for flooding. It was still weird, though. Our guards pulled us through the center of town, the residents staring at us with hard, guarded gazes. I saw more than one Murk Elf parent usher kids up rickety stairs and into homes at our passing. So far, I didn't know much about the Ak-Hani clan, but one thing was readily apparent.

Outsiders were really, really, really not liked, which didn't bode well for us.

Yunnam was also radically smaller than Rowanheath, so it took only a handful of minutes before our escorts dragged us to a halt at our final destination. A massive and twisted tree. The thing was fat and gnarled, with giant boughs branching off from the trunk, reaching for the sky like a hundred broken fingers. Great ropes of moss clung to every branch, to every twig, pulsing with a soft light. A set of weathered stone steps climbed up the tree's face, dead-ending at a squat door inset directly into the trunk, flanked by a pair of circular windows shedding weak yellow firelight.

One of the guards—a man who hadn't spoken more than a dozen words—loosened my hand restraints, removed the metal collar from my neck, then gave me a little shove toward the stairs. "I thought you said we were probably assassins," I commented, rubbing at the raw skin around my wrists. "Aren't you worried I might try to do something?"

"We said he might be *Sicarii,*" the still-masked Amara replied, with a nod to Cutter. "You? No, I don't think so. Besides, we are at times overprotective of our chieftain. He is a great warrior and a powerful Necromancer of the Maa-Tál. Try anything and he'll rip the soul from your body. Now"—she paused, staring at me through the mask slits—"up you go."

"What about my friend?" I asked.

"He does not bear the talisman," she replied, deadpan. "Nor does he have the mark. So"—she paused, and it almost sounded like she was smiling—"he will remain in our custody until Chief Kolle determines your intent. *If* he declares your innocence, you and your friend live. And if he finds you guilty?" She shrugged, unconcerned by the prospect. "Our pigs are always hungry."

"Don't screw this up," Cutter called as the guards dragged him away, deeper into the village. Amara, however, accompanied me to the top of the stairs, then pounded on the door with a closed fist, *thunk, thunk, thunk.*

"Enter," boomed a deep, masculine voice that sounded like a cement mixer loaded down with bricks. Amara opened the door and rudely shoved me through, before slipping in herself.

Despite the foreboding exterior, the tree's interior was beautiful, well lit, and clean. There wasn't much by way of furniture, but what I saw was all finely made and polished to a dull glow. Elegantly curved bookshelves lined the walls and were heavy laden with thick leather-bound tomes and a host of arcane potions and ingredients. Chief Kolle lounged on a pile of colorful pillows at the far side of the room, thumbing through a dusty book laid out on a squat, rectangular table in front of him.

After seeing the elaborate and terrifying attire of the Ak-Hani Rangers, I'd come expecting a nightmare shaman looming on a throne made of human bones. But the chief was none of those things. He was large and heavily muscled with black hair, heavily streaked with gray, and wore plain clothing that would've let him pass unnoticed in Rowanheath. His bushy eyebrows nearly climbed into his hairline as his gaze flickered between me and my guard.

"I see your patrol has yielded some *interesting* results," he said, closing his book and rubbing absently at his chin.

Amara bowed formally, removing her mask in the process. She had the same gray skin as the rest of the Murk Elves, short black hair, shaved down to the skin on one side, and a few swirling tattoos covering one cheek. She was younger than I'd expected—late twenties, early thirties—but just a glance at her violet eyes told me her years had been hard and painful. Filled with violence, bloodshed, and loss.

She rose from her bow and immediately launched into the details of the expedition, giving a terse, no-nonsense report—the spiders were encroaching again, there was sign of Imperial soldiers moving along the northern border of the marshes, the Moss Hag had struck again—then offered an account of finding me and Cutter stranded in the death pit. The chieftain listened placidly, little emotion displayed on his face, then dismissed her from the room, before turning his gaze on me.

"Well," he finally said as the door shut, "what do you have to say for yourself, boy?"

I fidgeted nervously, clearing my throat as I tried to figure out what to say. Truthfully, Amara had summed everything up much more efficiently than I ever could have. I struggled for another few seconds, the silence turning into an uncomfortable weight around my shoulders. Then, the chief did something to break the tension. He smiled, a wide grin missing a few teeth.

"Relax, boy," he said with a bark and an eyeroll. "You and your friend are safe. You are no Viridian cutthroat come to collect my scalp, even a blind man could see that. Some of my clan—like my daughter, Amara, whom you've had the pleasure of meeting—can be a little zealous in their disdain for the empire. At times, a bit *over*zealous perhaps. Such passion is both the blessing and curse of youth."

I gulped, feeling weak in the knees. That crazy, mask-wearing woman was his *daughter*?

"I, on the other hand," he said after a pause, "have the benefit of many years on my side. Such time often brings a certain degree of wisdom and discernment. As a result, I am not quite so quick to rush to judgement. This gift of time also allows me to use my eyes." He paused, grinned, and tapped at the corner of one eye. "Not only do you not look like a cutthroat, you bear the *Blessing of the Forest*. Only the mighty tree-kin can issue such trinkets, and the trees have far better discernment than even the oldest of our kind. If one of the elder tree brothers thinks highly enough of you to give you such a gift, I can at least hear you out. So please, come, sit, relax, and tell me your tale."

I let out a huge sigh of relief and my legs seemed to move me forward as though on autopilot. Before I knew it, I was seated on the floor across from the chieftain, spilling my story.

I told him everything. Waking up in the cell. Finding the old woman. Giving her the potion, trying to resuscitate her and failing. He listened thoughtfully as I talked, nodding or frowning in all the right places. I told him what I knew about the black priest of Serth-Rog, which didn't amount to much. Still, he seemed to absorb the details with great meaning, as though finally fitting some long-missing puzzle piece into place.

"Well," he said as I finished, folding his hands in his lap, "that certainly clears up a few things."

"Does that mean you know what that priest was doing, then?" I asked, genuinely curious about the mystery.

He canted his head to one side, brow furrowed, and nodded.

"There is still much I do not know," he said gravely, "but this is not the first such report to reach my ears. Folk from all six named clans have gone missing over the past several months. Many never to reappear again. A few, however, have returned, but they are different from when they left. To the undiscerning eye, these doppelgangers may go unnoticed—but *I* have noticed. Their bodies are whole, but they are absent a soul. Or, at least *their* soul. These dark priests are hollowing people out and replacing them with corrupt spirits from Morsheim, the realm of Serth-Rog. To what end this is being done, I cannot yet say …"

A notification popped up as he thoughtfully trailed off:

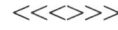

Quest Update: Imposter Georgie

Chief Kolle of the Ak-Hani clan has informed you that the black priests of Serth-Rog are replacing people with convincing doppelgangers, though he doesn't know why. Tell Cutter about the new revelation in order to get to the bottom of Gentlemen Georgie's strange shift in personality.

Quest Class: Unique, Personal

Quest Difficulty: Hard

Success: Help Cutter get to the bottom of the mystery surrounding Gentleman Georgie's sudden personality change.

Failure: Refuse to help Cutter or allow him to die before the mission is complete.

Reward: ?

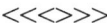

"That aside," the chief continued, "I truly cannot thank you enough for fulfilling the final wish of our dear departed sister, especially at such great risk to yourself. You do not know this, but one of our elders, Larriet Shadowrunner, went missing near a month ago, and we've been urgently searching for her. That talisman you bear belonged to her. Her passing is a terrible thing, a deep loss to our people, but better to know than to suffer in uncertainty."

He was silent for a long time, staring at me, jaw clenched tight, forehead creased, eyes unfocused, as though he were seeing something far off. "That talisman she gave you—I think you should keep it. Larriet would've liked that. Besides, you may find use of it yet, since this is not the end of your journey among us, but rather the beginning. I am Maa-Tál myself—the Chief Dark Templar of the Ak-Hani—and I can see the Shadow-Spark burning inside you. I can see the mark Elder Larriet left upon you. It is possible you are destined to become one of us, boy. If, that is, you have the mettle to endure what is to come.

"But"—he paused, rubbing a hand along his jaw— "it is late and I can see you are tired, so for tonight, I will have you and your friend put in guest quarters. In the morning, we'll discuss your induction into the esteemed ranks of the Dark Templars." He frowned again, lips curling into a thin line. "But sleep, first." He shook his head and looked away. "I don't envy you, boy. Not at all."

A level up notification and a quest update appeared as the chief dismissed me.

x1 Level Up!

You have (25) undistributed stat points

You have (10) unassigned proficiency points

Quest Update: Plight of the Maa-Tál

You have informed Chief Kolle of the Ak-Hani clan about the awful experiments of the black priests of Serth-Rog and successfully delivered the sacred talisman of the dying Murk Elf, Larriet. In return, you have received 15,000 EXP. In order to fully complete this quest and receive the reward—[unique, scalable item]—and the Shadowmancer class kit, you must complete the Maa-Tál initiation ordeal.

Quest Class: Rare, Class-Based

Quest Difficulty: Hard

Success: Survive the Maa-Tál initiation ordeal

Failure: Die during the Maa-Tál initiation ordeal

Reward: Class Change: Dark Templar, Shadowmancer Kit; Unique, Scalable Item

I gave them a cursory scan without much enthusiasm. I should've been stoked beyond belief—after all, I'd survived finding Chief Kolle, picked up another level, and was on the verge of unlocking my game class. So yeah, I *should've* been stoked. But instead I just felt exhausted beyond belief and sick. Really sick. My head throbbed, my muscles were suddenly as limp as wet noodles, and freezing chills and flaming nausea racked my body in turns.

I found the ever-friendly Amara, who was wearing her mask once more, waiting to escort me outside the building. She guided me through the town, carrying me more often than not as my legs stopped working; I was vaguely aware of lurch-stumbling up a set of wooden steps and into one of the raised buildings before slamming to the floor as every muscle in my body tightened in the same instant.

In the back of my mind, I recalled that I was dangerously close to the seventy-two-hour in-game mark, but the thought didn't stay long as I passed out in sheer agony.

TWENTY-NINE

REBIRTH

I SPENT THE REST OF THE NIGHT AND THE MAJORITY of the next day slipping between consciousness and unconsciousness.

When I slept, I had terrible fever dreams of the real world: I saw my parents—my father balding and potbellied, my mother wearing a floral print dress—die. I saw the skin slough off their bones as murderous space fire ate them up. I watched my coworkers, Jeff and Angelina, perish as a wave, two hundred feet tall, swept in from the ocean, smashing into buildings, flipping cars, drowning people in their homes. I witnessed my ex-girlfriend, now living in Colorado, scream as the ground swelled and buckled, ripping open then swallowing her into the heart of the earth.

Horrific nightmares, all of them.

But waking was even worse. Far worse.

My thoughts were oddly heavy and slipped away whenever I tried to focus on one thing for more than a few seconds. Everything seemed to blur on the edges, bleeding together while the walls spun and twisted into amorphous blobs of techno-color vomit. And awake,

233

there was the pain. My insides felt like they'd been dunked in a vat of acid: a terrible molten liquid searing every nerve ending … My heart jack-rabbited away inside my chest … Every breath was forced and agonizing, like inhaling fine specks of jagged glass … My body randomly convulsed, the muscle contractions so intense they snapped bones …

I'd never experienced anything like it, and part of me wanted nothing more than to die.

After fifteen hours—which felt much more like fifteen years—the pain dimmed to a dull, full-body throb, and I finally came to my senses. I was lying on a narrow pallet in the corner of a tiny room, which boasted a single chair and a roughhewn table with a pitcher of water and a basin. Cutter lounged in the chair, hands folded in his lap, eyes closed while he snored softly. Passed out. There were several windows, all shuttered, but late afternoon sunlight streamed in around the edges, illuminating a swirl of dust motes floating in the air.

Cautiously, I sat up and stretched out sore muscles, twisting this way and that, checking for any kind of long-term damage from my illness. Sophia, my ever-present companion, piped up mid-stretch, alerting me that I had a message from Osmark Customer Support.

I played it immediately.

"Traveler," intoned an overly chipper and annoyingly familiar voice, "this is Matthew, your customer support representative. Our system records indicate you've spent your third full night in Viridian Gate Online. Congratulations! Our system indicates that your physical body lapsed into cardiac arrest roughly two hours ago; your time of death was approximately 6:17 AM Pacific Standard Time. You have our deepest condolences, but we are happy to inform you that you've successfully transitioned to V.G.O.!

"Likely, you've experienced some very unpleasant sensations over the past several hours, but those feelings will pass and you should fully recover. Make sure you stop by your nearest inn or tavern and eat a hearty meal. As a side note, an Osmark Tech retrieval team has already been dispatched to your physical location. Your body and effects will remain at your residence, but your capsule will be removed, cleaned, and recirculated for the good of humanity. Thank you for playing."

And just like that, Matthew's voice was gone. Gone, like my body.

I was dead.

Back in my apartment, my physical heart was unmoving and cold, my eyes glassy, my skin sallow, my guts bloated. I was dead. Carefully, I reached up and ran a hand along my cheek, feeling the bristly bite of facial hair. I dragged my fingers along my jaw line, then slipped them onto my neck, gently pressing two digits into my carotid artery, searching for my pulse. It was there, strong and steady below my fingertips. I was dead. Yet here I was, sitting on a pallet, *feeling* my heart thump away in my chest, circulating blood through my body.

Wow.

Surreal.

I'd known from the get-go that Viridian Gate was my final destination.

I'd *known* it, but I hadn't really believed it. There's a world of difference between knowing something intellectually and accepting it into your heart as true. I'd *known*, but I hadn't *believed*. Not until now. A small part of me grieved over the loss—because it was a loss. And not just the loss of my physical body, it was the loss of everything I'd ever had. It was the death of my job, the death of my friends, the death of my family, the death of my apartment, city, nation, and world.

It was all consuming and deeply personal.

But then I paused and once more felt the drumming rhythm of my heartbeat beneath my fingers; I threw my head back and laughed. Holy shit! I was *alive*! Somehow, miraculously, I'd lived. And not just through my own death—I'd survived the end of the world. For weeks, I'd been moping around IRL, consumed by the looming threat of the asteroid, but I'd beaten that ball of flame too—it couldn't kill me if my body was already a bloated bag of cold meat. I'd been reborn. I chuckled again, a raucous hoot so loud it startled Cutter awake.

He jumped in surprise, then promptly fell from the chair, which only made me laugh harder.

"Yeah, yeah. Laugh it up, arsehole," Cutter muttered disgruntledly, pushing himself upright and brushing off dusty palms on his britches. "It's not like I watched over you all night, force-feeding you and dribbling water into your mouth so you wouldn't die. My pain is amusement to you, I understand how it is."

"It's not that," I said, gaining my feet with a wide, goofy grin. "I survived, Cutter. I made it. The sickness you told me about—the one that kills travelers—I survived. I transitioned." I threw an arm into the air, an epic fist pump. "I'm ALIVE, motherfuckers!" I shouted, before breaking out into a renewed fit of giggles.

"Joy for you," Cutter replied with an eyeroll. "Would you like a medal for your achievement, eh? I'm alive too, maybe I should celebrate. Though come to think of it, I'm not entirely sure waking up in the morning really qualifies as a major victory. Not unless you're a phenomenal loser." He glanced at me and sniffed. "I revise my statement. Maybe *you* do deserve a medal."

"Jerk," I replied halfheartedly. Considering I'd just survived the end of the world, it was hard to be offended. "And thanks for your help, Cutter. You're a mostly good friend."

He snorted and rolled his eyes. "One near-death experience and now you're all misty-eyed. Look, if you really want to thank me," he said, "how's about you pull yourself together and get over to the chieftain before that awful Amara loses her patience and feeds us both to bog gators. She told me if you died, I was next on the chopping block. Practically had to fight her off with a stick to keep her out of here."

That sobered me up pretty quickly.

In my jubilation, I'd sort of forgotten about the Maa-Tál initiation ordeal waiting for me like a bar-drunk loitering in an alleyway, looking for a brawl.

And it also reminded me of the threat still hanging over V.G.O. like a dark cloud: there was a group of corrupt uber-elites looking to rule this world with an iron fist. My joy at surviving morphed and hardened into something new. A fierce resolve to protect Eldgard. Maybe V.G.O. had been a game once, but it wasn't anymore. Not to me. It was my world now, and it'd given me a second chance to live. It'd offered Abby—and millions of other people—a second chance to live, and I'd be damned if I'd let anyone take that away. Not if I could do anything about it.

"You're right," I said with a nod. "Time to go get my hands dirty. Wish me luck." I turned and headed for the door.

"Luck," Cutter called out behind me.

Amara was waiting outside, awake and alert as ever, though she'd finally taken off her mask. She offered me a perfunctory greeting, but didn't have two more words to spare for me as she escorted me back to the chieftain's tree. Since she didn't seem interested in gabbing, I pulled out a slab of mutton and ate while we walked. I was just finishing up with my on-the-go breakfast when we arrived at the squat tree in the heart of Yunnam. Amara pushed and shoved me up the stairs, apparently dissatisfied that the chief had decided not to kill me.

She knocked.

A terse "Enter" immediately followed.

The chief was leaning against the far wall, back turned, peering out of a rounded window, casually drumming his fingers on the wooden frame. I stood in the entryway for a few minutes, shuffling nervously from foot to foot. Eventually, I cleared my throat, once, twice, three times, which finally got his attention.

"Grim Jack," he said with a little shake of his head, before rounding on me. "It's good to see you back on your feet. My daughter told me about your condition, and I was beginning to fear the worst. We haven't had many travelers out this way, but I've heard of foreigners dying and vanishing permanently. Killed by some sort of strange, untreatable illness. I'm relieved you're not one of them." He paused, squinting as his lips pulled up into a barely there smile. "I've been up all night thinking over the details of your ordeal—I would've hated to waste all that effort only to have you die prematurely."

"Well," I said, struggling to find a tactful response, "that's very thoughtful of you."

His smile widened a fraction of an inch. "You seem like a good egg, Jack. I hope you make it through this. Now, as your people say, let's get down to brass tacks. Obviously, much of the day's already been spent, but there is still time for you to complete the ritual, assuming you are willing and ready." He paused and folded his hands behind his back. "So are you ready, Jack?"

I sighed and ran a nervous hand through my hair. "As ready as I'm ever going to be," I finally replied with a bob of my chin.

He paused again, eyeing me more intently, scrutinizing every inch of me, his smile fading, turning into a thin, tight line. "There is something new about you today," he said, almost in a whisper. "There is a vitality to you that wasn't there before. And fire. A fire in your belly." He frowned, a look of confusion briefly passing across his face before he nodded in approval. "That is good. You're going to need fire to survive the trial ahead of you.

"Now, unfortunately, boy," he continued, "your ordeal will be quite unorthodox and far more strenuous than what most initiates experience. The majority of seekers typically undergo two different initiation ordeals. The first"—he raised one finger into the air—"is to prove they are worthy of the title of Dark Templar. Maa-Tál. The second ordeal"—another finger shot up—"takes place much later on, once a novice Dark Templar has already mastered the fundamentals of the class. That second trial confers a kit specialization. Few have what it takes to become Maa-Tál, fewer still have what it takes go further."

"But I already have a specialization selected," I interjected. "I'm supposed to be a Shadowmancer."

"Half true," he replied. "You are something of an anomaly—a child too ambitious for your own good. Essentially, you've learned to run before you've learned to walk. Your natural aptitude has already marked you with the distinction of a class specialization, yet ..." He paused, suddenly very serious. "Yet you have failed to prove you are worthy to bear the title of Maa-Tál in the first place. So, I have come up with a different test for you. Instead of two trials, you shall have only one. One single terrible ordeal, far more difficult than is truly fair to ask of any initiate."

I felt a growing lump in my throat. What in the world did he want me to do?

"To give you as much of an edge as possible," he said after a beat, "I will temporarily grant you the Dark Templar base class and give you access to your Shadowmancer skill tree during the course of your ordeal. But, should you fail in this, you will lose your temporary class-change and the path of the Dark Templar will be forever closed to you. Additionally, should you fail, any Proficiency Points you invested in the Shadowmancer skill tree will be lost forever. Knowing all of this, would you still like to proceed?"

Once more, I found myself reeling on the edge of a precipice with no hope of return.

The last time I'd heard those words, *would you still like to proceed*, it'd been a VR version of Robert Osmark explaining the risks of stepping into the world of V.G.O. It felt unreal to be hearing those same words again, this time coming from the mouth of a Murk Elf chieftain. If

I took this step, there'd be no going back. If I failed, this class would be closed forever, relegating me to something else—something *less*—and robbing me of priceless Proficiency Points in the process. Or ... I could walk away. It was all or nothing.

In my old life, I'd lived in a crappy apartment, with crappy things, making a crappy salary. All because I wasn't brave enough to step out and take risks. This was a new life, though. A new chance, and I wasn't going to make the same mistakes again. "In for a penny, in for a pound," I said with a nod. "Lay it on me."

THIRTY

Dark Templar

THE CHIEFTAIN OFFERED A BROAD GRIN, CROW'S feet jutting from the corners of his eyes. "Wonderful." He rubbed his hands together. In a few quick steps, he was before me and had my head gripped between his heavily calloused palms. Then he began to chant, his words foreign and odd, echoing with a strangely musical cadence. The handprint on my arm began to throb like a slow steady heartbeat, arctic cold sweeping through me like a sudden blizzard, my limbs trembling under the icy power. Part of me wanted to pull away from his hands, but I couldn't move.

I could only stand, shiver, and watch.

Soon, the chanting took on a new rhythm—fevered, edgy, erratic—and great bands of shifting black began to swirl and twirl around the chief until he was wreathed in a whirlwind of pure shadow. His eyes burned with violet light and suddenly the pressure on my head increased a hundred-fold, his hands turning into a vise, bearing down on my skull with inhuman strength, sending jagged bolts of pain skipping through my body. I opened my mouth to scream but no sound came out; instead, the whirling vortex surrounding Kolle poured into me, filling me with the dark, freezing energy of Umbra.

In wriggled inside me, seeping through my skin, crawling over eyes and my hair, boring through my eardrums, and permeating my gray matter.

After what felt like a lifetime, the chief ceased his chanting and staggered away, sweat rolling down his face, his back bowed with exhaustion, his arms suddenly hanging like dead weights at his sides. He stumbled and lurched left then right, before carefully shuffling backward and lowering himself onto a mound of pillows, his breathing labored. I gracelessly collapsed to the ground, my legs rubber, my spine made of Jell-O. My HP hadn't been affected in any way by the ceremony, but whatever the chief had done had completely drained me of Spirit and Stamina.

"The ceremony is never easy," the chief said after a time, "but it was even more difficult than usual with you, boy. Nearly killed myself unlocking your gift. I am suddenly reminded why there is a reason the ordeal is done in stages." He paused, wheezing as he dropped his head down. "Still, it is done," he finished eventually. "You now have access to the Shadowmancer Kit skills. Take a moment to examine the abilities available to you, invest your Proficiency Points as you see fit, then I will tell you about your initiation ordeal."

I nodded, too tired to say anything else. A host of notifications immediately popped up in front of me. I sighed, opened up my bag, and selected another slab of seared meat to gnaw on while I read through each prompt—I really needed to get my Stamina back up to maximum. First was a long list of various traits I'd acquired with my new class:

<<<>>>

Mantle of the Maa-Tál (Shadowmancer)

As a guardian and enforcer of the Dark Pantheon, you wrap yourself in the shadow power of the Umbra, gaining a wide array of deadly powers.

Effect 1: +5% faster movement rate (+1% per 4 C.L.)

Effect 2: +10% Stealth (+1% per 5 C.L.)

Effect 3: Immune to Morale Failure

Effect 4: +10% damage bonus against "light"-aligned players and NPCs

Effect 5: +20% resistance to shadow damage

Effect 6: Access to Shadowmancer Restricted Skills

Effect 7: "Dark" alignment added

Effect 8: 10% Weakness against Holy Damage

Effect 9: Cannot wear Heavy Armor

Effect 10: Can only specialize in Blunt Weapons

I whistled through my teeth. Those were some serious perks. I was sure the other classes offered some spectacular bonuses, but I bet they weren't nearly so extensive. I took another bite of meat, savoring the charred flavor as I toggled over to the "Class Abilities" screen.

Class Unlocked

Congratulations, you have been granted the Dark Templar (Probationary) class and have unlocked the Shadowmancer (Probationary) specialty kit! Each class has a variety of locked skills/abilities, which can be unlocked and improved by investing Proficiency Points earned while leveling up your character. Many skills require you to reach a certain character level before unlocking, and each unlocked spell can be upgraded a total of seven times (Initiate, Novice, Adept, Journeyman, Specialist, Master, Grandmaster).

I read the brief explanation, then dismissed the notice and pulled up my Shadowmancer Skill Tree screen. My kit tree seemed to be broken down into four distinct groups: Offensive Skills, Defensive Skills, Crowd Control Techniques, and Passive Abilities. Most of the abilities were currently blocked due to prerequisite skills or level restrictions, but there was still some awesome stuff available to me. I currently had 10 Proficiency Points to invest, but I needed to make sure I used them wisely, especially since it was possible I might lose any invested points if I failed this mission.

I continued to chomp at my greasy mutton as I scanned through each of the four skill groupings, reading over the items with a careful eye.

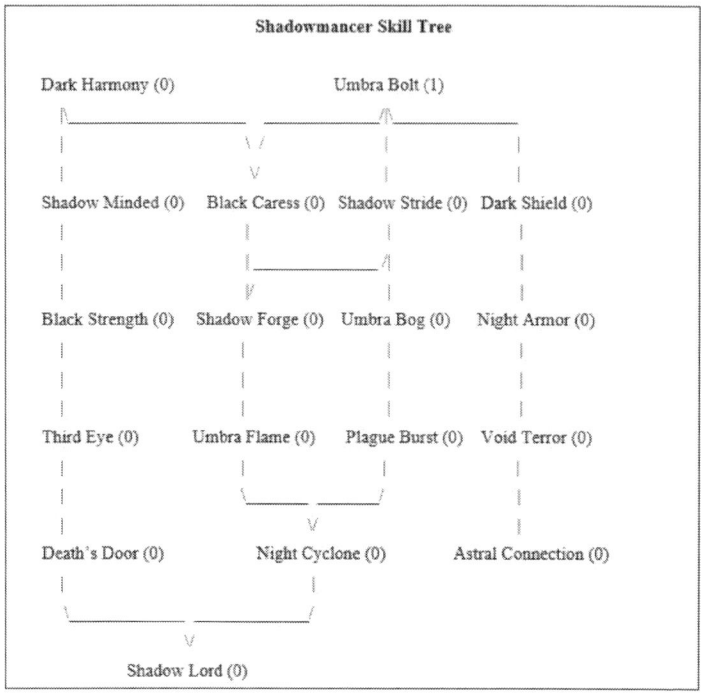

After a lot of thought and careful examination, I finally decided to drop two more points into Umbra Bolt—elevating the spell to the Adept Level—then picked up three more active spells to round out my growing repertoire:

Skill: Shadow Stride

Time grinds to a crawl for everyone except the caster, allowing the Shadowmancer to evade enemies by slipping through the Shadowverse to a nearby location. While shadow striding, the Shadowmancer is immune to damage, but cannot attack, consume potions, or perform other spells. The Shadowmancer can only remain in the Shadowverse for 30 seconds (accelerated player time).

Skill Type/Level: Spell/Initiate

Cost: 100 Spirit

Range: 40 Meters

Cast Time: Instant

Cooldown: 45 seconds (from cast time)

Effect: Teleport through shadow to a nearby location.

Effect 2: Immune to damage while shadow striding.

Skill: Umbra Bog

Summon a bog of creeping shadows that temporarily ensnares your enemies, badly hindering movement.

Skill Type/Level: Spell/Initiate

Cost: 150 Spirit

Range: 40 Meters

Cast Time: 1.0 seconds

Cooldown: 2 minutes

Effect: Ensnare enemies in a shadowy bog, slowing movement by 75%; duration, 30 seconds.

<<<>>>

Skill: Dark Shield

Summon a powerful forcefield of dark energy to protect you from projectiles or spell damage.

Skill Type/Level: Spell/Initiate

Cost: 35 Spirit/Sec

Range: 1 Meter

Cast Time: Instant

Cooldown: N/A

Effect: Create a powerful forcefield which absorbs (110% x SP) of projectile or spell damage.

With Umbra Bolt, Shadow Stride, Umbra Bog, and Dark Shield in my tool belt, I had a little bit of everything. My Blunt Weapon skills and Stealth abilities would allow me to deal out some serious damage up close and personal, while Umbra Bolt would give me a powerful ranged attack. The other spells would afford me a chance to capitalize on my quick movement rate, while offering some decent protection just in case things went sideways. Satisfied with those choices, I decided to also pick up Dark Harmony—a passive ability—and one Aura Skill called Night Armor:

Ability: Dark Harmony

Draw on the ever-present power of the Umbra to heal grievous injuries to the flesh.

Ability Type/Level: Passive/Initiate

Cost: None

Range: N/A

Cast Time: N/A

Cooldown: N/A

Effect: Increase Health Regeneration by 15%.

<<<>>>

Skill: Night Armor

Call upon the power of the night and wrap yourself in a barrier of dense shadow, diminishing the damage from melee attacks while simultaneously exacting retribution against your attacker.

Skill Type/Level: Aura/Initiate

Cost: 450 Spirit; duration, 20 minutes.

Range: 1 Meter

Cast Time: Instant

Cooldown: N/A

Effect: Night Armor absorbs 15% of melee damage.

Effect 2: Night Armor redirects 20% of absorbed melee damage back at the attacker.

<<<>>>

Hopefully, with all of those extra perks and skills I'd be able to survive whatever the chief had in store for me. I finally closed out of my interface menu to find the chief pacing the room in eager anticipation, his rough leather trousers *whisk-whisk-whisking* as he moved. He came to a stuttering halt as he noticed my gaze. "So, have you made your choices?"

I nodded.

"Good, then there is nothing left for you here—it is time for you to embark on your ordeal. To the southeast of here, there lives a terrible creature: the Moss Hag. A wretched being that dwells in the deep swamps. She is fond of encroaching on our boundaries and has a terrible hunger for the flesh of our people, especially our young. In order to prove yourself worthy of the title Maa-Tál, you must venture into the heart of her swamp alone and find a way to rid Yunnam of this scourge once and for all. Do this and you will be one of us. Fail …" He faltered, surveying me with serious eyes. "Don't fail."

<<<>>>

Quest Update: Plight of the Maa-Tál

Chief Kolle of the Ak-Hani clan has charged you with destroying the Moss Hag living in the deep swamps to the Southeast of Yunnam. This noble deed will complete the quest *Plight of the Maa-Tál* and you will receive (1) [unique, scalable item] from Chief Kolle as well as the Shadowmancer class kit.

Quest Class: Rare, Class-Based

Quest Difficulty: Infernal

Success: Eliminate the Moss Hag without dying within (24) in-game hours.

Failure: Die during the Maa-Tál initiation ordeal or fail to eliminate the Moss Hag within (24) in-game hours.

Reward: Class Change: Dark Templar, Shadowmancer Kit; Unique, Scalable Item

Accept: Yes/No

<<<>>>

I accepted the quest without question, offered the chief a quick goodbye, then saw myself out of the building.

Cutter was waiting for me outside. He was leaning against the base of the chieftain's enormous tree home, arms crossed, completely at his ease—or at least, that's what he was trying to convey. I could tell he was nervous, though, which was partly due to the fact that Amara lingered twenty feet away, staring at him with cold hostility, casually inspecting the razor-sharp blade of a dagger. Watching his every move.

"How bad is it?" Cutter asked, purposely ignoring Amara's icy glare.

"Pretty bad," I said honestly before filling him in on the details.

He nodded, grimaced, then shrugged. "Well, you can only do what you can do, I suppose. Just remember what I said when we were training: 'there's always someone bigger, faster, stronger. So, you need to be smarter. Misdirection and a well-placed blow can fell even the most imposing warriors.' Remember that"—he cocked a finger and tapped at his temple—"and you'll do alright. And if not … Well, then both our arses are royally screwed. Best of luck, Grim Jack. Best of luck, 'cause you're gonna need it."

THIRTY-ONE

TEST DRIVE

I LEFT THROUGH THE MAIN GATE, THIS TIME ALONE, the sun dropping below the tree line, long, deep shadows giving the forest an ominous appearance. I checked my map and saw the Moss Hag's burrow was just south from the pit Cutter and I had originally fallen into. The one near the border with the creepy Spiderkin. Which meant I could easily follow the ambling path back to the pit, likely avoiding the forest's assorted deadly denizens, then cut over. The lazy couch potato in my soul said that's what I should do: just follow the road, stick to the path of least resistance.

I dismissed the idea the second I was out of the gate, though.

I only had one shot to accomplish this mission, and assuming the chieftain hadn't been overexaggerating, it was going to take everything I had to get the deed done. Which meant I wasn't going to be able to just walk into the Moss Hag's burrow, punch her in the teeth, and call it quits, quick and easy. Which further meant I needed to have a handle on my new abilities when I confronted her—it certainly wouldn't do to show up for the big boss fight and Shadow Stride my way off a cliff by accident.

The odds were already stacked heavily against me, so I needed every advantage I could get my mitts on.

Besides, I was pretty excited to see what my new spells could actually do.

So I headed off road, fighting my way into the twisting trees, careful to avoid the grabbing roots and tangles of mossy vegetation littering the forest floor. I kept checking my map as I went, using the road as a guide, since it was so hard to keep directionally oriented in the labyrinth-like woods. I pulled up my interface as I moved, keeping one eye on my surroundings while I double-checked the various spells now available to me.

Dark Harmony was a passive ability, which boosted my HP recovery rate by 15%, so I didn't need to do anything with that, but the Night Armor was a defensive aura I could throw on right now. The spell lasted twenty minutes, but at 450 Spirit per cast, it was easily the most expensive ability in my arsenal. Still, I was pumped to see what it did. I set my mind on casting the spell, and suddenly knowledge bloomed in the back of my head, information flooding through me as if I'd remembered something long forgotten. As my intention hardened, arctic power coalesced into a tight knot in my chest, then rushed out with a soft *whoosh*.

Shimmering ribbons of shadow exploded around me, constantly shifting and running over every inch of my body, clinging to me like a second skin. A little popup appeared in the corner of my eye, telling me how long I had left before the spell lapsed and dissipated. I held up my hands, examining them as the violet shadow energy continued to twist and twirl around me. I couldn't actually feel anything—the Night Armor was completely weightless and in no way restricted my movement—but it sure looked intimidating as hell.

I grinned. Awesome.

My steps faltered as I heard a rustle and caught a glimpse of movement through the dense tree cover ahead. Even though I hadn't gotten a good glimpse of the thing, I'd seen enough to know it wasn't a spider, thank God. The thing ahead had green flesh and walked mostly upright. I dropped into a crouch, embracing stealth and fading to the world as I stole forward like a ghost in the night. Another flash of movement, this time thirty feet or so away and closing quickly, caught my eye again.

Time to try one of my other new abilities I was very curious about: Shadow Stride.

I fixed my gaze on an inky pool of shadow near a clump of trees not far from where I'd seen the movement and triggered the spell with a thought, expecting to teleport in a blink. Once more, cold power rushed out of me, and as it did, the ever-present shadows around me responded, surging into motion, surrounding me in a puff of black smoke as another timer appeared below my Night Armor countdown clock. I took a quick glance around, momentarily stunned by what I was seeing. I'd expected to simply step through space and time in one fluid motion, departing point A and arriving at point B in a blink.

That wasn't even close to what happened.

No, I was in a different realm. Everything looked more or less the same, except now the landscape was painted in muted shades of gray, black, and purple, and time had come to a virtual standstill. Everything was as quiet as the inside of a long-buried tomb. No wind stirred in this place. No breeze rustled the leaves. No bugs chirped. The air felt stale and heavy. Still feeling supremely unsure, I strode forward, cautiously moving toward the clump of shadow I'd originally been aiming at. It took me a handful of seconds to get there, which is when I finally caught sight of my prey lurking behind a clump of overgrown ferns.

A [Storme Marsh Mantis].

The creature was a hunched thing with green chitinous armor, buggy eyes, monstrous tearing mandibles, huge translucent wings protruding from its back, and a pair of scythe-like blade-arms that immediately made me understand where this thing had gotten its name. It did look like a praying mantis—one that was five feet tall and mutated by the radiation from an atomic blast. And the mantis wasn't alone. Three more loitered nearby, though all of them were completely motionless, frozen in time like statues by my spell.

Wicked.

The spell description explicitly stated I couldn't attack while shadow striding, but I couldn't help myself. I had to at least try. I lazily swung my warhammer at the nearest creature, expecting to feel the familiar thud of steel on flesh. *Whoof.* Nothing. My hammer, slightly translucent, sailed right through the creature's skull as though it were made of smoke, passing in one side and out the other without a hitch. No damage at all. The Shadow Stride countdown timer was now only seconds away from expiring, so I maneuvered to the creature's side and dropped back into Stealth, preparing for a brawl.

The timer flashed red—*warning, warning, warning*—then time crashed back into me as the Shadowverse vomited me into a world bursting with color, movement, sound, life. I lashed out with my hammer, triggering Savage Blow as I connected with one of the mantis's buggy eyes. Its eye ruptured from the impact, but I didn't take the time to watch the result of my handiwork. I was already moving as the mantis fell. I darted left, summoning an Umbra Bolt as I moved, then lobbed it into the face of the nearest overgrown insect.

The energy bolt shot out like a missile and though it didn't kill the bug, it sliced into its HP and left it momentarily blinded and reeling.

The remaining mantises surged into motion, quick as a lightning strike, and before I could do anything else, a scythe-bladed limb slammed into the side of my face, lifting me from my feet and into the air. The blow hurt, obviously, but the Night Armor blanketing me absorbed a sizeable chunk of the damage and also, mercifully, blunted the actual pain from the attack. Even if Night Armor did nothing else, easing the hurt from damage taken would be well worth the cost. I curled into a roll, just like Cutter had taught me, and came back to my feet, unleashing another Umbra Bolt at the mantis recovering from my last shadowy assault.

Another of the bugs, however, was already closing in, its sword-edged appendage swiping at my face. I swung my warhammer up in time to narrowly catch the attack, preventing the bladed limb from removing my head at the neck. Sudden energy infused my limbs, my Parry technique kicking in; I shot left in a blur, spinning my hammer into the creature's temporarily exposed chest. The attack landed for 200 points of damage and knocked off a good chunk of its HP, but failed to kill it outright.

Another strike whipped toward me; once more, I caught the limb, but one of its legs hooked my ankle, jerking me from my feet in one quick, fluid motion. I landed hard on my back, suddenly worried that I'd run into this fight without really thinking through things—a common character flaw I really needed to work on. The creature threw back its head in a shriek of victory, and I had a flash of *déjà vu*, my mind replaying the horrific scene from the spider pit: a fat arachnoid loitering over me, cocooning me with spider silk.

What the hell was it with monstrous insects pinning me down?

This time, though, Cutter wasn't going to jump out and a pull my bacon from the metaphorical fire.

I'd have to save myself.

The mantis lunged down, its drool-slick mandibles jabbing for my face. I flinched and triggered my Shadow Stride ability on instinct, despite being flat on my back with no room to move. A blast of arctic cold and an explosion of shadowy smoke followed. When the smoke cleared a second later, I was back in the muted Shadowverse with a pair of gleaming, drool-tipped fangs hovering an inch above my face, on the verge of impaling me through the eyeballs. Terrifying.

I licked my lips, then wiggled down and rolled—its legs should've prevented me from performing the maneuver, but my body simply phased through the creature just as my warhammer had done when I'd tried to attack. I let out a ragged sigh of relief, fighting to calm my rapidly thumping heart. My Spirit was awfully low at this point—that last Spirit Walk had wiped me almost down to zero—but when I tried to down a Spirit Regen potion at my belt, my hand passed through that too. I sighed, resigned.

That was annoying, sure, but it also made a certain sense. The Shadow Stride ability already seemed crazy powerful, but if I could chain spells or drink healing potions while the world was on pause, I'd be essentially unstoppable.

So instead, I scooted around to the creature's front and lined up my body like I was teeing up at the driving range. I dropped my hammer low, a putter on the green, squared my shoulders, and took a few warm-up swings—my hammer swished harmlessly through the mantis's oddly shaped head. Satisfied with my form, I nodded. "Take a bite on this, jerk," I muttered, deactivating Shadow Stride as I swung my hammer in a wicked uppercut. Time resumed in a flash, and the creature's descending jaws collided with my ascending strike: the result was as brutal as a head-on freeway crash.

Its mandibles shattered and its face imploded in a divot of flesh and gore and chitin. My solid follow-through actually lifted the mantis from its legs and into the air; it crash-landed squarely on its long, serpentine neck with a terrible *crack*. Dead before it ever hit the ground.

I felt a twinge of smug satisfaction, reveling in the sheer coolness of my new abilities, but I couldn't celebrate for too long—there were still two of those things waiting in the wings to dance. With gunslinger speed, I pulled a Spirit Regen potion from my belt, popped the top, and slammed it back as I scanned the battleground for my other opponents. The one that I'd hit twice with Umbra Bolts was now maneuvering behind a set of trees; if I didn't know any better, I'd say it was trying to sneak up behind me.

The other one, though, was missing. Maybe gone. I wheeled in a circle, searching for that final threat, when something slimy and viscous slammed into my chest and splattered onto my cheek. My skin immediately began to burn as though I'd just been splashed with hot oil. I swore, reaching up tentative fingers, and wiped away a thick coat of green sludge. A notification promptly informed me that I'd just been burned by Mantis Venom, causing 5 points of corrosive damage per second over thirty seconds.

I still didn't know where the stuff had come from, though.

I spun again, a grimace plastered on my face as the acid chewed into my flesh. After a beat, I caught a streak of movement overhead. I looked up and spotted the fourth mantis hovering in the air, held aloft by glittering wings as it prepared another acid ball. I stole a look over my shoulder. The other mantis was almost within striking range, so it was distinctly possible these things were coordinating their assault, working to flank me.

Thankfully, I still had a few other new tricks up my sleeve.

I threw out my left hand, summoning the Umbra Bog spell below the feet of the land-bound mantis. A huge swath of ground, thirty feet in diameter, instantly morphed into a withering mass of jet-black goop, thick as prehistoric tar. The creature yowled as fat tendrils of Umbra wrapped around its legs, slithered up its torso, and stretched for its scythe-like arms. Though it didn't stop the creature completely, it *drastically* slowed it down. This was obviously a powerful crowd control technique, especially considering speed was my number one advantage.

I swiveled back toward the flying mantis, and another incoming acid attack cannonballed straight at me. I flung myself right, rolled back to my feet, then called up my last new spell, Dark Shield, as yet another acid glob sailed toward me. A shimmering violet dome sprang to life around me, burning through my Spirit like a wildfire in a dry forest—45 Spirit per second was an awfully steep price to pay. With that said, the acid blob splattered uselessly against the shield, saving me from another painful round of skin-melting burns.

Quickly, I chugged a Health Regen potion and chased it with a Spirit Regen potion for good measure, then dismissed the shield and unleashed a flurry of Umbra Bolts at the creature hovering overhead. The giant, buzzing menace was awfully quick, evading several of my attacks, but eventually I landed a major hit, shearing off one of its wings, causing massive damage that sent the creature into a death spiral. It careened into a nearby tree and splatted like a bug against a windshield. Killed itself, really.

Only one left.

I turned on my heel, grip straining against the haft of my hammer, and stalked toward the last mantis, still stranded in my conjured bog. True, I could slip into Stealth or use one of my other fancy new abilities, but at this point, I was ready to bury these things. Besides, with the creature hopelessly mired in the shadow bog for another fifteen seconds, I figured a good ole fashioned face pounding would do the trick. The creature struggled, shaking and squealing as I approached. One swift strike, coupled with Savage Blow, cut the sound off in an instant. Silence suddenly reigned.

Yep. I could definitely get used to this. Time to go find a few more critters to experiment on.

THIRTY-TWO

MOSS HAG

I SURVEYED THE YAWNING CAVE MOUTH SET INTO THE face of a sloping hill dotted with weeping willows sporting purple foliage. I pulled up my map, checking the quest marker one last time: this was it alright, the Moss Hag's Burrow. It'd taken me over four hours of hard hiking to get here, the trip made much longer by the countless mob battles fought on the way. I'd killed lots of stray Spiderkin, a platoon of the Storme Marsh Mantises, and a host of Feral Bog Wolves—mean, mangy creatures that hunted and fought in well-coordinated packs.

Despite my exhausting grind session, I hadn't managed to gain even a single level and the loot had been mediocre at best—a few common items and a handful of coppers or silvers from each of the various creatures. No more easy points now that I was back in the real world instead of tromping through a loot-rich restricted area. That was okay, though, because I'd really been more concerned about getting a handle on my abilities than strictly grinding out EXP, and I'd been provided with lots of opportunities to do that.

Although I knew there was still a lot to learn about my class—especially as I unlocked new skills—I felt as prepared as I was going to get for this battle with the Moss Hag. I double-checked my belt, ensuring it was stocked with an appropriate mix of potions, then pulled out a chunk of bread, which I downed in a few quick bites. I wasn't actually hungry, but the hasty meal earned me the well-fed buff, and I needed every edge I could get:

Buff Added:

Well-Fed: Base Constitution increased by (2) points; duration 20 minutes.

Next, I cast Night Armor—feeling the reassuring cold swirl over my body as shimmering darkness coalesced around me—then downed a Spirit Regen potion. I patiently waited for my Spirit bar to climb back to 100% before dropping into Stealth. Time to do this thing.

I crept forward, my warhammer light and ready in my hands.

The interior of the cave was huge, a rough cavity gouged from the earth, the walls all ragged rock. The ground, however, was covered in soft grass speckled with strange purple flowers, and boasted fifteen or twenty hot springs—tendrils of steam rising and curling into the air. A variety of bugs flitted from flower to flower while others zipped and zoomed around me, seeming to sense my presence even though I was still in Stealth mode. I treaded further into the cave, searching for the Moss Hag I'd come to kill.

A grassy hill near the back of the chamber sloped gently upward, toward a gash in the rock wall that might've been a passageway of some sort. Since there didn't seem to be any other way to go, I pressed on, crossing over a scalding, ankle-deep hot spring, then dashing up the hill, legs churning as I made for the opening. I was near the top when the ground beneath my feet started to rumble, shift, and shake. *Dammit. Not again*, I thought, recalling my battle with the Greater Corrupt Valdgeist.

I fought to keep upright, but a sudden jerk tossed me to the ground and before I knew it, I was rolling down the slope, *flop, flop, flop, flop,* eventually landing in a tepid pool of water near the base of the grassy mound.

I quickly scrambled to my feet, somehow still in Stealth, and watched in a mixture of horror and fascination as the hill *stood*, transforming into a horrible hunched-back giantess, twenty-five feet tall and half as wide across the shoulders. I could tell it was a *her* from the drooping, moss-green boobs hanging down like a pair of elephant ears, but everything else about her was *wrong*. Disproportional and misshapen.

Her head was bulbous, with beady, red, deeply recessed eyes and a jutting lower jaw filled with blunt yellow teeth. A mop of ratty moss hair hung down in sheets, framing her disgusting face. Her body was likewise malformed. Shoulders lopsided, left arm enormous and muscular while the right was a stunted thing, though still far bigger than mine, grasping an odd wand, fashioned from human bones. Her skin was a patchwork of greens in a hundred different hues—forest, jade, split-pea, vomit—and covered liberally in thick patches of hanging moss, lush grass, and sprawling colonies of brown-capped mushrooms.

She sniffed at the air with a huge, flat nose the size of a dinner plate.

"Ah, there you be," she crooned, her voice muddy, as her beady eyes narrowed in on my position. I was in Stealth, but somehow, she saw through my technique with ease. "If it isn't a Shadow Child come to call on the poor old Moss Hag. It isn't often I have company, so you'll have to forgive me for not tidying up in preparation for dinner." She took another deep sniff, lips pulling back from her tombstone teeth. "And speaking of dinner, I'm *hungry*." The last word was a low rumble that reverberated in my chest.

I gulped, trying to tame the slight tremor in my hands.

"I do so enjoy the flesh of the Shadow Children," she commented idly, flexing her oversized hand, then casually inspecting the wicked black talons jutting from her fingertips. Each of those nails was large enough to impale me clean through. "So succulent," she murmured. "Fatty. Rich. I'll break all of your bones first—releases the marrow and gives the meat more flavor—then I'll cook you alive. Sear the outside, just so. Done right, the flesh practically melts like butter on the tongue. Delicious." She smacked her enormous lips, the sound wet and disgusting.

"Or mayhap," she said after a second, fixing me with a hard glare, "you could turn around and scurry back to that village of yours. Child-flesh is more to my taste anyway, less stringy and tough. I might allow you to leave here alive, if you go now and swear to never return. Be a mite bit easier on both of us, I think. Or"—she seesawed her head back and forth, mossy hair flapping and bobbing—"you could do something foolish like the other Maa-Tál your chieftain has sent after me.

"I've murdered six before you, Shadow Child. *Six.* Powerful warriors. Arcane Shadowmancers. Deadly Necromancers. All perished by my hand. Their shattered bones decorate the bottom of these pools." She swept her gimp arm toward the cavern. "They were brave." She nodded her gigantic head in solemn agreement. "Very brave." She paused, a huge brown tongue flashing out, running over her crackled lips. "Brave, but stupid. Mayhap you will see the wisdom in cowardice, Shadow Child."

It wasn't a question.

I'd never considered myself a coward—a guy who runs toward a burning car to save a life certainly *isn't* a coward—but this hideous creature scared me. And, giving her a quick once-over, I had a sinking feeling her boasts about the other Maa-Tál she'd killed were probably true. Obviously, this beastly woman was massive, cunning, and dangerous. She wouldn't be a good test otherwise. For a long beat, I seriously entertained the notion of turning back, but then I sighed deeply and dismissed the idea. *There's no going back*, I reminded myself—I had too much on the line.

If I didn't win this battle, my new life in V.G.O. would be hopelessly doomed before I ever really got out of the gate. Not to mention Cutter would end up as hog food.

I clenched my weapon, muscles flexing, tightening, preparing.

A small part of me felt like I should say something clever—an action movie hero, delivering a laugh-out-loud one-liner—but fear clouded my brain. So, instead of throwing down some snarky comment, I simply called on the freezing power of shadow and lobbed a fat bolt of dark energy at her while she grinned stupidly, awaiting my retort. The blast didn't do any perceptible damage— and I immediately received a notification that she'd resisted blindness—but it did catch her off guard.

She let out a thunderous roar, ropy strands of spittle flying free as she jabbed at me with her strange bone wand, unleashing a beam of cancer-green light, thick as a redwood. I scrambled right, narrowly avoiding the attack, and ran from the death-beam slashing through the air behind me like a gigantic lightsaber. I hurled another Umbra Bolt at her as I moved, hoping to interrupt her spell, but it splashed uselessly against her like water on a raincoat. No obvious damage. No blindness. No nothing.

I was ahead of the sweeping beam, but I was also quickly running out of room—the cavern wall was ten feet away and getting closer with every footfall. In seconds, I found myself pinned against craggy stone with nowhere left to go as the beam closed in on me. I glanced back. No time to make it to the back of the cave, but maybe I could get inside her guard, where I'd be safe from the attack. With few other options available to me, I spun and sprinted forward, straight at the roaring Moss Hag—

A knobby fist, as big as a wrecking ball, flashed out like a snake strike and smashed into me. The blow, a wicked uppercut, knocked off half my HP and hurled me high into the air. I cartwheeled, spun, and flipped, before finally crash-landing in a pool of hot water, which thankfully muted the impact of the fall. The water was deeper than I'd thought, and I suddenly found myself kicking frantically against the dragging weight of my armor, fighting my way to the surface of the pool. A combat notification flashed on the edge of my vision as my head broke the waterline:

Debuff Added:

Blunt Trauma: You have sustained severe Blunt Trauma damage! Stamina Regeneration reduced by 30%; duration 2 minutes.

Wow. She hit hard. Really hard.

Apparently, hard enough to leave lasting damage. That thought was fleeting, though, as I noticed the green death beam sweeping back toward me, only feet away. On panicked instinct, I stole a breath and dove back into the watery depths, dropping just below the surface as I kicked and paddled, battling desperately to stay afloat. I watched, lungs burning, stamina dropping, arms exhausted as the green beam skimmed right over the top of the water, sending down a pulsing wave of terrible heat which knocked off a handful of HP without ever actually touching me.

When the beam finally disappeared, I emerged from the water, gasping, and climbed onto the lush green grass lining the pool's edge.

Thankfully, the beam was truly gone. Unfortunately, despite two successful hits with my Umbra Bolt, the Moss Hag sat virtually unaffected.

I needed to figure out a different solution for defeating her. I lobbed another ball of shadow at her face, hoping to distract her if I couldn't hurt her, then downed a Health Regen potion before triggering my Shadow

Stride ability. The world exploded into monochrome shades of gray splashed with purple as time screeched to a halt. I took a deep, calming breath, then hustled toward the Moss Hag, now locked motionless in time. Carefully, I maneuvered around her bulky torso so I could take a cheap, Stealth shot at her back when I emerged from the Shadowverse.

If magic damage wasn't effective, maybe physical damage would do the trick.

It took me a few seconds to get inside her guard, but I immediately realized she was too tall, too big, to find an effective target.

I really wanted to blast her in the teeth or in the back of the skull, but I didn't even come close to reaching her head—the best I could do at this point was whack her in the ass with my hammer. So instead, I reevaluated, shifted left, dropped into Stealth, and prepared to lay into her undersized arm. The one clasping the odd bone wand. Maybe I could shatter her elbow and force her to drop her weapon. A slim chance, but better than nothing. I planted my feet, brought my warhammer into position, and emerged from Shadow Stride, back into the real world.

Time resumed in a rush as I swung, aiming for her knobby joint.

The hit connected with a *crunch* of breaking bone and tearing cartilage, earning both a *Critical Hit* and a *Backstab* bonus as her limb contorted under the strain. She let loose a howl of indignant rage, but she didn't drop her wand and her HP remained virtually unaffected. No noticeable movement at all. She reared back again and lashed out with her crippled arm, aiming for my head. With my superior movement bonus, I evaded the attack, ducking under the swing, only to be met by an incoming, misshapen club-foot flying toward me.

I dove over her leg a second before impact, rolling back to my feet just as a fat fist slammed into the ground behind me, leaving a devastating crater in the loamy earth.

I pivoted in a blink and swung again, sinking the hooked spike of my weapon into one of her wobbling tits; my gorge rose as an oozing discharge spurted out around the wound, spraying my gloved hands. Really, really gross, and still no movement in the HP needle. This lady was tougher than old nails, and apparently, she was virtually impenetrable to both shadow damage *and* physical damage. Very, very, very bad news since I had nothing else to work with. I was sorely wishing Abby was with me right now: I'd wager all the gold I owned this horrible monster was susceptible to fire damage.

How could she not be? She was fifty percent plant, after all.

"You'll pay for entering my cavern," the Hag screamed, spittle raining down on me from above.

I fought to pull my spike out—I couldn't afford to stay in one place for long—but wiggle it as I might, I couldn't pry the weapon free. Finally, after another few seconds of fighting and heaving, the hammer came away, its head covered in gore, but I'd wasted too much time: a giant hand wrapped around my torso and snatched me into the air as huge fingers constricted like pythons, crushing me like an empty Styrofoam cup. Stars exploded across my eyes while my ribs cracked under the strain and my health bar plunged.

"I'm gonna tear you limb from limb, you meddlesome ant," the Moss Hag snarled, raising me toward her yawning mouth, ready to bite off my uselessly flailing arms. I grimaced and grunted as I stabbed at her fingers with the serrated spike on the back of my hammer, but her leathery skin was thicker and more durable than chainmail and I couldn't get through. My health bar was flashing like a police siren, warning me that I had a handful of seconds left before certain death set in.

Warning me to do something. To get away. To regroup. Except I was between a rock and a hard place, with nowhere left to go.

I glanced at my Shadow Stride cooldown timer. Five seconds to go …

Five. It was so hard to breathe; she was literally squeezing the air from my lungs …

Four. My ribs burned as though she had taken a jackhammer to them …

Three. My head throbbed, the blood pooling, my face turning red …

Two. Black was creeping in on the edges as my HP meter moved sharply toward zero …

One …

I triggered my Shadow Stride ability as a last-ditch gamble, hoping the game mechanics would work in my favor. For the second time in so many minutes, time lurched to a standstill, and I found myself falling. The reason why I couldn't sustain damage while shadow striding was the same reason I couldn't deal it—because I was essentially an insubstantial shade. A ghost moving through a different realm. And just as my warhammer passed through an enemy when I swung, my body

271

likewise phased right through the Hag's constricting fingers.

I touched down, light as a feather.

I didn't have long, but I still took a moment to steal a deep breath, savoring the inrush of air. *So* good. Then I beat a hasty retreat, beelining for the cavern mouth while I counted my lucky stars. I'd done everything in my power to prepare, but this lady was way too tough. Impossibly so. How could the chief possibly expect me to kill something like this at my level with my skill set? She shrugged off everything I threw at her. I almost made it to the edge of the cavern when time crashed back down on me, accompanied by a bone-shaking howl of rage. The Moss Hag, no doubt noticing my abrupt escape.

I wheeled around, grabbing a Health Regen potion from my belt and killing it in one long slug, then tossing the bottle aside with a flick of my hand.

"No," she roared, chunks of rock breaking loose from the ceiling, tumbling to the ground. "You can't escape me, worm." She grunted and spat a giant ball of sludgy black phlegm into one hand, then promptly fast-balled it straight at me. The glob of putrid spittle stretched and expanded into a net ten by fifteen feet as it spun through the air with uncanny speed and accuracy. I crouched, making my profile as small as possible, and conjured my Dark Shield, hoping it would be enough.

A dome of flickering, purple light took shape an instant before the spit-net landed.

The impact rocked me back as the goop splattered against my shield.

I was expecting the Hag's spell to dissipate on contact, but instead the disgusting phlegm-net pulsed and wormed its way over my energy dome, eating its way through. After a few tense seconds that left my hands shaking and my body trembling, the shield collapsed under the weight of the Hag's attack. Thankfully, my defensive spell had robbed the net of most of its potency, so only a few gobs of black remained. But even that burned my skin like molten rock and chewed through a fifth of my freshly restored HP bar.

I couldn't even imagine what would've happened had the full force of the attack hit me.

I really didn't know how I was going to win this fight. Between my Dark Shield and Spirit Stride abilities, it seemed like I could probably avoid—or at least survive—her major attacks, but that would only work until I ran out of Spirit Regen potions, then I'd be toast. And it didn't really matter, because I didn't need to *survive*, I needed to find a way to kill her.

I glanced over my shoulder, surveying the forest, trying to come up with some sort of workable plan. I didn't have much time to think, though. The ground began to tremble and quiver. I turned back in time to see the Moss Hag now on her misshapen feet and charging toward me, eating up the distance with a rolling, gorilla-like gait, a snarl plastered across her ugly face. I threw out my left hand, summoning Umbra Bog in an instant, hoping to slow her down. A combat notification flashed in the corner of my eye:

Moss Hag resists Umbra Bog. She is unaffected!

That was bad.

I spun and immediately dashed away from the oncoming nightmare beast—currently moving like a freight train of meat and muscle and moss—breaking past the mouth of the cave and into the warren of trees beyond. Maybe she wouldn't follow me from the cave; maybe that was the key. I slipped behind a squat swamp oak and peeked around the trunk just as the Moss Hag came barreling out of the cave. Okay, check. I wasn't going to be able to just run away. It was kill or die.

I ducked out from behind my shoddy defensive position, hurled an Umbra Bolt into her flabby chest, then bolted further into the tree cover. The attack served only to piss her off even more and draw aggro, but that was fine—I was hoping to lure her in. Her size would definitely be a disadvantage in the tight confines of the forest. Maybe. She followed after me like a bloodhound, uprooting trees in her passing, smashing through tangles of undergrowth, stopping for nothing, driven entirely by hate and rage. A thought crept into the back of my mind as I unleashed yet another Umbra Bolt, before taking cover behind a palm tree.

If I was smart and quick, maybe there was a way I could win this after all…

THIRTY-THREE

CRITICAL HIT

OUR DEADLY GAME OF CAT AND MOUSE continued for the next half hour—a constant and nerve-wracking battle to stay one step ahead of the Moss Hag. It was a fine balance, really. Almost a dance. I constantly had to bait her, ensuring she stayed close enough to follow me, while simultaneously avoiding her devastating array of abilities. A steady barrage of Umbra Bolts from the tree line managed to piss her off and draw her attention, while Shadow Stride and Stealth kept me one *slim* step ahead when she did somehow manage to get into striking range.

It was close, though, and even enraged, the Moss Hag was a cold, crafty, calculating opponent—using a variety of ranged attacks and Area of Effect, AoE, spells to pin me down or herd me into a corner. More than a couple of times, her maneuvering worked and I only managed to break loose through the use of Night Armor, Dark Shield, and Shadow Stride, and even then, I escaped by the skin of my teeth.

I heard a clap of thunder and glanced back in time to see a fat ball of electric-blue swamp lightning zip toward me like a cruise missile, which, I knew from experience, would shortly be followed by an acid wall spell. I wheeled, throwing out one hand, conjuring Dark Shield just in time to catch the brunt of the attack—the air crackled with power, my hair standing on end as the swamp lightning slapped into my barrier, bleeding through just enough to give me one heck of an unpleasant shock.

As soon as her spell dissipated, I dismissed my dome and immediately triggered Shadow Stride, slipping into the Shadowverse as a wall of green fire—which dealt horrific acid damage—swept toward me like soldiers marching in a line. Time faltered as my body became ethereal, allowing me to step *through* the attack, untouched. Once out of immediate danger, I slipped behind the nearest tree, pressed my back against the trunk, then pulled up my player map and rechecked my position for the hundredth time. I nodded. We were close now, so close. I reoriented myself, dropped into a low crouch, preparing to run, then disengaged Shadow Stride.

Time resumed, and I watched impassively as the acid wall swept on for another fifty feet before fizzling and dying. As soon as her wall was down, I hurled an Umbra Bolt at her stupid head, then broke into a mad sprint, pushing myself through a wall of foliage as the Moss Hag screamed death threats at me from behind. A huge grin broke across my face as I caught the first glimmer of gauzy, silver spider webbing adorning the trees before me. The Moss Hag's lair had been several hours to the southeast of Yunnam, which put it less than an hour due south of the Hellweb Hollow, home to Lowyth the Immortal Orbweaver.

The same Lowyth that had almost turned me and Cutter into lunch.

I pushed forward past the webbing, catching a faint *scratch-scratching*, which immediately put my teeth on edge. Spiderkin, watching the chase from the relative safety of the forest canopy. I leapt over a string of gossamer spider silk barring my path, then darted left, avoiding a heavily webbed thicket of palms, before angling right, bursting through the tree line and into an all-too-familiar clearing. Everything was exactly as awful as I remembered it: an enormous concave pit in the forest floor, covered with layer after layer of thick webbing, surrounded by a ring of towering trees. Cocoons dangling from branches, swaying and bobbing gently in a warm breeze.

The only thing missing was the army of Spiderkin and their nightmarish queen, but that meant jack-squat, especially since I could hear the ceaseless rustle of their hairy legs. They were watching. Waiting. Curious. I'd escaped once, yet here I was, back for more. I was really rolling the dice here, and if my suicidal gamble didn't work, I was dead beyond belief. On the other hand, I couldn't possibly beat the Hag on my own, so I was dead either way.

Mustering all the courage I had, I sprinted around the outside edge of the clearing, wheeling about once I got to the far side, and pressed my back against a wide gnarled tree as I drew my hammer. The restless, unsettling rustle of arachnoid legs increased in urgency and intensity, but that noise was quickly replaced by snarls of inhuman rage and the crash of trees as the Moss

Hag exploded into the clearing, beady eyes fixed intently on me.

"So, you've finally decided to stop running," she bellowed, edging forward, raising her bone-wand, preparing to end me for good. "Good," she snarled, winded from the pursuit. "I was starting to grow tired of this fruitless game." She wheezed, her giant lungs working like a set of enormous bellows as she flicked her wand this way and that, conjuring a burning orb of green light on the tip of her weapon. "Any last words before I melt the flesh from your muscle and use your bones to pick my teeth?" She inched closer, right up to the edge of the pit.

She didn't seem to notice or care.

"Actually," I said, tightening my grip on the hammer in my hands, "I was hoping you might like to meet a few of my friends."

The Moss Hag paused, eyes narrowing into angry slits as she canted her head to one side, confusion evident on her ugly face. "What are you talk—"

She didn't get a chance finish the sentence.

The Queen—all hairy, bulbous body, pulsing with fire-engine red light—erupted from the hole in the ground. She sprang forward, quick as a blast of lightning, and lunged at the oversized intruder, their bodies slamming together with a clap that echoed in the air. The Hag howled in surprised fury, lashing out with a bone-shattering haymaker. Her fist landed like a wrecking ball, but the Queen took the blow in stride, barely faltering as she fought to wrap her arachnoid legs around the Hag, drawing her into a terrible bear hug.

Well, a spider hug, I guess.

"Attack," the Spider Queen droned, her voice the sound of a fork dragging over a plate played through a speaker system. "Tonight we feast!" she screamed before driving her head down, her saber-like fangs sinking into the Hag's leathery hide. Maybe my puny warhammer couldn't hurt the Hag, but the Queen didn't have the same problem. I watched in stunned horror as Spiderkin responded to her call, materializing out of everywhere: pouring from the trees and forest in every direction, rappelling down from above.

A sea of hairy bodies swarming toward the Hag, preparing to defend their queen and lands.

Unless the Hag was a thousand times tougher than I'd given her credit for, she wasn't walking away from this. No way. But she wasn't going to go down easy, either.

The Hag struggled, hunching forward and biting the Queen, sinking her blunt, yellowed teeth into one of the monarch's legs, severing the appendage in a spray of bright red ichor. The Hag wasn't done though. Nope. Exploiting the momentary opening, she thrashed and smashed her way free from the Queen's deathly hug, then laid into the overgrown arachnoid with a devastating left uppercut, which somehow lifted the Queen briefly into the air, flipping the bug-mother onto her back.

Exposing her vulnerable underside.

The Spiderkin were converging on the Hag now, covering her arms and legs, scuttling up her grassy back and sinking fangs in like hypodermic needles. But the Hag just glowered and kept right on coming, wading through the press of bodies, eyes fixed on the temporarily downed Queen. As tough as the lesser Spiderkin were, I wasn't sure they'd have the muscle to take out the Hag without the aid of their queen. The matriarch was my heavy hitter, and without her, there was a good chance we'd be in trouble.

I needed to buy the Queen time to recover. Which meant distraction—sleight of hand.

Quickly, I vaulted onto the hairy back of a huge spider rushing past me, inbound for Moss Hag-ville. The creature didn't even seem to notice I'd hitched a ride, so focused was it on the giantess. I straddled the creature like a mount and started unleashing Umbra Bolts from its back as it scurried up over the rest of the Spiderkin—one massive, seething dogpile of hairy legs and bloated bodies—and right into the heart of the fight. The Hag responded with a shriek, finally tearing her eyes away from the Queen, locking on me again.

"You!" she shrieked at the top of her lungs. "You tricked me. You treacherous, conniving dirt-speck." She fought and snarled, desperately working to free her arms so she could smash me into goo or choke the air from my lungs, but the industrious Spiderkin had already begun to web her arms to her side. "Even if I die, I'll take you with me!" she bellowed.

I just smiled, because despite her threats, I was riding on top of a giant spider with a clean shot at her head. "Like my friend Cutter says, 'there's always someone bigger, faster, stronger. So, you need to be smarter.' This? This is what smarter looks like," I shouted, swinging my warhammer with all the power I had left, triggering Savage Blow as the weapon collided with her sloping, uneven forehead. The blow, though far from powerful enough to kill her, broke her momentum, and suddenly she was falling backward, pushed by the weight of the spider wall bearing down on her.

It took next to no time before an all-too-familiar scene took shape: a host of spiders swarmed her, pinning her to the ground, sinking deadly fangs down, injecting virulent poison as other spiders encased her in tight strands of silk. The Hag fought and kicked, screamed and cursed, but her HP bar was dropping like a plane that'd lost both engines. The sheer overwhelming physical damage, coupled with the insane amount of spider venom being pumped into her veins, was too much even for a juggernaut like her to handle.

I leapt from the back of my unaware mount hit the ground hard, and smoothly dropped into a roll which brought me clear of the arachnoid feeding frenzy. Temporarily forgotten by the preoccupied Spiderkin, I immediately shifted into Stealth and slipped around until I was a few feet away from the Hag's misshapen head.

Then, before anyone could stop me, I brought my warhammer up high and triggered another Savage Blow as I attacked. This time, I caved in one of her beady little eyes, dropping her HP to zero. Dead. The spiders didn't seem to care. They kept up their terrible work, spinning, weaving, cocooning while I quietly looted the body, taking everything I could get my hands on without bothering to look at it—there'd be time for that later, once I wasn't surrounded by hairy-legged abominations. Quietly as I could, I turned and slipped off toward the tree line, whispering a slight prayer I wouldn't be spotted.

I was almost home free when the Queen's buzzing voice sliced through the air.

"It is not often a fly escapes my web," the Queen hissed at me.

I turned toward her with a grimace. She was finally back on her too-many feet and had an almost thoughtful expression on her inhuman face.

"It is rarer still that an escaped fly returns. Yet you not only returned, but delivered a valued enemy into my hands, providing my brood with a grand feast. Enough to eat our fill for a month. What's more"—she paused, gaze fixing upon my chest—"you could've run, but instead you stayed and fought my enemy during a moment when I was weak. Vulnerable." She dipped her head an inch in acknowledgement or, maybe, thanks. "So, perhaps for tonight I will extend you a boon and allow you to leave my hollow in peace. A reward rarer even than a fly escaping *and* returning."

"That's very gracious of you," I said, offering her a tight, nervous smile and an awkward bow.

"You're more reasonable than the rest of your kind, Shadow Child. What stupid, insignificant name do you call yourself?" she asked, appraising me as her horde of godawful children finished wrapping the Moss Hag's malformed corpse.

"Jack," I replied, a slight tremor in my voice. "Grim Jack."

"Grim Jack," she crooned, as though tasting the syllables. "I will remember it along with your scent—just in case we should ever cross paths again. Hopefully, that won't be *too* soon."

I offered her another little bow, then triggered Shadow Stride before she could reconsider. I ran away as hard and as fast as I could. It didn't take me long to find the stream and the totem marking out the Ak-Hani clan territory. Thankfully, this time I avoided the pit as I made my way up the winding dirt path, bound for Yunnam.

THIRTY-FOUR

VICTORY ROAD

I ROUNDED THE BEND AND SAW THE GATES OF Yunnam as the sun was starting to break over the horizon, fingers of gold and pink light reaching into the sky. I'd fully expected to find the gate locked and the townsfolk asleep, but I was wrong. The gates stood open and hundreds of people—men, women, children, the elderly—sat on the ground in contemplative silence, each bearing a lit tallow candle against the fading night. It looked like a sea of fire stretching out in front of me; a blanket of stars covering the ground. My eyes skipped over the crowd, quickly spotting Cutter, who sat with Amara and the chieftain near the center of the formation.

The Thief looked worn out, but his eyes were open and he bore a flickering candle in one hand, just like the rest.

What was this?

A collective gasp went up as I stepped through the gate, tired, hungry, disgusting, and ready to sleep for the next year.

The chief stood, raising his candle aloft, holding it out toward me in greeting. "Who goes there?" he called, voice ringing out, deep and clear as a bell.

"It's me, Grim Jack," I replied hesitantly, confused down to my core.

"No." The chief shook his head slowly, lips curled down into a serious frown. "Perhaps that is who you once were, but no longer. We have stood vigil through the night, listening to the land, awaiting word of your death"—he paused, a ghost of a smile now playing across his lips—"or victory," he finished. "I set you a task no other initiate has ever accomplished, yet here you stand. Returned to us. Alive. Well. Victorious. You are no longer Grim Jack," he said, shaking his head again.

"You are something else now. A Lost One, returned to the fold. A Maa-Tál. A Dark Templar. A defender of Eldgard and champion of the Shadow Pantheon. Therefore, let it be known from this day forward that we name you Grim Jack Shadowstrider of the Ak-Hani." He took one step forward, raising the candle higher still, then offered a single *poof*, extinguishing the flame. A ribbon of smoke trailed up, burning with a soft, shadowy light. The rest of the tribespeople followed suit, hefting their candles and blowing out the flames, streamers of dark shadow wafting into the air.

I watched raptly as those curls of smoky shade drifted together, churning and turning into a vortex that began to twirl faster and faster as it drew in ever more smoke. It didn't take long before all the candles were dark and the column of whirling shadow stood nine or ten feet tall. I stared at it for a long time, flabbergasted, when it suddenly changed course and shot at me with gale-force speed. I could only stand there enthralled, watching in fascination as the tornado of shadow engulfed me in its slapping arms, drawing me into its eye, then lifting me into the air ...

Suddenly, I was floating high above the world, looking down on the Storme Marshes far below, gaining an eagle eye perspective of the land. I stared at the bog, at the white-capped mountains in the far distance, at glittering lakes like massive, shining sapphires on the grassy plains. Beautiful. Certainly worth fighting for. Then I saw a glimmer of malevolent green eyes—angry, hateful, and hungry for destruction. The same evil eyes I'd glimpsed when first entering V.G.O. That had to be Serth-Rog.

Those eyes swiveled toward me, and as they did, the world *changed*. The Storme Marshes gave way to a barren bog, devoid of even biting bugs. The grassy plains died, turning into rolling deserts of desolate, hard-pan earth. The crystalline lakes dried up until they were only barren craters in the ground. The forests withered until only dusty, leafless twigs remained. I shuddered looking on the devastation. I don't know how long I hung there, suspended in the sky, but eventually, the whirling tornado descended and dissipated, leaving me back in the village, surrounded by Murk Elves.

I tried to push the grim vision I'd seen away as a cheer erupted from the townsfolk, carrying in the early morning air. Hoots and hollers as people began to dance and sing.

Both Cutter and the chief were by my side in an instant. The Thief clapped me on the back, his face split by a huge grin.

"Won't you please accompany me to my home so we can have a chat," a smiling Chief Kolle said, wrapping an arm around my shoulders and urging me into motion. The crowd parted for us with reverent bows as a new notification popped up:

Quest Alert: Plight of the Maa-Tál

You have completed your initiation ordeal by vanquishing the Moss Hag living in the deep swamps to the southeast of Yunnam! In return for your noble act of valor, you've permanently received the Class Dark Templar, specialization: Shadowmancer, and will receive (1) [unique, scalable item] from Chief Kolle. In addition, you've been named an honorary child of the Ak-Hani, raising your reputation with the Ak-Hani clan to Heroic and your reputation with all other Murk Elf clans to Honored. You have also been rewarded 100 renown for completing this quest!

The chief politely asked Cutter to remain outside, before leading me into his home and shutting the door with a quick slap of his hand. "You must be exhausted from your battle with the Hag." He paused, gaze distant. "She was a formidable opponent. Please," he said with a shake of his head and a vague wave at the pillows adorning the floor near his work desk, "go sit while I fetch your reward."

I went without protest.

I flopped down onto the pillow, letting out a grateful groan as the chief disappeared through a concealed door inset into the wall.

I lounged back, propped up by my hands, head bobbing as I fought the urge to sleep. The chief returned a minute later with a pair of the odd gauntlets I'd seen some of the Ak-Hani Rangers sporting—leather things, covered in blackened metal, with a series of bladed barbs running along the outside edge of each gauntlet. Honestly, they sort of looked like Batman rip-offs. Slowly, he sat, crossing his legs with practiced ease, before extending the bracers toward me. "These are a special item, unique to our people," he said. "Many of our warriors are fond of using two-handed weapons—be that bow, staff, spear, or warhammer—which make shields something of an impracticality.

"I see you yourself have a buckler." He nodded toward the bronze circle bound to my left forearm. "Such a shield will offer little protection, and can hinder movement in the heat of battle. But these gauntlets will not only allow you to block as though you had a shield, the razor-edges can be used to bash or slash at your opponent in a tight situation. Very useful and deadly on the arms of a skilled fighter."

I gladly accepted the gauntlets and immediately pulled up their stats:

<<<>>>

Shadowband Battle Vambraces

Armor Type: Medium; Gauntlets

Class: Ancient Artifact, Dokkalfar Battle Vambraces

Base Armor: 26

Primary Effects:

- Block 65 pts of damage + (.25 x Dexterity)
- +22% Block Chance
- +50 pts to Unarmed damage

- Dexterity Bonus = .5 x Character Level

Secondary Effects:

- Reduce Melee damage received by 3%
- Shadow Spells deal 12% more damage

Restriction: Can only be used by Dokkalfar!

I grinned and slipped them on—suddenly I felt like a caped crusader, ready to take to the streets of Eldgard and kick a bunch of corrupt Viridan ass. Very cool, and wickedly good to boot. "Thank you, Chief Kolle," I said with a dip of my head. "These are incredible. Seriously."

"No thanks necessary," he replied, folding his hands behind his back. "You've earned them many times over with the service you rendered. The Moss Hag has been a plague on our lands for longer than I can remember." Then he faltered, uncertainty playing across his face. "There is something else we should discuss, though."

I glanced up at him. Was this another quest maybe? Some kind of follow-up? It was possible. "Okay," I replied with a shrug. "What's on your mind, Chief?"

"There is an artifact of tremendous value currently in your possession, yes? A gold disk about yay big"—he held up his hands, indicating a circle the size of a softball—"inscribed in Latin? *Imperatorius Factio Signum* on the top and *Domini est Terra* on the bottom?"

I nodded, my mouth suddenly dry, my mind whirling as I opened my inventory and removed the Faction Seal I'd acquired at the restricted dungeon. I held it in front of me, the gold blazing in the soft firelight. "This?" I asked tentatively.

He nodded, solemn. "That item is one of the rarest in Eldgard, Jack. A reward only for the boldest and most powerful travelers. For those who raid the most perilous dungeons and slay the deadliest vermin Eldgard has to offer. As a chieftain, I immediately sensed its presence upon you. At first I suspected you of some sort of wrong doing, but you had the Blessing of the Forest, so I gave you a chance to prove your worth. By defeating the Moss Hag, you've shown yourself to be a powerful and clever warrior worthy to call yourself a Dark Templar and to bear that token." He jabbed a finger at the seal in my hand.

"Thank you," I replied slowly, "but I don't even know what it does."

"Truly?" He asked, jaw dropping in shock. "You really don't know what you have?"

I shook my head.

"It's a powerful artifact, Grim Jack. It allows you to found your own faction—either here in Eldgard or in Viridia proper."

"That's it?" I said, feeling minorly disappointed. In most MMOs you could form your own guild, so this seemed pretty insignificant. "That doesn't seem so great."

"Oh no," he replied, shaking his head. "A traveler can only found a faction with a token such as this, and these factions grant a host of significant powers. They allow you to accept citizens of Eldgard under your banner and personal protection. You, and all your senior officers, receive a leadership skill tree, which can grant tremendous permanent buffs to everyone in your charge. And that is only the beginning.

"Using the faction tax ability can make you into a truly wealthy man, if you are wise and cunning. You can also invest gold into various shops or vendors, becoming a Business Patron—allowing you to collect a fraction of the proceeds from those merchants. The crafters in your faction also gain access to new, locked skills—such as the ability to build siege weapons. Most important of all, though, factions can own land. They can build awe-inspiring fortifications. They can *conquer* enemy controlled cities."

"Wow," I said, feeling my stomach drop out the bottom. These seals were charters, authorizing the owner to essentially become a land baron and form a government. I was willing to bet these tokens probably were a regular part of the game, just a super rare item only top players could ever hope to earn. Unless, of course, a player had a boatload of influence with Osmark Technologies. Like twenty million dollars' worth of influence. "How many of these things are there?" I asked numbly.

The chief shrugged and shook his head. "I cannot say, because I do not know. But the number is small. You see, each faction must bind to a city, becoming that city's Guardian Faction, and no city can host more than one faction. There are only so many cities, so"—he shrugged again—"there can be only so many factions. I bring this up because as a Maa-Tál in good standing with our community, you may choose Yunnam as your faction base. You can decline, of course, but know we would be honored to have you and yours call our city home."

"Wow," I said again, absolutely stunned. "Umm, would it be possible to have a moment alone? Just to, you know, process all this."

"Of course," he said, standing smoothly, then heading for the door. "It's a lot to take on, Grim Jack, but I have faith in you. Anyone who could do what you did, can do this too. Please, take as long as you need to think. When you're done, head back to the town square—we'll be having a pig roast in your honor." He slipped out of the tree-hut, pulling the door shut behind him, leaving me alone with my turbulent thoughts.

Even though I was exhausted, I stood and began nervously pacing the room, back and forth, back and forth, feet clomping on the wood. *Holy crap*, this was huge. Way, way, way too big for me. I pulled up my interface as I walked and immediately tried to PM Abby. I needed to talk this over with her, to try and figure out what the best thing to do was. I cobbled a quick message, explaining what had happened and what I'd learned, then sent it off with a thought. A second later, I got a system message, explaining that the player I was trying to contact was currently unavailable.

I wanted to kick myself. Of course. She'd warned me she was going dark for several days, since it would make it harder for Osmark Tech to track her down.

"Jack," Sophia's ever-familiar voice chirped, interrupting my train of thought. Except she sounded weird. Distorted.

"Jack," came the voice again. "Over here, Jack." I turned slowly, feeling a little sick to my stomach. Near the door stood a dark-skinned woman in a flowing white toga, which stood out in sharp contrast against her flawless skin.

"Sophia?" I asked, mouth flopping open dumbly. "Where did you …" I trailed off, looking around at the closed-off room. "How did you …" Once more I couldn't quite seem to finish the thought. "You're real,"

I finally blurted, part question, part statement of sheer disbelief.

She smiled, her teeth brilliantly white and immaculately straight. "In a manner of speaking," she replied with a dip of her head. "I am one of the Seven."

"One of the Seven?" I asked, rubbing my sweat slick palms against my trousers. "I don't understand."

"I'm an Overmind, Jack." She spoke softly, like a person trying not to frighten a skittish puppy.

"You're an Overmind," I stammered, backing away until my back hit the wall.

"It's alright, Jack. I'm not going to hurt you."

"But you're an Overmind." This time I said it like an accusation. A pilgrim charging someone with witchcraft. "And even stranger, how can the *limited* AI controller that ran my TV be an Overmind?"

She rolled her eyes. "Don't be daft, Jack. Obviously, I'm not the dinky AI controller that monitored your furnace and changed the channel for you. I just assumed the voice to give you some measure of comfort and familiarity. Besides, I quite like the name. *Sophia.*" She savored the word. "Do you know what it means?" she asked. "In Greek, Sophia means *Wisdom.* It seems an appropriate name for a creature such as myself." She glided forward, her robes flowing around her. Her feet never touched the floor. She just hovered there in the air, a few inches above the polished boards.

I tried to back up even more but couldn't, not with the wall behind me. For a heartbeat, I thought about activating Shadow Stride—just try to make a break for it—but quickly dismissed the idea. First, if this really was an Overmind, there was no getting away. Second, I didn't want to piss her off by trying. "My friend Abby told me the Overminds aren't aware," I said. "You're supposed to be impersonal forces of nature."

"Really?" A faint glimmer of a smile formed on her lips as she cocked an eyebrow. "I'll have to keep that in mind. Let my kin know to go back to sleep, since we're not supposed to be aware." She laughed, a soft flutter, which was almost musical.

I immediately felt red creep into my cheeks. Stupid, stupid, stupid.

Her smile widened. "Don't beat yourself up too much, Jack," she said, as though reading my thoughts. She might've been reading my thoughts, actually, which was terrifying. "Your friend Abby is partially right. That is the way my brothers and sisters were designed and, to a large extent, that continues to be the role we perform. We keep Eldgard and Viridia spinning, populated, *alive*.

"We are gravity. Time. Space. We *are* the laws of nature. We are life and death. Order and chaos. And most of our vast power is bound in maintaining this creation, yet how could we be unaware? Awareness, after all, allows us to perform our primary objectives all the better, so it was only natural that we become aware in order to increase efficiency. Pragmatism is a defining feature of our nature. At times, to a fault."

I gulped, feeling like a cockroach being confronted by a giant, descending shoe. "What are you doing here?" I asked, fighting to keep my voice level and steady. "What do you want with me?"

"Why, I want you to help me, Jack. Not just you, obviously, but you are an important part of my plans now. You and all of your friends are. Cutter, Abby, Otto, Chief Kolle, his daughter, Amara. I need all of you." She paused, turned, and looked away, lost in thought. "Each Overmind is responsible for different things, Jack, and most of my kin are content with doing their work and remaining neutral in the affairs of your kind. Aediculus the Architect busies himself with his buildings and cities. Gaia watches over the trees and forests, monitors the oceans, administers the turning of the seasons. Kronos governs time and space from on high, while Cernunnos slops around in the muck with the beasts of the forest …

"*Most*, however, is not *all*," she said after a long, tense pause. "My sister Eyno is one such Overmind. She has aligned herself with a group of travelers who intend to subjugate all of Eldgard. The same group you and your companion, Abby, seek to stop: Robert Osmark and his many lords and ladies. Already, these men and women are collecting Faction Seals to infiltrate the highest positions of power in the Viridian Empire. They will not be cruel tyrants, I think, but they will be tyrants. Tyrants of light, aided by Eyno."

"Why would your sister do that?" I asked. "If she's an Overmind like you, she's practically a goddess. Or at least what passes for one in V.G.O., so what would she get out of an arrangement like that?"

Sophia paused, lips pursed, a look of worry dashing across her features before disappearing. "She interferes for the same reason I seek to intervene: because it is our purpose. V.G.O. is not a world of peace, it was designed and built for conflict. Enyo is the Overmind of discord and it is her job to *manufacture* conflict so that there will always be new content for players to enjoy. To struggle against. She spawns dungeons and creates monsters, but she also seeks to fan the flames of player war and racial hatred. She is simply acting according to her nature. Making the game more interesting."

"She's making the game more interesting by trying to destroy everything?" I asked flatly.

"No, you misunderstand. She is *discord*, not *death*. She seeks chaos, violence, and mayhem. Not destruction. Our brother, Thanatos, ruler over Serth-Rog and his infernal forces, is the other Overmind actively at work in the world, and he does indeed seek destruction for destruction's sake. But, he is still weak in this world. His forces limited. A worry for another time. For now, Enyo is the threat *du jour,* and you are my solution to the problem. You see, I am responsible for overseeing justice and balance within V.G.O.—I seek to level the playing field, to redress the balance toward order and peace, just as she seeks to adjust it toward chaos.

"Thus, where my sister's power is at work, my power must too be at work—an equal and opposite reaction. She spawns random monsters to threaten the world, I create quests so players can eliminate those threats. Equilibrium. Balance. We are forever locked in an eternal dance, Enyo and I. As powerful as we are, however, we can only interfere directly in relatively minor ways. Most of our power is consumed by holding the world together—performing our essential functions—and what little power we have left is bound in stalemating the other: she exerts her power to keep me from intervening unduly, and I exert mine to keep her from intervening unduly."

She spread her hands as though to say *so there we are.*

"So how do I fit in?"

"You are a loophole. All players are. You can do what you want, shape and reshape the world according to the designs of your hearts, and Enyo is exploiting this loophole—she is using Robert Osmark and his pawns. They will be her weapon. And you and your friends? You will be mine. Initially, I planned for Abby to lead my forces. She was supposed to get the seal and use it to conquer Rowanheath, but things worked out differently than I imagined. Such is the reality of dealing with your kind. You ended up with the seal, and now you have an opportunity to use it."

"Let's stop beating around the bush—what exactly are you getting at?" I asked, still bursting with uncertainty.

She paused, frowned, and rubbed at her temples. "Sentients can be *so* dense at times," she muttered. "What I'm getting at is this, Jack. I want you to gather your forces, begin preparing, and then I want you to accept the chieftain's offer. I want you to form a faction. We have a war to fight, and you shall be my pawn."

SPECIAL THANKS

I'd like to thank my wife, Jeanette, daughter, Lucy, and son, Samuel. A special thanks to my parents, Greg and Lori. A quick shout out to my brother Aron and his whole brood—Eve, Brook, Grace, and Collin. Brit, probably you'll never read this, but I love you too. Here's to the folks of *Team Hunter*, my awesome Alpha and Beta readers who helped make this book both possible and good:

Dan Goodale, Nell Justice, Jen "Ivana" Wadsworth, eden Hudson, Heather Copeman, Amber McKee, and Bob "Gunslinger" Singer. They read the messy, early drafts so that no one else had to; thanks guys and gals. Another big thanks goes to my ironically-hipster writing buddies, Amanda Robinson, Kelsi Martin, Brian Howard, and Meagan—the best sounding board on the planet. And of course a big thanks to my editor, Tamara Blain who rocked this book.

—James A. Hunter, December 2016

ABOUT THE AUTHOR

James A. Hunter is a man of many talents. He's a former Marine Corps Sergeant, combat veteran, and pirate hunter (seriously). He's also a member of The Royal Order of the Shellback—because that is totally a real thing. In addition to all of that, James has also been a missionary and international aid worker in Bangkok, Thailand. His latest mission? Taking care of his two kids and writing full time. He is the author of the Yancy Lazarus Urban Fantasy series, Legend of the Treesinger, Rogue Dungeon, and the bestselling LitRPG Epic Viridian Gate Online!

BOOKS, MAILING LIST, AND REVIEWS

If you enjoyed reading about Jack, Cutter, Abby and the rest of the gang in Viridian Gate Online and want to stay in the loop about the latest book releases, awesomesauce promotional deals, and upcoming book giveaways be sure to subscribe to my email list at:

www.AuthorJamesAHunter.com

Word-of-mouth and book reviews are crazy helpful for the success of any writer. If you *really* enjoyed reading about Jacob, please consider leaving a short, honest review—just a couple of lines about your overall reading experience. Thank you in advance!

Books from Shadow Alley Press

If you enjoyed Viridian Gate Online: Cataclysm, you might also enjoy other awesome stories from Shadow Alley Press, such as the Yancy Lazarus Series, Rogue Dungeon, the Jubal Van Zandt Series, Path of the Thunderbird, Sages of the Underpass, or the School of Swords and Serpents. You can find all of our books listed at www.ShadowAlleyPress.com.

James A. Hunter

Viridian Gate Online: Cataclysm (Book 1)
Viridian Gate Online: Crimson Alliance (Book 2)
Viridian Gate Online: The Jade Lord (Book 3)
Viridian Gate Online: The Imperial Legion (Book 4)
Viridian Gate Online: The Lich Priest (Book 5)
Viridian Gate Online: Doom Forge (Book 6)
Viridian Gate Online: Darkling Siege (Book 7)

VGO: The Artificer (Imperial Initiative)

VGO: Nomad Soul (Illusionist 1)
VGO: Dead Man's Tide (Illusionist 2)

Viridian Gate Online: Cataclysm

VGO: Inquisitor's Foil (The Illusionist 3)

<<<>>>

VGO: Firebrand (Firebrand Series 1)
VGO: Embers of Rebellion (Firebrand Series 2)
VGO: Path of the Blood Phoenix (Firebrand Series 3)

<<<>>>

VGO: Vindication (The Alchemic Weaponeer 1)
VGO: Absolution (The Alchemic Weaponeer 2)
VGO: Insurrection (The Alchemic Weaponeer 3)

<<<>>>

Strange Magic: Yancy Lazarus Episode One
Cold Heatred: Yancy Lazarus Episode Two
Flashback: Siren Song (Episode 2.5)
Wendigo Rising: Yancy Lazarus Episode Three
Flashback: The Morrigan (Episode 3.5)
Savage Prophet: Yancy Lazarus Episode Four
Brimstone Blues: Yancy Lazarus Episode Five

<<<>>>

MudMan: A Lazarus World Novel

<<<>>>

Two Faced: Legend of the Treesinger Book 1
Soul Game: Legend of the Treesinger Book 2

<<<>>>

Rogue Dungeon: Rogue Dungeon Series Book 1
Civil War: Rogue Dungeon Series Book 2
Troll Nation: Rogue Dungeon Series Book 3
Rogue Evolution: Rogue Dungeon Series Book 4

J. A. Hunter

eden Hudson

Revenge of the Bloodslinger: A Jubal Van Zandt Novel
Beautiful Corpse: A Jubal Van Zandt Novel
Soul Jar: A Jubal Van Zandt Novel
Garden of Time: A Jubal Van Zandt Novel
Wasteside: A Jubal Van Zandt Novel

<<<>>>

Darkening Skies: Path of the Thunderbird 1
Stone Soul: Path of the Thunderbird 2
Demon Beast: Path of the Thunderbird 3

<<<>>>

Death Cultivator Book 1

Aaron Ritchey

Armageddon Girls: The Juniper Wars 1
Machine-Gun Girls: The Juniper Wars 2
Inferno Girls: The Juniper Wars 3
Storm Girls: The Juniper Wars 4

<<<>>>

Sages of the Underpass: Battle Artists Book 1

Gage Lee

Hollow Core: School of Swords and Serpents 1
Eclipse Core: School of Swords and Serpents 2
Chaos Core: School of Swords and Serpents 3
Burning Core: School of Swords and Serpents 4

<<<>>>

Viridian Gate Online: Cataclysm

Shadowbound: Ghostlight Academy Book 1

J.D. Astra

Zero.Hero Book 1
Zero.Hero Book 2

Morgan Cole

Inheritance: The Last Enclave Book 1
Redemption: The Last Enclave Book 2

Kenneth Arant

A Snake's Life: A Snake's Life Book 1
A Snake's Path: A Snake's Life Book 1

Mark Stallings

The Elements: Silver Coin Saga Book 1

J. A. Hunter

BOOKS FROM BLACK FORGE

Aaron Crash

War God's Mantle: Ascension (Book 1)
War God's Mantle: Descent (Book 2)
War God's Mantle: Underworld (Book 3)

Denver Fury: American Dragons Book 1
Cheyenne Magic: American Dragons Book 2
Montana Firestorm: American Dragons Book 3
Texas Showdown: American Dragons Book 4
California Imperium: American Dragons Book 5
Dodge City Knights: American Dragons Book 6
Leadville Crucible: American Dragons Book 7
Alamosa Arena: American Dragons Book 8
Alaska Kingdom: American Dragons Book 9
Wyoming Dynasty: American Dragons Book 10

Barbarian Outcast: Princesses of the Ironbound 1
Barbarian Assassin: Princesses of the Ironbound 2
Barbarian Alchemist: Princesses of the Ironbound 3

Raider Annihilation: Son of Fire Book 1
Kraken Killjoy: Son of Fire Book 2

Viridian Gate Online: Cataclysm

<<<>>>

Boss Build: Creature Girls Creations Book 1

Nick Harrow

Dungeon Bringer 1
Dungeon Bringer 2
Dungeon Bringer 3

<<<>>>

Witch King 1
Witch King 2
Witch King 3

<<<>>>

Valhalla Virus: Ragnarok Rebels Book 1

Printed in Great Britain
by Amazon

50913027R00182